Shifter's Journey

Laura Hawks

DEDICATION

As always, this is for my mom who passed from cancer in 2015, but I'm also dedicating this book to my Aunt Donna who was a huge supporter of my writing. She always had to have the first copy of my latest book. Her passing has left a huge emptiness as she was the last of my Mother's sisters. At least they are now all together and probably playing cards. I miss them all very much and am very grateful for friends and fans who have helped me during this very trying time.

NOTES

Dear Readers,

Although the places do exist, I've taken some artistic licenses with the timeline in order to make them fit the storyline. The Colorado Springs Harvey House didn't open until 1917, but in my 1895 story I already have it in operation as early as 1894. The Cripple Creek & Victor Narrow Gauge Railroad didn't officially begin until 1897. The Midland Railway began in 1885 but sold to the Atchison, Topeka and Santa Fe line in 1890, which ran it as the Colorado Midland Railroad. These lines did connect to the later Cripple Creek line.

As always, most of the people are fictional. Any resemblance to anyone, live or deceased, is purely coincidental. The Governors of Colorado, as well as Fred Harvey, are actual historical figures.

I hope you enjoy this third book in the Spirit Walker's Saga. If you are interested in learning more about the Harvey Houses, the Railroads, the Cripple Creek's gold era, the Cheyenne or Seminole Native Americans, please check the back of the book for more information.

Prologue

2018:

The jutting mountain peaks surrounded the town, slightly capped with a touch of pristine white snow while the lower areas ranged from gray to brown then green. The jagged pinnacles contrasted against the azure empyrean. Lying at the eastern foot of the Rocky Mountain Range, the city of Colorado Springs is situated near the base of Pikes Peak, carved by ancient glaciers. The sun illuminated the area, held high in a cloudless sky, and cast shadows of the multiple buildings positioned along the roads. A crisp breeze blew across the streets, seeming to foretell of things yet to come.

It wasn't often than Sierra Hall felt anxious or nervous, especially in such a beautiful location that inspired tranquility. Coming from Illinois, Colorado Springs was an immensely diverse juxtaposition to the mostly flatlands filled with corn and soy fields, which she had temporarily left behind. True, Chicago was only a few hours from where she lived, allowing her the big-city life when she desired it, but she preferred the quietness of a small town surrounded by lush greenery and her nearest neighbor being a couple of miles away. It allowed her an almost hermit existence without actually being one.

Although not quite as large as Denver, Colorado Springs felt like the big-city life to her, with tall buildings and structures close to one another. However, what started out as an idyllic vacation was rapidly turning into something more, and not all for the better. Ever since she was a child, she had the ability to occasionally have a strong sense, a premonition if you will, of something she needed to do, a place she needed to be or of imminent danger. At the moment, she was feeling the latter.

The past couple of weeks, her dreams had influenced her to come to Colorado Springs and the surrounding area. Although she'd never been here before, she knew instinctively this was where she needed to be. Her senses were often the gauge for the path she needed to embark upon, but they had never before been so dark, mysterious or even cryptic as they currently were. In her visions, she saw snow-capped mountains, men on horseback and what appeared to be Native Americans in traditional dress. She was being pulled by them in opposing directions. Each time she awoke in a sweat, gasping for air. Her premonitions called to her. *They* called to her. She didn't understand, but then she rarely did. She just had to follow her instincts and find the hidden meaning that her dreams were trying to relate to her.

She wasn't exactly sure why, but she knew it had something to do with her destiny, her future lying in wait. When they became even more persistent, she took a last-minute vacation from her work and packed a small, rolling suitcase as she booked her flight. She rarely did anything so impulsive, but the need to get to Colorado grew increasingly imperative with each passing day. Her senses screamed at her to travel by train through the mountains and she needed to get there as soon as possible to fulfill the strong intuitions. She had no idea what it might entail, as her feelings had never been quite so distinct before, but she knew she needed to be here, for something big was about to happen. Something important that would affect her life in a once-in-a-lifetime opportunity, and if she missed it, she would forever be lost. A part of her would cease to exist in some significant way.

Chapter 1

The fresh, brisk air seared its way into her lungs. Sierra closed her eyes for a moment, letting the sun warm her face, lost in the pleasurable sounds and scents that surrounded her. However, something was off. It was an odd sensation that trickled over her like a thousand ants crawling on her skin, but she couldn't quite put her finger on why she suddenly felt that way. She had followed her intuition, the implications of her dreams that sent her here, so why was she feeling uneasy?

Arriving here, she felt there was a mystery to solve, a need for her skill set, and maybe that was what she was currently feeling in the pit of her stomach. She'd always listened to her gut, not that she minded because it had enabled her to succeed as well as she had as a reporter. Her feelings kept her on edge, made her alert and inquisitive, looking for the story it might bring. Besides, she really did need a vacation and she certainly couldn't have asked for a prettier spot to visit with a lot to see—the Garden of the Gods, known for their spectacular red rock formations; the U.S. Olympics training facility; the cog-wheel train up Pikes Peak; as well as the old mining and railroad town of Cripple Creek. She knew it was imperative to be on a train, and the only one that seemed to meet the requirements of her omens was the Cripple Creek Narrow Gauge. What was supposed to happen, she was still vague on.

Today, she just hoped to walk around the town a bit, allowing herself to get acquainted with the altitude and her general surroundings. Maybe have her nerves would calm down slightly, even though it might just be a reaction to the altitude. She was certainly not used to being over 6,000 feet. She was told to drink lots of water and minimal coffee and alcohol until her body adjusted, which normally could take months, and she certainly wasn't planning on being in Colorado that long. Two weeks was the amount of time she had off, but something told her she didn't need quite that much time for whenever her destiny was to become salient.

However, the nervous energy she was feeling

didn't seem to be solely from the higher elevation. She just couldn't comprehend why she was feeling so anxious. If she had to name it, Sierra would venture the apprehension was akin to having someone walking over one's grave. At least, that was how the feeling had been described by others. Small hairs on the back of her neck stood up as a cold shiver went down her spine. She wondered if it was part of her sensitive nature, a premonition of something to come, although none of her previous experiences had made her so susceptible to outside stimuli in the past. Why she was so vulnerable now was a complete mystery.

Sierra stopped to look at a menu in the window of a local restaurant. She frowned as she saw her mirror image: auburn hair whipped into a tangled mess by the breeze, hazel eyes gazing back at her from a pale face with freckles sprinkled across her nose. She hated those freckles! Forcing herself to look away, she happened to catch the reflection of a man observing her from across the street. He was tall; his long, dark hair was pulled back in a ponytail. His eyes were dark and piercing. Although it was just a reflection, they seemed to sear into her very soul. He wore a black leather jacket, opened in the front to show a plaid shirt over blue jeans. At first, she didn't pay much attention to him, but when her eyes focused again on him instead of the menu, she noticed he hadn't moved. He seemed to be staring at her, and it made her heart race. She didn't think she looked like a vulnerable tourist, but then she wasn't sure why or how criminals chose their victims. She was carrying a fairly expensive digital camera. Maybe he thought she was wealthy enough to rob. She decided to quickly move on. Maybe if she moved out of his line of sight she'd be okay. Sierra was sure it was just her overactive imagination combined with her aforementioned uneasiness that was playing such a negative role in her skittishness.

Swiftly walking down a couple more streets, she couldn't help but turn and see if he was following her. He was!

Chapter 2

Her heart sped up as her fear increased. She was becoming a bit panicked as she looked around for assistance or a safe place. Seeing the Broadmoor Hotel half a block away, she ran towards it, checking behind her every few steps only to see him increase his pace so he wouldn't lose sight of her. She hoped she wouldn't trip and fall as she headed towards the public venue, which seemed a good place to find sanctuary. If nothing else, there'd be witnesses should he try anything. Would he trap her there? Wait for her to leave before he picked up her trail to follow her? She needed assistance and the Broadmoor should be an excellent place to get it.

Sierra glanced behind her again as she neared the building. He seemed to be quickening his stride and closing the distance between them, but he wasn't running. In a panic, she turned and burst into the lobby, causing others to turn and gaze at her questioningly. She hurried to the front desk, pushing past the line of people.

"Please, someone, help. There's a guy

following me."

But no one stepped up. Instead they looked at her as if she just said an alien ship landed on their rooftop. She turned. No one had come inside other than her, but she knew he was out there…waiting.

Turning back to them, she implored the employees to call the police. Finally, a young woman wearing a blue dress-suit stepped away from the counter and approached her. "Come on over to the concierge desk. We can call from there. You're safe in here. It'll be okay."

Sierra nodded, grateful someone was going to come to her aid. She followed the young woman, whose name tag said Caroline. Caroline pointed to a chair in front of a walnut desk while she moved behind it and reached for the phone.

"What's your name?" she asked as she started to dial the non-emergency number for the local police.

"Sierra Hall." She pulled her camera and purse onto her lap, clutching them tightly.

While Caroline was talking to the police, Sierra

kept a nervous watch on the doors. She was sure the mysterious man wouldn't enter such a public area, but she was wrong. She gasped as he came in, looked around and headed right for her.

Sierra stood and backed up, terrified. Caroline noticed her sudden fearful movements, and as she watched the threatening man approach Sierra, her own desperation came into her voice as she spoke to the police, indicating the extreme emergency this had become. Caroline waved a couple of bellmen over who tried to stop him, holding him back as best as they could in hopes the police would arrive soon. A struggle ensued as he tried to get past them in order to get to her. Sierra didn't know what she did to attract such single-mindedness from a man she never saw before, but he was determined to reach her. She screamed in terror as he continued to struggle against those preventing his way, punching out the bellmen and anyone else who attempted to stop him from reaching his goal.

Sierra was cornered against a wall with nowhere to go to escape him. She screamed again as he grabbed both of her arms, leaning into her. She wasn't sure what he was going to do to her, especially in public, but he didn't seem to care there were multiple witnesses around them. His sole focus was on getting her and he'd succeeded. She struggled, twisting and turning, punching him as best she could, first with her purse, then with her fists when the strap broke, everything inside scattering about the floor.

As he gripped her upper arms, he leaned in close, and though she didn't think it possible, somehow she began to panic even more. Was he going to bite her? Was he going to strangle her? What could he possibly want? She had never seen him before noticing him in the restaurant's window. This couldn't be happening. Her destiny was to come to Colorado for something new and exciting, not to be killed. This didn't make any sense. None of it did.

"Sierra. I need you," he growled low, his intense, amber-gold eyes flashing with darkness. Then he cried out in pain as he let her go, collapsing to the floor.

She hadn't noticed nor heard the police come in, calling for him to release her, but when he didn't, they tased him, sending 50,000 volts of wattage into his thigh. He convulsed, a look of pained surprise on his face. She must've been truly unnerved, because for a brief nanosecond, she would've sworn his face took on the appearance of a cougar just before he dropped to the floor.

The police ran up to him. One of the uniformed men knelt on the assailant's back and put cuffs on him before they hoisted him to his feet. He was groggy from the tasing, but as he was dragged away, he turned his head to look back at her, his eyes pleading. "Don't leave me again."

She watched as he was dragged out and stuffed into a police car. It was only then she realized an officer and Caroline were by her side.

"Would you like an ambulance?" the officer asked.

"Are you hurt? Did he hurt you?" Caroline inquired as she bent to help her get the stuff back into her now-broken purse.

"No. No ambulance." Although she rubbed her arms slightly, the worst thing she'd have to remind her of this experience would be bruises. He hadn't had a chance to do anything else to her. "I'm more upset than physically hurt."

The officer nodded and indicated for her to return to the seat by the concierge desk in order to talk to her. Sierra hesitated a moment, then followed his silent instructions on shaking legs. She was grateful to be sitting, because she didn't think her knees would support her much longer. Thanking Caroline for gathering her tossed items and returning them to her, she gripped her camera and purse as if they were a lifeline. Caroline gave Sierra a reassuring smile, then left the officer and Sierra alone, focusing on getting the bellmen to keep the gawking onlookers back so the two of them could have a bit of privacy as they talked.

"Hi. I'm Officer Crandall. And you are?"

"Sierra Hall." Her voice was shaky from the trauma.

"Okay, Ms. Hall. You're safe now. Where are you from?"

"Galesburg, Illinois."

"What brings you to Colorado Springs?"

"Vacation. I heard how beautiful it was and I just had to see for myself." There was no sense in her going into detail about her dreams indicating this area was where she needed to be. She didn't want them to think she was more nuts than she currently felt. She could still see his cougar face in her mind's eye, and she questioned her own sanity.

"Why don't you tell me what happened?" He jotted down notes as he talked to her, looking up on occasion to watch her responses when he asked her questions. She'd dealt with enough police to know he was checking her answers for truthfulness.

"I just landed early this morning. I thought I'd spend the day getting acclimated to the elevation, explore the city a bit leisurely. When I looked at a menu displayed on a window, I noticed him watching me. At first, I didn't give it a second thought, but when I looked again, he was still watching, and it kind of spooked me. So, I walked away. He started following me. I then ran in here, hoping to find safety and some help."

"You did a smart thing. Staying in the eye of the public but someplace that can also assist you was a good move. Do you know him? Had you ever seen him before?"

She shook her head. "No. Never. I have no idea who he is. He might've been following me longer, I'm not sure. I only noticed him at the restaurant." Although she didn't know him, the man seemed to know her, at least her name. How? Why did he tell her he needed her, like they were friends, maybe even something more? His final plea still reverberated in her head: "Don't leave me." It was said with such longing and sadness, as if she had known him and had left him. It just didn't make any sense. Who was this man who had stalked her into the hotel? Would she ever know?

"Where are you staying while you are in town?"

"The Mining Exchange." She smiled slightly.

"I love historic hotels. Do you think that's why he followed me? He was planning on robbing me?" Although the Mining Exchange Hotel was not the most expensive property she could've chosen, it was older than its counterpart, the Broadmoor Hotel. The Broadmoor was built in 1918, whereas the Mining Exchange was built sixteen years prior. It was still a grand building and more in her price range than the Broadmoor. True, she could've gone with less expensive, there were certainly plenty of motels and hotels to choose from, but she enjoyed the elegance of a bygone era, and it was a luxury she didn't mind splurging on every once in a while.

"How long are you staying there?"

"Only a few nights. I'm then changing hotels to the LaQuinta. Cheaper rates."

Officer Crandall jotted everything down, then flipped his notepad closed and peered at her. "We will have him in custody for a while."

"I appreciate that."

Sierra appeared nervous, still jumping at the slightest of sounds. Officer Crandall leaned towards her. "If you would feel more comfortable, I can drive you back to your hotel."

She gave him a weak smile. "Actually, I'd like that. I think I've had enough drama for one day. Ordering room service and chilling in my room while enjoying the view sounds like a great way to spend the rest of my day. Hopefully by tomorrow I'll feel up to exploring other parts of the city."

"You should. Don't let one man spoil all we have to offer."

He stood and waited for her to follow suit before he led her out to the car, holding the back door open for her. She gave him a look. "I've never ridden in the backseat of a police vehicle before."

He tried to lighten her mood slightly. "Consider it an adventure, then. Thankfully, you're riding as a passenger and not someone under arrest. It's the handcuffs that are cumbersome."

Sierra slid into the car. Why she couldn't calm down, she wasn't entirely sure. Her mind kept replaying his words. They seemed so personal. She also kept seeing the face of a cougar for that split second, wondering why her mind was playing tricks on her.

Chapter 3

Sierra's first full day in Colorado Springs wasn't what she'd ever contemplated, nor would she consider relaxing. After Officer Crandall returned her to the Mining Exchange Hotel, she visited the brochure rack and talked to the hotel concierge to get some idea of what to do the next few days. Anything to get her mind off the day's terrifying event.

She'd always been the kind of person who, although she thought about situations incessantly, was aware she needed to move on with her life. She had two choices: either run back home with her tail between her legs or move forward and try to enjoy her trip to Colorado as planned. She wasn't one to run away scared, and she wasn't about to let today's events cloud her much-needed vacation or her purpose.

Spending her time to plan her itinerary, she hoped it would alleviate the jitters she was feeling. She enjoyed looking at the various brochures and tried to get excited once again in being in such gorgeous surroundings. Sitting on her balcony overlooking the Rocky Mountain Range, the beauty spread before her didn't fully dissuade her from analyzing who her mysterious stalker was and what she had done to cause him to select her to harass.

She ordered room service and decided she needed to move on with sightseeing. There were so many choices it was almost hard to select which ones she wished to do, and then what should be first. After rereading the tourist pamphlets a few more times and selecting those she was most interested in, she planned out her next couple of days, starting with a train ride through the mountains in Cripple Creek and the old mining camp. A definite requirement on her to-do list, Sierra knew that was one of the reasons she'd come to Colorado. She hoped the tranquility of the area and the calming motion of the train would settle her still-jumpy nerves. Because the train had outdoor seating, she opted for a pair of jeans and a pale-blue blouse. It was simple, but she wouldn't care if they got dirty as they were easy to wash.

Before she arrived in Colorado, she'd been unaware of how many casinos were available in the town of less than 1,200 people. Yet, for so few, there were nine casinos in Cripple Creek. However, that did allow her to cheat in getting transportation there, not having to rent a vehicle. Thanks to the Mining Exchange concierge, she was able to sign up for a player's card for the Wildwood Casino and then utilize a free shuttle bus between Colorado Springs and Cripple Creek. It saved her $25, and she figured she would gamble a little anyways, so it wasn't entirely cheating. More like being frugal.

The motorcoach picked her up at Borriello Brothers Pizza and, with several others, they drove down the highway to the historic mining town 44 miles away. Once she was let off, she went inside and dutifully played $10 in one of the machines, using her new player's card. She then walked around a bit before leaving the casino and getting her bearings. There were too many other things she wanted to explore in the quaint town before she departed.

A short walk brought her to the Cripple Creek and Victor Narrow Gauge Railroad. She entered the historic terminal and purchased her ticket. It would be a couple of hours before the steam locomotive would depart the station. Although she could've gone within the next thirty minutes, she'd been informed of a rare, unique opportunity to ride in an antique Midland Railway car. It appeared the Cripple Creek and Victor Railroad was making an exception to the normal schedule by hooking up this special coach for a once-in-a-lifetime excursion. The normal ride on the C.C.V.R. lasted 45 minutes, but this particular journey would take twice as long as they would travel as far as Victor, the neighboring gold-mining town. Sierra couldn't believe her luck in being there at such an opportune time, despite knowing it was fate that brought her here for this adventure. Excitedly, she decided to continue her exploration of the town while she waited.

There was a shuttle that would take her about the area for $1, and it sounded like the perfect way to get out and explore a bit before she settled on visiting some of the museums. She wasn't much of a gambler, so visiting the other casinos wasn't something that appealed to her.

Like most of Colorado she had seen thus far, Cripple Creek was picturesque, albeit a bit more rustic than Denver, or even Colorado Springs. The town was surrounded by rolling hills dotted with evergreens. Although there were a few streets with houses on them, the majority of the town stretched along Bennett Avenue, where red-brick buildings consisting of hotels, restaurants and casinos were located.

Riding the shuttle to what appeared the farthest point of the tourist area to visit the Cripple Creek Jail Museum, she kept an eye out for other things she'd want to do either before or after her train excursion. The whole downtown area didn't appear to be more than a few blocks and easily walkable. Had she known, she would've just hoofed it. However, the shuttle was nice, and once she finished at the old jail she would just stroll back. It was a beautiful day to be outside and she liked to walk. She kept a look out as the trolley made its way along the street, making mental notes of a couple of shops, as well as a place to grab a bite to eat, she wanted to be sure and visit.

She had to smile to herself as she noticed all the donkeys meandering around the streets. She soon learned from the trolley guide that they were descendants of animals brought in for the mines and have since been left to wander on their own since they were no longer needed after the gold rush. As she could be a bit claustrophobic, visiting the Kathleen Molly Mine, which offered excursions into their depths, was a bit daunting. Even though it was one of the largest mines in the area, the fact that she'd be several hundred feet underground was more than she could contemplate.

Instead, she decided to start her visit with the Outlaw Museum located in the Cripple Creek Jail. Gazing at the various pictures and reading all the materials, she soon found herself staring at a particular picture placard just above a ball and chain. Chuckling softly, she read it three times just to be sure she was seeing it correctly. The informational card stated, "It is illegal to hitch a horse, burro, or mule to a lamppost, hydrant or tree." However, what got Sierra amused was the following line that there was an equine "speed limit" in the city not to go in excess of six miles per hour. How in the world would they know if the horse was going seven or eight miles per hour? Did they hire someone to stand there with a stop watch and check all the horses moving at a good clip through the streets to see how long it took to get from one end of Bennett to the other? Regardless, she did find it comical and the whole thing lightened her spirit.

By the time she finished the small two-story museum, she realized she'd still have the opportunity to grab a quick bite and visit the Old Homestead House Museum. The place intrigued her, as it was once a brothel. During its heyday, Pearl de Vere, who owned and operated the establishment, charged $250 a night, and got it, during a time when the average wage was $3 a day.

However, the latter didn't take quite as long as she thought, so she decided to peak in the Cripple Creek District Museum. Sierra considered herself an amateur photographer, so she was especially interested in the photograph gallery. Maybe after the train she would return for a more in-depth visit, but a quick run-through of the photos would be time enough before she needed to be at the C.C.V.R. terminal. As she walked around the gallery, she stopped in front of one particular photo. It was similar to one she had seen in the jail, but from a different angle.

This time, something about it seemed more familiar. She couldn't quite put her finger on it, but it was more than just having seen the same picture earlier. The photo was a group shot, yet it was the Native American in the background against the building that caught her attention the most. She realized in the jail display he wouldn't have been caught as easily, but here, his image was more conspicuous. He was tall, his long, dark hair was braided over his shoulders, with a single thin braid in the center intertwined with feathers. However, it was his eyes that caught her attention and made her take notice. They were haunting, dark, almost sad, and she realized she'd seen him before. Those eyes. That man. He was the one from yesterday. She was sure of it, yet it was impossible. This picture had been taken in 1896—over 100 years ago. The only thing that made any sense was the man yesterday must be a direct descendant of the man in the picture. Yet, it was uncanny how similar they were. Peering at the sign again, she realized there was no information about him, but then, since he was in the background of a group shot, she didn't expect there to be any. Staring at the picture just a bit longer, she finally pulled her eyes away. She was left with an eerie feeling she just couldn't shake and, after exploring a bit more but not really seeing what she was looking at, she left the museum.

Chapter 4

Sierra walked the few blocks to get back to the train station and sat on the bench, watching as they hooked up the Midland car to the steam locomotive. The engine was black trimmed in gold with the words "Goldfield Engine" emblazoned on the side in gold trim. Compared to the other engine she noticed, a bright blue trimmed in red that was a bit too gaudy for her personal tastes, she was happy they were hooking up the more elegant engine. The original viewing cars were a brilliant green and yellow with back-to-back long benches, which ran down the middle of the two cars, one covered and one open. Considering it was a coal-burning engine, she could only imagine how full of soot the passengers must get traveling in those cars. How she ever lucked out in getting the specialty car, she'd never know, but she was very grateful.

Although she enjoyed watching the mechanics of hooking up the coach to the train, she found she couldn't stop thinking about that picture. Getting frustrated, she stomped her foot and stood, just as the train blew its whistle. The sound reverberated through the crisp, still air. She turned to look at the conductor, who was ushering the passengers up the couple of steps onto the train, and slowly made her way to board, taking her seat against the shiny, wood-trimmed window. The red-cushioned seats were covered in soft velvet and, considering the age of the accommodations, they were in great condition. Whoever owned the car took good care of keeping it pristine. Only the red-and-gold oriental-style runner in the aisle looked a bit worn.

She stared out the window, watching the others board the historic train. In minutes, the stairs were removed and the doors closed. As she scanned the town beyond her window, she gasped, her hand covering her mouth in shock and fear. Standing near the red-brick station was the man who harassed her yesterday. She'd assumed he'd make bail, but she had no idea he would've realized where she'd come and find her so easily.

Her heart plummeted to her stomach. She knew he'd seen her, as their eyes met just as the train lurched, pulling out of the station. She turned to watch him as the train moved away and his eyes followed her until she was out of sight. What in the world was she supposed to do? He was in Cripple Creek, and he'd be waiting for her when the train returned. Checking her phone, she didn't have a signal. She looked around in fear, hoping there was someone, anyone, who might be able to aid her once they returned to the station.

Since the car was attached separately, there had been no hook-up for the speakers to allow the conductor of the train his narration. Sierra noticed a young woman who was calling for the attention of the other passengers to describe the area they were traversing and motioned to her to speak somewhat privately. Frowning, the young woman approached her, and Sierra quickly informed the woman of her situation.

"I'll take care of it. Don't worry. When we make our first stop, I'll call the CCPD and make sure they're at the station when we get back. In the meantime, try and relax and enjoy the ride. You're safe on here." The young woman turned and headed back to the front to begin her spiel of the gold mining history and the birth of the town.

With reaffirming words of protection and nothing more she could do at the moment, Sierra leaned back in her seat. She tried to relax as much as her worry would allow. She did the best she could as she calmed her slightly racing heart by taking long, slow breaths to move past her fear.

Closing her eyes, she concentrated on the commentator talking about the terrain. Every now and again she would open her eyes to behold the old ghostly remnants of the mine shafts and the dark stones chiseled beside the tracks. In other areas, the topography was filled with rolling brown hills laced with evergreens. Puffs of billowing clouds from the steam engine would roll past their windows and she was again glad she was inside. Even though a few opened their windows for fresh air from stuffiness, they were much better protected than they'd have been in the green-and-yellow sightseeing cars.

The trees seemed to close in on them in some

areas. In others, the red-and-black rocks seemed to be from another world. As they traveled, Sierra became a bit colder and wrapped her arms around herself, trying to find a bit of warmth. The others she was traveling with seemed to be unaffected, so she assumed the cold she was feeling was a type of shock with regards to seeing that man at the station, as well as the stress and worry of being chased yesterday.

Another huge blast from the coal engine surged past, the coldness catching her off guard. A burning sensation in her throat caused her to cough, and she squeezed her eyes closed as she tried to breathe during her fit. She felt lightheaded, shaking slightly, and focused on her breathing exercises, paying no attention to the voices around her. At least not until there was a lot of shouting as the train came to a sudden stop. Sierra sat up quickly, trying to discern what the commotion was all about.

Some costumed cowboys wearing bandanas to cover the lower portion of their faces were waving their guns around asking for everyone's money.

Sierra rolled her eyes. A fake train robbery wasn't what she was anticipating whatsoever and certainly not what she needed.

She watched the drama play out as the costumed men moved closer to her location, pulling some of the other passengers from their seats, grabbing their money and jewelry. As she continued to look around, Sierra became more puzzled. She didn't remember any of these people who were now in the car with her and they were all dressed in vintage styles of clothing.

As the bandits approached her, the man in front of her, wearing a brown bowler and matching suit, stood up to block their path. He was a spindly man, lanky and thin. He reminded Sierra of Don Knotts, almost comical in his appearance. *If they were going to hire a hero,* she thought, *one would think they'd find someone who was a bit more burley and carried some weight to his words, as well as look like he'd be able to back them up.*

"You don't have the right to rob this train or steal from these hard-working people. It's part of the government and therefore under its protection. Leave these people and be gone." His raspy voice tried to have some semblance of authority, even though his overall manner was a bit weak to provide any sense of strength behind his words.

"The government ain't here and ain't gonna be anytime soon. Hand over yer wallet quickly and I'll let ya live."

"And if I don't?"

The bandit didn't waste any breath on an answer and shot the brown-suited man, who crumbled at his feet. The gunman turned and looked at the others in the train car.

"Anyone else got any complaints?" The bandit raised his voice over the screaming women, but even they quickly became quiet when he started waving the gun around. Sierra watched as a woman fainted when the robber looked directly at her.

Turning back to the robber as he focused on her, clarity set in. This wasn't a show, but something far deadlier. She gazed down at the Don Knotts look-a-like. The man's blood stained his otherwise pristine suit, as well as the red-and-gold carpet. While Sierra watched in horror, the bowler hat rolled down the narrow aisle between the train seats.

Chapter 5

1895:

Staring at the dead man sprawled on the floor by her feet, she was trying to contemplate what was occurring. *This isn't right. None of this is right!* her mind screamed over and over, as if she were caught in some devilish nightmare she couldn't awaken from. She felt a hand push against her shoulder and her attention was drawn away from the body to stare into the barrel of a six-shooter. Her breath caught in her throat. She was going to die. This was it. It was all over and her dreams of needing to be here for something special were a colossal farce. Never had her senses steered her so wrong. She heard the robber speaking, but she was so frightened her mind couldn't make out the words.

The gun was cocked back and Sierra couldn't blink, couldn't move her eyes away from the barrel of the gun aimed directly at her head. She heard a shot ring out and she waited for the pain to seep in, the blood to drip down her face, but neither occurred. Instead, the robber fell to his knees, then flat on his face, over Don Knotts' legs. The gun dropped from his hand and she stared at his prone body, trying to sort out what just happened. A deep, red stain spread across the back of the robber. She was still too shocked to move. Everything occurred so quickly, her mind just couldn't comprehend the enormity of it all. Only when her arm was grabbed and she was dragged through the car to step outside did she fully take in what was occurring, even though she still had a difficult time accepting it. Outside, the small group of people she'd noticed being robbed stood in a small huddle. Some of the women were crying, being comforted by men who looked totally uncomfortable in the role.

"Are you okay, ma'am?" A deep voice drew her attention to the man who still gripped her bicep. "Ma'am?" he asked again when Sierra didn't answer.

She nodded. "I'm unhurt. I'm not sure what happened, but I'm not physically injured. Thank you. I really thought he was going to shoot me." Sierra was still trying to fathom what occurred, the atrocity just boggled her mind. She actually watched a man be shot! And somewhere in her brain was the reality of something odd in general. The people, the clothing, everything just felt off. The sound of horses' hooves thudding against the ground caught her attention and she turned towards the approaching group of riders. That's when she noticed there were no motorized vehicles. No telephone or electricity lines. Even more surprising was the fact there wasn't anyone on their cell phones calling friends and relatives or filming everything with the built-in cameras.

He released his hand from her arm and tipped his hat to her. "Yer welcome, ma'am. He won't be shootin' anyone ever again."

He turned away from her to meet the small party reining their horses in, walking towards them to discuss the situation, leaving her standing there in bewilderment. Grateful for the moment to breathe, she took in her surroundings.

She wasn't sure where she was. It looked familiar and yet so very different. Vintage in appearance and yet new looking. Nothing made sense. The group from the train stood in a huddle, peering at her and whispering. They barely paid any attention to the others arriving on horseback. She had assumed cars would find the terrain difficult, but there were jeeps and ATVs that could have easily made it. Maybe even some trucks, so she didn't understand why they were on horseback.

Sierra turned her attention back to the small group and frowned. Why were they staring at her? It made her feel as if they were talking about her with all their whispering and looks. She looked down at her clothes wondering if maybe there was something more than the blood splatter from the Don Knotts look-a-like on her that would create such stand-offish attention. Then she realized something. She had noticed it before, but in the terrifying moments on the train, she had overlooked the fact all the others were in period outfits...the period being the turn of the Twentieth Century. The women were in long dresses, bonnets and shawls. The men in pants, some with suspenders, most with a gun belt. Even the few that were in a suit and bowtie also wore a holster.

Sierra turned around slowly, examining her surroundings. She appeared to be the only modern one in the area. She pulled out her cell phone, but there was no reception. Not that it was a surprise, since it was spotty at best when she was in town. Lord only knew where in the middle of nowhere she currently was.

"Hey! Is anyone's cells working out here?"

They all stared at her as if she spoke Greek. She grumbled and turned away, trying to get any indication of picking up service as she waved her phone all over, attempting to get a signal. When she had turned 180 degrees, she stopped. In front of her was Cripple Creek. If she'd any doubt, the sign above the station in the distance was a clear indicator.

"This can't be," she mumbled under her breath. "It's totally impossible." She looked back at her phone, then at the town she'd left only an hour ago. She felt someone at her arm, touching her elbow lightly.

"Are ya sure yer doin' okay, ma'am? You weren't hurt none, were ya?" The man who had saved her from the gunman was again at her side.

"What year is this?" Her voice was hoarse, unsteady.

He gave her a quizzical look with his steel gray eyes. "Ma'am?"

She looked at him again, more closely. He was taller than her 5'7", maybe 5'9"? His skin was tanned from the sun. His eyebrows were a light brown, but his hair was under his cowboy hat. He was handsomely rugged, and she amusingly thought he would be great in a western movie or as a model for Levi jeans. His shoulders were broad and, albeit, not totally Vin Diesel muscular, but no slouch either. He was built more like Captain America's Chris Evans. His eyes were unblinking as he watched her. For a moment his gaze was unsettling, like he was watching prey, but the look swiftly subsided. He had on one of those long dusters you see in the movies, and maybe that was what was happening. Somehow, she stumbled onto a movie set, but she doubted it. There were no cameras, no directors, no make-up artists to replenish the actors' faces for the film. Nothing made sense. "What year?" She was desperate and clung to his lapels.

"1895, ma'am." He gazed at her as if she was out of her mind.

She let him go, almost deflating in her stature as she peered around again. "1895," she repeated softly, trying to adjust to the comprehension he was right, and, somehow, she had managed to travel back in time.

"Do you have kin yer meeting at Cripple Creek?" he asked her softly. There was something about her that made him concerned. It was more than just saving her life only a moment ago. She seemed lost and vulnerable. He wanted to take care of her, though why, he had no clue. Her clothing set her apart, out of place, even though they weren't overtly unusual. Especially since the train had connected from one out East and Easterners wore strange things. Albeit, usually more flamboyant. He would've expected her in a luxurious gown more than jeans and a blouse. Outside of the blouse, to see women in pants was unusual to begin with, but the blouse gave her a bit more feminine appearance and he didn't even know they made something like that, even out East, for women. Not that he paid much attention to women's fashion, but he couldn't help noticing hers.

"No. No kin," she mumbled. She felt lightheaded, discombobulated. She was sure she'd wake up to find this was all just a strange dream and she had missed the sights of the narrow-gauge train ride, having slept through it all.

"Do you have a place to stay? Cripple Creek ain't got much, being a mining town since gold was discovered five years ago. Y'all here for prospecting?"

Rubbing her temple, she closed her eyes for a moment. She wasn't sure what to do or, worse, how to even get back to her own era. *Think,* she admonished herself. *You're not stupid. You can figure this out.* After a moment, she looked up to see him still watching her closely. He was a very handsome man and his concern for her touched her deeply. With everything that had been happening since she came to Colorado, nothing seemed normal, nothing seemed right.

"I have a hotel room waiting for me in Colorado Springs."

Now it was his turn to appear perplexed as he scratched the back of his head, tipping his hat forward slightly as he did so. "With this robbery, it's doubtful the train will get there until tomorrow. Sheriff Grissom will want to investigate and speak to all of you before he lets you leave. But afterwards, if ya need help getting to Colorado Springs, just ask for me. I'm well known in town. Name's Bartholomew Higgins. Most 'round these parts call me Bart." He tipped his hat to her and headed over to the small group of other passengers.

"Thank you," she called after him. Sighing, she looked around again. She'd have to remember to not say anything about the future, no matter how normal it seemed to talk about it.

Chapter 6

The interview seemed to take forever. Sheriff Grissom was very thorough in talking to each of the passengers one by one. By the time she was finally released, it was late and she wasn't sure what to do.

Just before she departed the office, the sheriff pointed to a small brown case near the door displaying a cream-colored tag with the initials S.H. and the words Colorado Springs on it. "Don't forget yer belongings, Miss Hall."

Sierra was about to deny they didn't belong to her, but everyone else had departed and taken their items with them. Even stranger was the fact it had her initials, as well as her destination, on the tag. Since it was the only bag left, she thought there might be something in there to help her. Maybe it was meant for her to have since she arrived in this time so strangely. That alone didn't make any sense. Why would a bag with her initials and destination be any more logical? Picking it up, she headed outside.

She realized, belatedly, that any money or

credit cards she had were useless. With no way to buy anything, even food or a place to sleep, she was unsure how to obtain even the basics of life, unless there was something in the bag she was now holding, but she certainly didn't want to open it up while standing in the street.

Stepping off the porch, she looked around, unsure of where to go next. She'd already had her panic attack, her anxiety of not being able to return home and her nervous breakdown, thankfully all before she met with the sheriff, and the little nervousness she experienced during the interview he associated with the fact she'd almost been shot.

She jumped about ten feet when Bart appeared at her side. "Do you got someplace to stay? Money for food?"

She put her hand on her chest, feeling her heart pound rapidly, and took a couple of deep breaths to calm down. "No," she finally managed to get out.

"Come on." He turned and started to walk away. Did he think she was just going to follow him blindly? Then her stomach growled in major protest, despite her nervousness. Unlike most people who lost their appetite when they were upset, she had a habit of nervously eating. She didn't want to, had no desire to, and yet, she would find her stomach would disagree with her entirely and complain about wanting food. Sighing, she moved to follow him, albeit reluctantly.

She watched him walk away and not even glance behind to see if she was following. She didn't know what to do, but he'd saved her life and she had no finances to speak of. Sierra had always been a fighter. She didn't fear much of anything, mostly snakes, at least until she was staring at the business end of a gun thrust into her face and realizing she was no longer in Kansas, wondering where her Toto was. If she could, she'd probably hit herself upside the head for doing a poor imitation of The Wizard of Oz. Instead, Sierra ambled after him while she looked around. Cripple Creek was vastly different. Before she left, there were quaint boutiques, hotels, sweet cafes and restaurants, some with boisterous signage for their gambling parlors.

Well, the latter hadn't changed much, except for the lack of neon and colorful signs. Now there were more brothels, opium dens, lots of banks and trading for the miners who would come in town for rest, restocking supplies and obviously lots of fun ways in which to spend their newfound wealth.

During the walk, she realized she'd been lagging even more and quickened her step to catch up. She focused on Bart, his coat flapping behind him as he strutted down the almost-empty road. His shoulders were broad, his hips narrow, although from her current angle it was hard to tell from the flaring duster.

As he approached a small shack, he opened the door, holding it for her to enter first. She should be frightened to enter the home of an unknown man—who knew what he'd do to her?—but she wasn't. She was too tired and too hungry and far more concerned with figuring out how to get back to her time. The most logical idea would be to get back on the train, but she'd probably need currency for that—money she didn't have. Besides, as she reminded herself often during the saunter through town, he did save her life. Why save it only to take it now? It seemed reasonable he wouldn't harm her. At least that's what she hoped. He could expect payment for saving her life, but she could defend herself from male advances. She'd little doubt of that.

Years ago, she'd been attacked on her way to her vehicle after an evening of drinks and fun at a local bar. Although she was extremely lucky to have the bar's security staff show up before anything happened other than having her ID and credit cards stolen, she knew she'd need to protect herself better. Especially because she was scared since the robber knew where she lived, but she wasn't about to remain frightened the rest of her life. She was a fighter and determined to fend for herself any way she could. She'd signed up for self-defense classes and continued with Taekwondo when the aforementioned courses were completed.

She'd berated herself for not reacting better to the robbers on the train while she waited for the sheriff, but she also realized it was more than just a gun shoved in her face. When would anyone be prepared for traveling through time? It was too much all at once, her brain trying to understand one thing while another physical threat was occurring, but she'd calmed down since her close encounter. Handling herself against any unwanted advances Bart might make shouldn't be too much of an issue.

Slowly entering the house, Sierra let her eyes adjust while Bart set about lighting the lanterns to illuminate the darkened inside. The place was small, two rooms. The first she'd entered contained a small table, two chairs, a couple of shelves for some pantry essentials, a couple of hooks for coats or other clothing, an open doorway and a pot-bellied cast-iron stove.

Bart pulled off his duster and hat as he pointed to a chair, commanding for her to sit. "I'll fix up some vittles and you can have the bed in the other room. Tomorrow, we'll figure out what's to be done with ya."

"Thank you. I know those words are

inadequate, but they're very heartfelt."

Bart gave her an odd look. "Must be yer Eastern ways that explains yer speech and yer clothes. Or are ya thinking yer a man?"

She shook her head and tried to alter her speech pattern slightly, remembering childhood westerns, and hoped it would quell any further suspicion until she could get back to her time. "You mean my britches? They're worn when traveling. As I told the sheriff, my personal items are in my bag, but any money I had with me, as well as my ticket, was in my purse, which seems to have disappeared since the robbery."

"We'll figure everything out, but it's been a long day. Tomorrow'll come soon enough." Bart busied himself lighting the pot-belly and opening a can of beans and preparing a pot of coffee. Carrying an empty bucket, he went outside for some water. Returning, he left extra water by the stove. She didn't know what to do or how to help, and he didn't seem to want it. He reached for a container where he pulled out some hard, rectangle-shaped, tan-colored items and placed them on a plate. She was curious, unsure what the items were, but waited patiently to see if she could figure it out without asking and raising more suspicions from him.

"Your speech is interesting. Were you born here?" she asked.

"What do you mean?"

"Sometimes you say ya and yer and others you and your. I was just curious."

Bart turned to look at her, a smirk teasing his lips. "You're perceptive. Born in Pennsylvania. I moved to Kansas before I headed out here with the rest of the prospectors. I get lazy every now and again in my speech, picking up the local colloquialisms."

"I apologize if I was being personal. I tend to be like the curious cat, always wanting to know as much as possible."

"It's alright, ma'am."

"Sierra. My name is Sierra."

"Pleasure."

She found it surprising how men in this era

were different from what she expected. In general, people helped each other more than she was used to, though it made sense in order to survive the otherwise harsh environment. At least that was what they'd always been taught in school. It wasn't something she was used to—blind helpfulness and compassion. Although things have changed for the better since she was a child, it still seemed strange.

Bart brought the plates of beans and the strange items over before he turned and poured them each a cup of coffee. While his back was turned, she tested the rectangle and found it as hard as a brick. She was supposed to eat this? No wonder most people didn't have teeth left if this is what they ate on a daily basis.

She watched as he sat in the opposite chair and dropped his hard thing into his coffee and let it sit there. It was then she figured it out. It was hardtack. She'd heard about it, read about it being a staple item for soldiers, mostly, or those who weren't home much, because it would last almost as long as a cockroach and probably be as indestructible. She mimicked his movements and let her hardtack soak in the coffee. They ate silently for a bit, and though it wasn't the worst thing she'd ever eaten, it certainly would take care of the immediate hunger she was experiencing.

As they concluded their meal, Sierra started to become a bit anxious. She stood to help clean the dishes, feeling it was the least she could do for his hospitality. He indicated the bucket he'd carried in earlier was to be used to wash the dishes. Bart showed her where a knife was for the bar of soap. She quickly figured out the knife would scrape soap shavings into the water and that could be used with a rag to wash the dishes. He had split the water into another bucket. One for washing and one for rinsing. As she worked on cleaning the dishes, she watched as he took her bag into the other room that she hadn't gone into yet.

"Where will you sleep?" There wasn't much to the shack, and certainly no couch or cot in the room they were currently in for him to sleep on.

"I don't sleep much. I'll give you some alone

time and head over to the saloon. When I come back, I'm good with my bedroll on the floor."

Although he didn't say it, she assumed he implied he'd be getting one of the many female companions seemingly readily available for a fee.

She'd overheard some of the other train passengers discussing the high price of Pearl de Vere and how she appealed to the miners. "If'n she twern't so 'spensive," one of them said, "I'd be able to enjoy Mable more oft'n."

"If'n Pearl wasn't getting the $250 a night, she'd lower her prices or go outta business, but it ain't happening, 'cause she's got talented gals."

Sierra remembered this from her earlier visit to the town's museum. It was better known as a Parlor House, and a very notorious one at that. Which made her wonder about Bart's finances in order to be able to afford a parlor-house girl and yet live in a shack.

"As long as you're sure I'm not putting you out." She attempted to give him the ability to remain discreet. Again, she wondered about the women of this era, knowing how limited they were in what they were allowed to do for jobs. A working woman was not the norm or readily acceptable in 1895. Never had she thought about the women's revolution and the fights they had throughout history, from gaining a vote, to gaining freedom in the work force, equal pay and so much more. Being thrown back to an era when women were the weaker sex, she could understand the ability to want some control, and she had to admire the woman who ran a business, even if the business was the oldest occupation in the world. Pearl put herself in a man's world, insinuating herself with an area that she was allowed when so few opportunities were otherwise unavailable to women.

"If I thought you were, I'd never have brought you to my humble home."

She asked him about washing up, and he gave her an odd look, then pointed towards the bedroom.

"There's a pitcher and basin in there, as well as a chamber pot. More water is outside." He seemed anxious to go, so after making sure Sierra had no further questions or concerns, he quickly departed, leaving her alone.

Once she finished taking care of the dishes, she brought the lit kerosene lamp into the other room. Thank goodness her latent Girl Scout camping skills were remembered, making the adjustment to this rustic era a bit more tolerable.

She stood staring at the bag he'd laid on the bed for her. Sierra felt horrible, like a thief or a voyeur, as she contemplated going through someone else's belongings, and yet, it wasn't claimed, wasn't taken by anyone else. Even the dead man's belongings had been identified. The bag was too strange of a coincidence for her to not at least see what was inside. Right?

Taking a deep, resolving breath, she steeled herself and opened the valise. It was impeccably packed, every piece within folded with a crisp preciseness she'd never encountered before outside of a store. This surprised her as well, since the bag had been jostled about on the train and again while she carried it to the cabin.

Black dresses lay on top. Lifting one with great care, she was surprised it appeared as if it would fit. The next layer contained a large envelope, which she set aside for the time being. She'd come back to it later. Under the envelope were a couple of crisp white aprons. Beneath those were two simple dresses, one brown and the other gray. Not her style, but it would help her blend in better for the moment. A couple of undergarments, a hair brush and comb set, which matched an ornate hand mirror, lay on top of a white nightshirt. There was also a small towel and matching cloth used for washing. A bone handle with holes bored into it, which contained some sort of animal bristles tied onto it, made her realize it was a very crude toothbrush. It looked new, like it'd never been used before. It wasn't her preferred electric toothbrush recommended by four-out-of-five dentists, but she couldn't be picky at this point. Next to the brush was a jar of something. She wasn't sure, but upon closer examination she realized it was a type of cleaning solution to brush her teeth with.

With great and meticulous care, she replaced most of the items, keeping out the nightshirt, wash rag, towel, toothbrush, solution and envelope. Putting the case on the floor and leaving the rest at the foot of the bed, she sat on the edge of the horsehair mattress and opened the envelope.

First there was a letter of assignment addressed to House Mistress Florence DeVoe with regards to Elizabeth S. Hanley having completed training under the tutelage of Mistress Calhoun for the Harvey Girls employment at the Santa Fe Station's Harvey House Eating Establishment in Colorado Springs. Included in the envelope was a contract stipulating the terms of employment, which included a pay of $18.50 a month, as well as room and board during her one-year term at the station.

That would certainly take care of living, and even grant Sierra a bit of money in order to buy a ticket on the Midland Railroad. She hoped if she could get back on it, it would transport her back to 2018.

Reading the letter a couple more times, she

realized she would, essentially, be waiting on tables when the trains came in at the Eating House so the passengers could eat and get back on board before the train departed. Should be easy enough. She was in the service industry, both as a waitress-then-hostess during college and currently in her position as a local newspaper reporter. How difficult could being a Harvey Girl possibly be?

True, she felt a bit sick to her stomach at the thought of replacing Elizabeth, but circumstances were dire, and Sierra was desperate. Putting all the papers back into the envelope, she put it on top of the case for easy access, hoping Elizabeth S. Hanley wouldn't show up later and accuse her of identity theft. If that was even a thing in 1895.

Noticing the pitcher and wash basin, she was again grateful for her wilderness and camping skills. They were certainly coming in handy. Who would've thought?

Sierra headed outside to find the water and realized it had to be drawn from a well. Huh! That was something she'd never had to do before. It had been getting dark and she was appreciative for the kerosene lamp she'd brought with her. Setting it down, she took a cursory look at the contraption, then unhooked the bucket from its tie, lowering it until she heard a soft splash. She continued to lower the bucket a bit more to make sure it contained plenty of water, then cranked it back up. Success! Stupidly, she felt proud she was managing so well under such foreign conditions.

Pouring the water into the pitcher, she started to head back into the cabin when an eerie feeling came over her. She stopped, holding the lamp aloft as she peered around. For no particular reason, she looked up into a tree and a pair of golden eyes reflected back at her. Sierra's heart raced in fear.

Slowly, she backed up, not wishing to make any sudden moves. She prayed the mountain lion watching her wouldn't pounce and attack. Thankfully, the animal didn't move, seeming content to just watch her.

Her back hit a wall and she realized it was the cabin.

"Just stay, kitty. I won't hurt you, so don't attack me." She knew it was a ridiculous thing to do, but who thinks logically when threatened twice in one day?

They stared at each other for a few heartbeats, then she turned to set the kerosene lamp down to open the door. In her fear, she was shaking so much she was having difficulty getting the latch open. She kept expecting to feel sharp claws dig into her back and was slightly surprised when she didn't.

Finally, she managed to get the door open, grab the lamp and dash inside, slamming the door shut and leaning heavily against it, desperately trying to calm down.

She didn't know how long she'd rested against the door, but it was several minutes before she got her legs to work enough to move into the bedroom.

Should she let others know there was a dangerous animal so close to town? But without phones, she'd have to go back outside and that sure as hell wasn't going to happen!

And that's when she broke down. Everything

that occurred since she boarded the airplane for an adventure came bearing heavily down upon her and she just couldn't handle anything else. She crumpled on the bed, weeping inconsolably. She wasn't sure if she was ever going to get home, or ever going to see her friends and family again. She was just an ordinary person forced into extreme circumstances. Her phone was useless, even to get info on Wikipedia on what this era would expect of her or how to get theories of time travel in order to figure out how to return to the 21st century. And worst of all, she was about to attempt the duplicity of pretending she was someone else in order to survive the harshness of the era. She liked voting, having a say in things, having a career reporting on the news and more. Sierra knew she'd attain none of this in the 1890s. A total despair overwhelmed her, and she couldn't help the complete disintegrating collapse of emotion, which rendered her powerless to stop the flood of tears.

Chapter 7

The red-bricked, green-roofed building, trimmed with white around the multitude of windows, was extremely impressive. Bart rode alongside her as they approached the Colorado Springs AT&SF Station and Eating House. He had appeared relieved when she informed him of the position waiting for her in Colorado Springs and he willingly leant her a steed with which to travel to her destination.

Her stomach was all over the place as they approached. Would she be caught in her lie? Would someone actually *know* the real Elizabeth Hanley? Was Elizabeth already there? The saving grace was Elizabeth had a middle name that began with an S, but would someone know what the S stood for? Sierra was going to be physically ill from all her concerns. She shouldn't be doing this. It was important to find her way back on the Midland to try and go home. Hobos did it, right? Just sneak on a train and ride for free? Why couldn't she? *Because there were no freight cars on the Midland.*

It was a passenger train. It was plainly obvious to her: she'd never get on without a ticket, and she couldn't get a ticket without money. There was also the issue of her intuition and needing to be here. Maybe this was what her premonitions were telling her. If that was the case, then what mystery was she supposed to solve? Regardless, never had she missed the use of her credit cards so much. It was right up there with missing her cell phone. Who would've believed she'd go through Facebook withdrawal in keeping contact with her family and friends? Everything in this time period was so primitive compared to what she was accustomed to.

Thankfully, she was sitting on a horse that had no qualms about moving towards the impressive structure, unlike her legs, which quivered even as she sat in the saddle. She knew they wouldn't have made it on their own if she had to walk. She was scared—no, terrified. This era was so foreign to her; she could get shot for blinking the wrong way. Her sole advantage was she was a woman in a time when women weren't considered much more than soft decorations with hardly a brain that needed to be cared for. However, she was from a time when women had major positions in the world, an advantage as far as she was concerned. She'd figure this out, and if working at the Santa Fe Eating Establishment to earn the finances she'd need to buy a ticket in hopes of getting home again was what she needed to do, then so be it.

As she was so busy contemplating everything, she'd not realized how quickly they were moving, because one moment she was dreading the approach, and the next, Bart was by her side to assist her off the steed. Looking down at his hand, she mumbled to herself, "Do or die." Now was the time to face the others and see if she can get by with the lie or if she'll get caught. Lord only knew what would happen to her if she was discovered.

An older woman with brown hair and deep gray eyes came outside. She wore a black dress and white apron, similar to the ones Sierra carried with her. The woman stood on the porch, her hands clasped in front of her as she patiently waited for

Bart and Sierra to draw near. Sierra had removed the envelope from her bag and held it out as she approached the woman, wondering if this was Florence DeVoe, the House Mistress mentioned in the letter.

Upon closer inspection, Sierra realized the woman was probably younger than she first seemed. Her appearance was stern, her mouth in a tight frown and her mousy brown hair pulled back in an austere bun.

The woman took the package without a word and opened it to read the letter, peering up occasionally, her look grazing over Sierra disapprovingly. After several tense minutes, and Sierra visibly sweating, the woman spoke, disdain clearly lacing her voice. "I assume you have your uniform with you? We don't accept laxing rules here."

Sierra wasn't sure what rule would consider her lax, but she'd deal with it. More importantly, the woman accepted her as Elizabeth, and that was a huge hurtle achieved. "Yes, ma'am. They're packed in my case. I didn't feel it was congruous to wear on my travels."

"We're not pretenders here."

Sierra's heart skipped and almost stopped entirely, but she said nothing as the woman continued.

"We are ladies and we will act with the proper propriety at *all* times. That includes the proper attire of a woman, as well as the female position when riding a horse."

Sierra breathed with a sigh of relief. She was wearing the jeans from yesterday and she rode astride like a man. "Yes, ma'am. I'll endeavor to remain proper the rest of the time I'm here."

The woman gave a curt nod. "I'm House Mistress Florence DeVoe. I run the Santa Fe Eating House." In a louder voice, she called behind her, "Anna!"

Within moments, a young woman with auburn hair also pulled tightly back and attired in the black-and-white uniform appeared at Florence's side. "Yes, Mistress?"

"Please show Elizabeth to her quarters and tell her to prepare for the 12:30 train."

"Actually, I prefer Sierra."

Florence looked at the letter. "Your middle name, I presume? Very well. Anna, show Sierra to her room."

"Yes, ma'am." Anna didn't wait but expected to be followed and immediately returned inside, but Sierra hesitated and turned to Bart.

"I can't thank you enough for everything you've done for me."

Bart tipped his hat. "Pleasure, ma'am."

"Will I see you again?" She didn't know why she asked, but she had to know.

"Most likely. Although I have the shack in Cripple Creek, I actually live here in Colorado Springs." He couldn't help noticing her perplexed look and added, "You're surprised?" He grinned. "A story for the next time we meet." With another quick tip of his hat, he turned, gathered the reins of the horse she rode in on and swung up onto his own steed. Turning the horses, he headed down the road.

Sierra watched his retreating back a moment longer, then headed inside, hoping to find Anna and thereby her room.

Anna was standing by the staircase waiting for Sierra to come in. Sierra carried her bag in one hand, looking around the establishment. Mistress Florence was nowhere about. Sierra noticed a large ornate dining room off to her right as she walked down the hallway. Off to the left was the train station's waiting room lined with wooden benches. Reaching the staircase, Anna led her upstairs. Only when they reached the second floor did Anna smile. "Welcome, Sierra. We've been expecting you. Kinda been shorthanded."

"Oh? Have you been shorthanded long?"

"No. Some of our gals, though, have been breaking the contract and leaving with the gold miners or pioneers even though their year ain't up. Ain't made Mistress Florence none too happy. She really ain't all that bad, once she gets to know you, that is."

"Good to know she can be more pleasant than

what I've encountered thus far."

Anna giggled lightly. "Yep. She mellows when she knows yer serious about doing the job." She opened a door and waited for Sierra to enter.

Sierra moved past Anna into the small room, furnished with a single bed, an armoire, a chair, small writing table and a walnut washstand, which supplied the washing basin and pitcher, along with a mirror. Simple but sufficient.

"You're lucky in that you get a window. We had two of our girls depart in the past month, so the nicer rooms have become available and you get one. We need to be dressed and down in the dining room in thirty minutes. Mistress Florence likes us there a half hour before the train is due in for prep work. Do you need any help?"

"No, thank you, Anna. I'm going to wash up quickly and change in order to be ready. I'll be down in a few minutes."

Anna gave her another beaming smile and closed the door, leaving Sierra alone in the room. She pulled out the contract and took another glance at it. The rules seemed simple enough. Curfew was at 10. Considering all the work and the early mornings, she didn't think that would be a problem. No make-up or chewing of gum. Well, she didn't have makeup with her, or gum, so again, not a problem. Must work as a Harvey Girl for one year, minimum, or forfeit half the base pay. Most important, they had to remain professional, courteous and ladylike at all times. Considering she rode astride up to the establishment and dressed in men's attire by wearing pants, Sierra could understand why Mistress Florence wasn't too happy with her. She made a mental note to make sure to remain proper during the rest of her stay. It was hard enough to be in a place and time she was unfamiliar with, she didn't need to isolate herself from the other women here. She was grateful Anna seemed so pleasant when she first arrived. Anna would never understand or know how much her simple smile and welcoming presence meant to Sierra. Although Bart was kind, he seemed happier not to be around her. She wasn't sure why he helped her when he seemed averse to having her about, quickly leaving her vicinity as soon as possible.

Quickly washing the dust off her face and arms, she changed into the black dress. Tying the white apron around her waist, she quickly brushed her hair, pulling it tightly into a severe bun as she noticed both Florence and Anna had worn. One final look in the mirror before she headed downstairs into the dining area. Rapidly, she assessed the room and what might need to be done.

Florence met her and pointed to a section at the counter. Her job was to keep the coffee urn full, fill the coffee carafes for the other servers and feed those at the counter. At first it seemed a bit overwhelming. However, Anna came by her side every moment she could, beaming enthusiastically and checking on Sierra to make sure she was doing okay during the rush, quietly prompting her for things she needed to do and generally helping Sierra feel more at ease during the onslaught of the unfamiliar work.

When the train blew its whistle, the passengers

hastily departed. The room became eerily quiet. At least for all of three minutes. Anna came towards Sierra, bringing another young woman with her blond hair pulled up in a bun.

"Sierra? This is Louise. She is going to help you deal with the dishes and prepping the salads before the next train arrives in two hours. Louise, be gentle. Remember your first day. If you need anything, just holler." Anna was gone before either woman could reply.

Louise chuckled, shaking her head while she played with a medallion around her neck. "That's Anna for you. A whirling dervish. Come on. Have you actually seen the kitchen yet? The first time I saw it, I was flabbergasted. It's the most efficient and modern kitchen in the world, I think."

"That's a pretty necklace, and unusual."

Louise stopped fidgeting, tucking it back under her dress collar. "It's actually a medal my father was given for his service in the War. After he passed, I had a necklace made, so I could always have a piece of him near my heart."

"That's a great idea. You must've been proud of him."

"I am. I was. He was always one for adventure, and I like having a part of him with me."

Sierra followed her into the kitchen. It really was rather impressive, even to her. The expanse was immense. There were several long tables, sinks, stoves more modern than she expected and large ice boxes. She had learned that Fred Harvey had a deal with the railroad to have a car of ice and fresh food delivered a couple of times daily so as to have the best food on hand for their customers. Due to the time limits, the customers would purchase their meal tickets on the train, then place the tickets on the table after they were seated. Meals were then served immediately, as the vouchers were picked up for accounting's inventory.

When they entered the kitchen, the cooks were already starting to prep more food. Louise and Sierra waved a general hello to the others before heading to the sink to start on the massive pile of dishes, pots and pans. As Sierra washed, she couldn't help but take several glances around. Despite the amount of preparation, the dirty dishes and the cooking being done, she was amazed with how clean the room was. The chefs were quiet as they got the food ready, moving like a well-oiled machine in perfect harmony. She'd heard how Harvey had hired women to work and run the Eating Houses along the AT&KC line, but she had no idea until now how they changed the West. Good, healthy, fresh food daily; clean, respectable places in areas that were just opening to new settlers and explorers. It wasn't something she readily considered when learning about this era in school. She knew the settlers who came to the West had to build everything from primitive aspects, but unless one experiences it first hand, one can't explain how major the differences were. Of course, it was vastly different than the time she'd come from or the modern conveniences taken for granted.

By the end of the day, she couldn't remember being so exhausted, but she'd finally settled into a routine that flowed along with everyone else. The male cooks headed elsewhere while the women headed up to their quarters. The next train would be through Colorado Springs at 6:30am, so they would have to be up and ready for work by 5.

Sierra couldn't remember a time where her body ached as much as it did, and she gave a silent kudos to the various women that did this on a daily basis and still had energy to spare. One woman, named Sophie, pulled out a guitar and started to play in the common area while another, named Alice, joined her on the piano. Sierra sat and listened for a while, having casual conversations with Louise and Anna. She'd learned Sophie's guitar was the one major thing she refused to leave behind. It was an heirloom she loved, and it meant the world to her. Sophie would rather starve than have anything happen to her guitar.

Finding her eyes growing extremely heavy, Sierra decided to head to bed when Florence came in and scowled at her.

"There's a Mr. Bartholomew Higgins here to see you. Please be aware curfew is in fifteen minutes." Sternly, she turned and left.

Somehow, Sierra didn't think she'd ever get on the woman's good side, but even more surprising was Bart being there to see her. She thought she'd never see him again, especially since he appeared glad to be rid of her earlier today. Had she forgotten something? Did he need her for some reason? She couldn't fathom why he was there. Heading downstairs, she found him waiting for her in the train station lobby. There were a couple of people milling about, but Bart was definitely easy to spot. Tall and distinguished looking, the familiar duster made him stand out. His back was to her as she approached him. She cleared her throat slightly. "Bart?"

He turned to gaze down at her, a smile touching his lips. He was impeccably dressed; she almost didn't recognize him. A black suit, with his shirt buttoned up to the collar. When he turned, he pulled his hat off his head and held out a single daisy. "I wanted to check up on you. How was your first day?"

She grinned as she took the daisy. "Such a sweet gesture. Thank you. My day was hectic, but good."

"Do you think you'll be staying?"

"My contract is for a year." She kept it general, not wanting to admit she wanted to leave as soon as she could.

"I'd like to ask you to accompany me to dinner whichever night you're not working."

She brought the daisy up to her nose, almost hiding behind it. She shouldn't even consider starting something with anyone here in a time that wasn't her own, yet she found herself wanting nothing more than to be with Bart. "Okay. Although, I'm unsure which day I'll be off just yet. I'm still getting settled into the routine of things."

"I'll check back later when you've a chance to get more acquainted being here and find out your schedule." He put his hat back on, tipping it slightly before he took his leave.

Sierra stood there, watching him. He turned around once, as if to see if she were still watching, but he didn't look at the waiting room of the station. Instead he scanned the rooms above where the girls were staying before he looked at her standing right where he'd left her. Tipping his hat, he disappeared around the corner. He must've thought she headed upstairs before he saw her.

She brought the flower up to her nose again as she turned and headed to bed.

Chapter 8

Over the past two weeks, Sierra had settled into a routine of getting up at 5am, being downstairs by 5:30 and prepping for the arrival of the trains six days a week. The seventh day, Bart came and took her to dinner and a pleasant walk about town. Her body was getting used to the long working hours and the strain, but she had to admit, she looked forward to her day off and spending it with Bart.

Smoothing over one of the plain dresses she had, she took a last look in the mirror. It certainly wasn't her style, but beggars couldn't be choosers. Thank goodness, because she would *never* have chosen something like this on her own. Sierra started to head downstairs when a commotion in the common room caught her attention. Concerned, she headed over. Alice was weeping in the corner. Florence paced angrily. Anna was just staring out the window. A couple of the other girls were just sitting and watching the others or staring at their feet.

"What's going on?" Sierra asked, hoping

someone would answer that wasn't Florence.

Florence turned on her. "Sophie has broken her contract and left. That makes the fourth one in just as many months. Seems each time we get a new girl, one decides it's time to leave and marry one of the yokels." Florence stormed past her but stopped alongside of Sierra in the doorway. "This means we all have to work harder to make up her workload. I suggest you don't stay out too late. You're going to need the extra rest." Florence moved past her and into her office at the end of the hall.

Sierra moved into the common room and over to stand next to Anna, who hadn't moved. "Is this normal? Girls just leaving?"

Anna sighed and turned to face her, shrugging her shoulders. "For this house, it seems to be. Lately, Mistress DeVoe has had to replace almost a girl a month. The thing is, we don't really even see them with a particular gentleman caller before they just up and disappear."

"Do they leave a note saying where they've gone? Or who they're with? Do they pack up their personal belongings?" Sierra noticed Sophie's guitar was sitting against the wall by the piano. She thought it odd that Sophie would leave behind such a treasured artifact. During their conversation just a couple weeks ago, Sophie had told her the guitar had belonged to her mother's family and had been passed down to her. She hadn't known how to play, so she taught herself. Playing the guitar made her feel closer to her mother. She made a point of carrying it with her coming out West; why would she forsake it now?

Anna shook her head. "No. They wouldn't want to take these uniforms of ours, but even their meager belongings get left behind sometimes. I think if they packed, it would be more noticeable, and they wouldn't be able to sneak off as easily. Although, it does seem strange to just sneak away when we wouldn't stop her from packing and departing appropriately. Heck, we'd even throw her a party to help her celebrate the beginning of a new life. We might've asked she stay long enough for us to get a replacement, but we wouldn't have stopped her from leaving." She patted Sierra's hand. "Many women come out here looking for a husband and don't have the money to get here, so they apply with the Harvey Houses. It's not unheard of. It's just frustrating because we always seem to be shorthanded. We've managed before; we'll continue to do so. Go enjoy your dinner with Mr. Higgins. As Mistress DeVoe stated, I'd recommend that you don't have a late evening. It's going to be exceptionally hectic without Sophie here."

"I understand. I won't be long. Just a light dinner and I'll be back."

"Sierra?"

"Yes?"

"Sophie was about your size. She has a couple of dresses that are a bit nicer for dinner dates. I'm sure the extra uniforms will come in handy as well. You seem to be lacking with both compared to the other girls here."

"That's very kind of you. Yes. That would be very helpful. I know my wardrobe is a bit lacking. Thank you. I'll help you when I get back?"

"No. I was going to pack up her things anyway. I'll just leave what I think you might like in your room. If she didn't take it with her, I doubt she'll come back for it. At least it'll go to good use and won't be wasted. Have a nice dinner."

"Nothing wasted. Thank you, Anna. Good evening, ladies." Sierra headed out of the room and down the stairs to find Bart waiting for her.

She couldn't help but admire him. He was the perfect-looking traditional cowboy. She'd learned he was well-to-do, having found a good-sized gold vein shortly after he first arrived four years ago. Not that it mattered to her, and she was sure he sensed that about her. She enjoyed his company; who wouldn't with his classic good looks and kind personality?

"Sorry if I kept you waiting long. We had a bit of a situation." Sierra hastened towards him.

He tipped his hat and frowned slightly as she approached. "Situation? What happened?" He held a single daisy out to her and, after she took it, he crooked his arm for her to take.

She breathed in the daisy before taking his arm. "Thank you for the flower. It's amazing how they seem to last for about a week. They die just as I am about to get another one from you. Do you plan it that way?" she teased him lightly.

He didn't seem quite sure what to make of her sense of humor. "Just works out that way. Daisies are a hardy flower. They remind me of you. Strong, beautiful and enduring."

"Enduring? I don't think I've ever heard a person described that way."

"I just mean you came out here against all odds, faced a gunman and still remain here in Colorado instead of running back to your home."

"When you explain it like that, enduring seems the correct word." She giggled lightly as they walked down the street to one of the local saloons for dinner.

"You were going to explain what situation occurred in the house?" he asked again after he pushed in her chair, then sat across from her.

"Oh. One of the girls, named Sophie, departed,

leaving us shorthanded."

"Is that unusual?"

"No. I guess not. I'm told she's the fourth one in as many months. Mistress DeVoe isn't happy about having to find another girl so quickly. I just find it strange that Sophie left without a word to anyone, even about whom she'd been seeing. She also left without taking anything with her, which I find highly peculiar."

"Why? Mostly likely she probably met up with a newly wealthy miner who discovered gold in the area and wooed her to depart with him, promising to take care of her."

"Maybe. That's what the others believe also. However, I could see that being true with leaving behind her clothes, but she had a guitar that she told me belonged to her mother. It was a family heirloom. I just find it strange she wouldn't at least take that with her, especially since she told me she'd never leave it behind."

"She was probably just in a hurry and didn't think about it. What would you like to drink?"

She knew from experience the water was not the best choice, so she quickly developed a liking to coffee and tea. Most saloons didn't appreciate serving such items, but this particular one served more than just hard liquors and loose women. "Tea, please."

He stood, and she couldn't help but notice how quickly he changed the subject from Sophie's guitar to leave the table. Her investigative suspicions clicked into overdrive, warranted or not. He returned a few moments later with a beer in hand. "They'll bring your tea with the food. I told them to serve whatever was the freshest. I hate paying for that rancid stuff they try and feed the others who can't pay for a better product. I refuse to eat poor fare and I wouldn't expect you to either."

"Thank you. I'm sure it'll be fine."

"Does anyone know who Sophie was seeing?"

"No. As I said, it was all a surprise to the women in the house. No one knew she was entertaining any man. She just disappeared without any warning."

"What about the others? You said this was the fourth one leaving in as many months. Did the others depart as secretively?"

"I'm not sure. I only know there were three others before Sophie, but they were gone before I arrived, so I know nothing about them."

"Probably just as well. Most likely nothing more than harlots to leave with the first male who flashed a shiny object at them, wooing them with promises of a life of leisure."

She gave him a strange look. His words were so harsh, she almost didn't recognize the voice of the man who spoke them. "I'd hate to think that's true. I prefer to think of them as being in love so much, nothing would keep them apart any longer and she had to leave with him."

"Rather a romantic notion for this hardened place."

"Don't you think women leaving the comforts of Eastern civilization to be a romantic notion? Or men, for that matter? To make their way out to this area of Natives, wildlife and other unknown dangers have a romantic appeal?"

"They could just be escaping from Victorian boredom and high society pressures."

"That may be, but I believe it still falls under the idea of romantic notions." Sierra looked up as a waiter brought her tea and three platters laden with food to their table. He also set down a couple of dishes and some utensils, as well as a cloth napkin for each.

Bart changed the subject and they discussed lighter themes while they dined. Once completed, Bart escorted Sierra back to the Eating House, lightly kissing her hand goodnight.

Chapter 9

Returning to her room, she was surprised at how still and quiet the floor was. She knew many were going to bed early due to the extra work they were preparing for as a result of Sophie's untimely departure. Entering her private chamber, Sierra was surprised at the amount of clothes delivered to her from Anna after packing Sophie's things. She expected a few uniforms and maybe an additional couple of everyday dresses, but there were several more than she anticipated. There were five other uniforms, which meant Sierra didn't have to worry about not having clean ones for work. There were also eight dresses. Two were flowery, not really her style. The two she liked the most were a little dressier than the rest. One was a solid green and the other was a solid blue. The rest were more somber in appearance, one gray, one brown, one cream, and one a mustard yellow. She quickly tried all of them on to make sure they fit okay and was excited when the blue looked the best. With its light blue silky material over the skirt and a high empire waist, it quickly became her favorite. She was grateful for having something different to wear for Bart than the same dull dresses she'd found in the suitcase. On top of the dresses were two hats and a sun bonnet.

She couldn't help but let her reporter instincts shine through, curious about Sophie and the three others who just left. If not for the guitar, Sierra probably wouldn't have given it another thought. She'd be sure to ask more questions starting in the morning. Putting the clothes away, she hurried through her nightly ministrations before she climbed into bed. As tired as she was, however, she couldn't sleep. Her mind was racing about why Sophie left so quickly and who might have the answers to the questions she knew she was going to be asking. She had hoped talking to Bart about it would've settled her mind, but it didn't. It may have been her imagination, but there were times when he seemed extremely curious and others when he quickly changed the subject with regards to Sophie. She wondered if he knew the young guitarist or if he was just being polite in listening to Sierra's concerns. Either way, she had a multitude of questions to ask, hoping to get to the bottom of not only Sophie's disappearance but also the other three.

Flipping around, she punched the thin pillow, trying to reshape it to being comfortable before she tried to fall asleep. Why was it when one wanted to sleep, they were wide awake and when one wanted to be awake, they couldn't keep their eyes open?

Somehow, she must've dozed, for the next thing she knew the sun was starting to rise and Florence was knocking on all the doors to make sure everyone was up. Rubbing her face, Sierra got up and poured water in the wash basin, cleaning up as best she could before she headed downstairs and to the kitchen to get new directions from Florence on what she needed to do to help cover a portion of Sophie's duties. For the first time since she'd arrived, she'd wait on eight tables, as well as her original duties, which were already significant. Immediately, she wished she'd had the additional sleep she knew she was going to need before the end of the day.

Being busy prepping for the first train would've been an understatement. Soon, the locomotive pulled in and Sierra was busy filling the coffee pots for service. As she mingled about the tables, gathering food vouchers and pouring coffee, she couldn't help overhearing some of the conversations. Mostly she ignored them, focusing on her work and not screwing up the orders, but one table's discussion caught her attention.

"I heard another one just up and left. That's why they're so shorthanded," a young, thin man told his companions. It was a table of four men, the other three were older.

One had a grey beard with big bushy eyebrows hiding his squinty brown eyes. "I remember her. The one who took leave. She was the blonde mousy one with those penetrating green eyes and eerie quietness. Don't know who would want her so desperately to have her leave before her contract was up. That was the good thing about the men that were here before Harvey started hiring all his girls."

The third was heavyset, his oily brown hair pulled back in a ponytail. He had a horseshoe mustache, which was what she learned they called it. In her time, it was known as a trucker's mustache. "The men were rude and unpleasant to deal with. They make good cooks, but they don't appeal as servers. Women are better for that position."

"And better to gaze upon, eh, John?" The fourth gave Sierra a wink as she leaned in to pour his coffee. She was sure he would've slapped her ass if not for the fact they'd been warned the Harvey Girls were proper women and would be treated with respect. As such, she was also aware many outside the confines of the Eating Houses and train stations thought the girls as immoral, at best, or worse, prostitutes.

The heavyset nodded. "Definitely more enticing than men. I'm rather glad they are coming out west to offer the miners some pleasant distractions. That said, I don't appreciate them absconding with them. Listening to Mr. Harvey rant about his employees disappearing does not make for pleasant conversations. I should be expecting a post from him in a week or two reminding me how remiss I am in not controlling the miners better."

"Do you know which one might have the young woman?" The young one sipped his coffee before dabbing his mouth with the napkin.

The heavyset one shook his head. "That's just it. I can't figure it out. I'm sure I would've noticed if any men were missing before we left the camps this morning. I'll have to check with the foreman when we get back next week."

Sierra found their conversation informative, but time was short and she needed to finish her service before the train blew its whistle. She moved out of earshot, but the men's conversation replayed itself in her mind every moment she had a chance to think.

Taking some of the dirty dishes away, she was surprised to see Bart come in and sit at the lunch counter. The dining room was full and, despite the lack of Sophie's presence, the girls were still able to meet the requirement of serving a four-course meal in the thirty minutes allotted for it. She knew some of the locals would come in to sit at the counter because the food was prepared well, and it was fresh. Even though towns with Harvey Eating Houses fared better in getting fresh food, other restaurants and saloons just couldn't keep up with Harvey quality. Basically, Fred Harvey made contracts to get the food brought in fresh for him, and every other business obtained whatever was left over.

She smiled and waved at Bart, but he didn't seem to see her. He was focused instead on Louise, who was currently handling the counter.

That bothered her, and she berated herself for caring. She wanted to get back to her own time—an era when he was dead and dust. What was she hoping for? To have him love her? To have her in his life? Did she think this was why she needed to come to Colorado—so she could travel back in time just to be with him?

She thought of those dreams that propelled her

to Colorado and she realized the overwhelming sense of her destiny lying here was all that still remained of her urgency to come. A feeling of needing to accomplish something important still resided within her. The only thing she knew for sure was this wasn't it. At least, it didn't feel like it. No, her premonitions were normally about others, not things for herself. Plus, Sophie was on her mind a good deal of the day. That seemed more likely to be the cause of her current presence in 1895. Sierra was here to find, and maybe even help, Sophie. This was where the strongest impressions came from.

True, she'd not gotten any intuition from Sophie before she left, but since she's been gone, Sierra just knew it wasn't of the woman's own volition. Sierra felt it in the deepest recesses of her soul. So lost in her thoughts, she'd almost forgotten Bart was there until she turned around to see him. Her work was mechanical, cleaning the plates, pouring coffee, checking on the clients to make sure everything was okay while her mind was mostly on Sophie with occasional drifts to Bart.

However, Bart was busy talking with Louise, who was giggling at their conversation. Were they flirting? *Ugh!* Why should she care? She turned back to her customers, putting Bart out of her mind, and Sophie too.

Florence checked on her just before the train whistle blew. It was almost comical the way everyone stood and dashed back to the train to re-board before the second whistle. The train was moving once the second whistle sounded and if they weren't on it, they'd be out of luck.

Sierra stood against the table to remain out of the way so the passengers could move past her without interference. Once they'd cleared out, she turned towards the counter and found Bart had departed. A wave of disappointment coursed through her.

She felt a light touch on her shoulder and turned around. Bart's face was shadowed by his wide-brimmed black hat as he gazed down at her. "Greetings."

"Hello, Mr. Higgins. I'm surprised to see you

here." She was conflicted, both excited to see him and upset remembering his flirtatious behavior with Louise. Unfortunately, the latter currently prevailed, even as she tried for hospitable civility.

"I had a desire for a good meal and some delightful company."

"I noticed you seemed to be enjoying your...lunch." Her tone was far snider than she intended, with a strong emphasis on the final word, but she couldn't seem to help herself. Why spend time with her and take her to dinner, then flirt with someone else? She didn't need a player in her life, even if she wasn't going to spend it here. Just the idea made her furious. She'd been played once before. Well, twice really. She just didn't ever want to be in that situation again. No male or female would ever get close enough to betray her. True, she was relying more on those here, Anna, Alice and yes, even Bart, but watching him and Louise reminded her to protect her heart and be more cautious. Honestly, she blamed the disorientation of time travel for her weakness. She'd never thought it was possible to go through time as easily as walking through a door. It felt like she was living an H.G. Wells novel, it was too fanciful to be reality.

She caught a brief look of disgust, or maybe hurt in his eyes at her caustic remark. She was immediately regretful of her tone, knowing it stemmed from her previous betrayals. Maybe, one day, she'd tell someone about them, but now was not the time. "I'm sorry. You didn't deserve that."

For a moment, he had the look of someone caught with their hand in a cookie jar, but that guilty expression disappeared as quickly as it came, and she wasn't sure if she'd imagined it or not.

He spun on his heel without a word. She grabbed his arm. "I'm sorry. That was truly uncalled for. You really didn't deserve that," she repeated.

Bart took a step closer to her, his jaw working. After several disquieting moments, he growled low. "If you were a man who took that tone with me, I'd've shot you dead where you stand."

She dropped her hand. She'd apologized, but

she'd be damned if she begged for forgiveness, especially when he was so blatant about flirting in front of her. Something about that tense moment scared her and she wasn't quite sure why. Feeling like prey being sized up by an apex predator, she was greatly unnerved. She watched his retreating back, then turned to finish clearing the table. Not sure if she'd ever see him again, she spent the time resetting the tables and making more coffee, reminding herself of why she shouldn't have let him get as close as she had.

Chapter 10

She worked herself up to being angry and annoyed. Since Bart left, she gave the cold shoulder to Louise, which, of course, just made the day exceptionally long despite the busyness. The iciness continued for several days, and Sierra was in no hurry to change the situation as she realized she shouldn't get close to any of them. This wasn't her place. These people were long dead before she was even a gleam in her mother's eye.

After the last train of the day pulled out of the station, they prepared the tables for the morning. Sierra headed directly to her room as she had the previous few nights, avoiding everyone, as her mood was extremely dour and she'd no desire to be around anyone in her frame of mind or pretend to be sociable.

When she woke up the following morning, there were some undertones and commotion in the house. She was still in a fairly crappy mood, more determined to figure out how to get away from here and return home, that she didn't pay much attention to the whispers nor even the side glances cast surreptitiously her way.

Sierra focused on her work until mid-afternoon. The train left, and it was her first chance to relax and get a bite to eat. Anna sat next to her, though she picked at her sandwich. Sierra didn't think it possible for Anna to be so quiet. Putting her own feelings aside, as well as her meal, Sierra turned to Anna to give her full attention. "Okay. What's going on?"

Anna stopped pretending to eat, giving her head a slight shake. "I just can't believe it! How could she? How could she leave like that? Especially when she knew how shorthanded we already were? I just don't understand it." She pierced Sierra with a stare. "Some think it's because of you."

Sierra was truly perplexed. "Me? What did I do? Who is she? Sophie? That's week-old news. I don't understand what you're talking about."

"Haven't you noticed? Haven't you heard the news?" Anna realized Sierra had no clue what had happened, so she continued. "Louise departed the house last night."

"Departed? Why? Because I was upset with her? How? Did she leave with…Bart…I mean, Mr. Higgins?"

Anna gave a soft snort and shook her head. "No. Not because of you, and I don't think with Mr. Higgins, either. I saw him earlier this morning in the train station and he didn't have Louise with him."

"What was he doing here then?"

She shrugged her shoulders. "Business, most likely. He was meeting a train and I saw him head off with a man in a suit. He does that a couple of times a month. Meets a man from the train for business of some sort or other. I can't imagine he was the one who left with Louise today if he had a meeting planned."

"That does seem logical. Louise hadn't talked about anyone else, though, that I'm aware of."

"She didn't talk about Mr. Higgins, either. Why did you think she left with him anyways?"

"I saw the two of them flirting over lunch a few days ago."

"Is that why you thought she left because of you?"

"She knew I was upset. I gave her the cold shoulder after that and I know she saw Mr. Higgins and I have a disagreement immediately after his meal. I've not spoken to either of them since, but I did see them together again the following day."

"I'm sure whatever it was about, you misinterpreted it. Mr. Higgins seems smitten with you and anything he was enjoying the other day with Louise was strictly platonic, I'm sure. Which is why Louise leaving is so surprising. She didn't talk about anyone either. There've been no mention of any gentleman callers. Knowing how shorthanded we are, I can't believe she'd leave us without warning. It doesn't make sense to me."

"What does Mistress DeVoe say? Was there a note? Did she speak with Louise before she departed? Did she take her things?"

"Her room was empty of all its belongings. I'm

told Mistress DeVoe found a note under her door when she got up this morning saying she was breaking her contract and leaving early. I'm just confounded by all of it. Why did they leave like they did? Where did they go? Why did Sophie leave all her belongings behind and yet Louise took all of hers?"

Sierra patted Anna's hand. "I know. I'm as confused as you. We'll figure it out. It's just going to take some time."

Anna leaned over and gave her a quick hug. "Will you disappear on us too? I'd hate to have you leave as well. I feel like I'm losing all my friends."

"I promise I won't leave without proper goodbyes." But Sierra got to thinking how she mysteriously turned up in 1895. Could Sophie and Louise have been transported through time as well? Although, that wouldn't explain how Louise packed up all her belongings and took them with her. Again, Sierra's reporter instincts kicked into overdrive, her mind darting around with dozens of questions about Louise leaving and the note she'd left behind. Was there more information than what DeVoe was telling them?

"Train in 20 minutes," Florence called out.

Scooping up their unfinished lunches, Sierra headed into the kitchen to drop them off and get ready for the next group of customers about to arrive.

She prepared the dishes of food to be brought out for service and stopped short when she reached one of her tables. Bart was there with a man she didn't know or recognize. Anna had been correct. If he'd been the one Louise had taken off with, he wouldn't be here.

"Sierra. This is Mr. Wainwright. He's a business client. I thought it best to take him to the most delicious fare around for lunch. May I have a moment of your time?"

"Hello, Mr. Wainwright. Pleasure to make your acquaintance. I'm currently busy, Mr. Higgins. Train lunch crowd, you know. Would you like coffee or tea?"

"Coffee, ma'am." Wainwright's voice was

deep, which belied his nerdy, thin appearance. She had a brief flash of the Don Knotts look-a-like and she shivered. She forced a smile and turned to Bart.

"I meant, may I see you for a moment once the train crowd departs. I'd like to speak to you privately. And yes, coffee would be fine."

"I'm sure I can accommodate your request after service. I'll attend to your beverages and food. Excuse me." Sierra went to get the other orders for her set of tables. When she first arrived, she had to caution herself to speak properly for this era. It was a bit getting used to to not to use modern colloquialisms, but now her speech seemed almost natural and she was grateful she didn't have to constantly think about her words before speaking.

Service was soon completed, the train whistle sounding off and the hustling crowd quickly departing the dining room for the train. Starting to clean up, she turned to find Bart at her elbow. "May I have that word with you now?" he asked quietly.

She looked around. There was still so much to do, but just as she was about to say not yet,

Florence was beside her. "Take a break. I'll clean up your area."

Blinking in surprise, she wasn't sure what to say. For Florence to tell her to go so she could speak with Bart wasn't something she was expecting, and she had to wonder if Bart had spoken to Florence to enlist her aid in doing so.

Bart waved his arm for Sierra to precede him, which she did after she put down the few bowls and dishes she had previously gathered. Stepping outside, she felt the cool breeze instantly. Taking a deep breath, she waited for him to move beside her and begin speaking. Truthfully, she knew she was pushing the cold shoulder and she should just let his flirting go, especially with Louise absent, but she found it difficult to do.

"I'm sorry. I hope you'll forgive me."

She turned to face him. "Forgive you for what?" She needed to know he was aware of what she felt he had done.

"The other day. In retrospect, I understand how you'd think I was being flirtatious, which was a disservice to you."

"You know she's gone, right?"

"Mrs. DeVoe informed me of such when I asked for her assistance in being able to talk to you. I admit, I was a bit taken aback."

"Some think she went with you."

"You're still upset. I can hear it in your voice. Sierra, I really don't care if Louise is still here or not. If she found someone who makes her happy, then I'm very glad, but her happiness or lack thereof is not my concern. You are."

Sierra visibly deflated, her anger evaporating. She didn't want to remain annoyed or upset any longer, having already carried it for days. She was just trying to get through each day waiting for a payment so she could buy a ticket on the Midland, although she'd have to say goodbye to some who had become friends. Worse, she'd be leaving the ladies here at the Santa Fe Eating House shorthanded again. She knew firsthand how difficult it was to get everyone served and back on the train in the small amount of time they were allotted. It was important to have a fully staffed establishment in order to complete their duties in a timely fashion and not be super exhausted in the process. However, his last statement had softened her resolve. Despite the occasional impression something was off about him, though she couldn't put her finger on what, she liked him. He might be worth staying in 1895 for. He was handsome, strong, caring, and he could be loving towards her. Would she really miss her life in the 21st century? Would anyone really miss her? This was a whole new world for her, one which seemed simple, albeit, rustic and unhurried. She liked the slow pace of life here; even busy as she was serving the passengers of the train, life wasn't harried or rushed. Instead it was serene and quiet. Living with him wouldn't be half bad.

"Why?"

"Why what? Why have I appointed you as my concern?"

"Yes. And if that's really true, then why were you so into Louise a few days ago?"

"Into? I'd never heard it put that way, but to

answer your first question, I saved your life on the Midland and I feel as if it's a never-ending job. Second, Louise and I were just talking. Nothing more. I had hoped you were working the counter, as I know that's where you'd been assigned since you arrived, but with Sophie's departure, I was unaware of your reassignment. Despite my disappointment, Louise was kind enough to keep me company during her dutiful service."

That riled Sierra up again. "You consider me your never-ending job? I don't need your attention because you feel obligated. I can take care of myself. The train incident and the difficulty in getting to Colorado Springs was unfortunate, but not a cry for your continued assistance. When I get my first paycheck, I can reimburse you for your inconvenience."

"You've misinterpreted. I didn't mean it as you stated. I don't need you to reimburse me for anything. I only meant it was fortuitous I was able to assist you and I'd like to continue having the opportunity to do so." He grabbed her arm to pull her closer. "I want to continue to take care of you."

"Bart." She didn't know what to say. How could she tell him that, even though she found him extremely handsome and kind, she didn't want to hurt him when she left.

"I know, Sierra. You're not ready. You're still trying to get your bearings here and you have a signed contract that you have to fulfill. In the meantime, won't you let me be by your side? Let me continue to spend time with you? Getting to know you? Trust me, Sierra, I only wish to be your beau."

"Trust. That's a strong word."

Bart lifted her hand to his heart. "Trust can be easily given, though. It only takes faith in believing what's right in front of you."

She wanted to. She wanted to tell him everything. Not so much because she was in love with him, but because she needed to confide in someone she could gamble on. Placing confidence in someone was hard to do, especially for Sierra. "I don't trust people easily."

"You've been hurt. I can tell. Is that why you came out West? To escape from whoever hurt you? To find a safer place where you can start your life again?"

"Not exactly, but it might be an underlying cause."

"Will you tell me? Will you let me help you begin a new adventure? Become part of my journey through this life?"

Sierra looked around and pointed to a tree. "May we sit down?" This was normally her break time and getting off her feet was something she always looked forward to. She also needed a moment before she could answer without giving away she didn't belong in this era. Again, his words made her wonder if staying behind with him wouldn't be so bad. When he gazed upon her with those steel grey eyes of his, she had to admit her insides melted like warm butter.

"Of course." Bart led her to the tree. He took off his coat and laid it on the ground for her to sit upon before joining her.

"As you suspected, I was hurt. To be truthful, I've given you more faith than anyone else in the past few years."

"How did he hurt you? What did he do to betray you?"

"There were two actually. The first was a woman. My best friend, or so I thought. We grew up together. Attended school together. She got married to an abusive husband and needed a place to regroup while she got back on her feet. She had two young sons, and I felt I needed to help her however I could. I let her come live with me to get away from her husband. When she finally left, I realized she had stolen from me. Took my savings and charged massive bills to accounts in my name that she opened, of which I was unaware. It took years to clear up the mess she left me with. I trusted her. Like I said, we were as close as if we were sisters and then she did that to me. It cut like a knife and I found it difficult to believe in anyone after that." Truth was, Tracy had used their friendship to open credit cards in Sierra's name. Charged up to

$75,000 and ruined her credit. However, they didn't have credit cards yet, so telling Bart about what awful things Tracy really did seemed ridiculous. "Somehow, I did though. I figured I had to let it go. I cleared up everything she'd done to me, and it was time to move on with my life. That's when he came into it. He'd been a friend too. We confided with each other, told each other almost everything. So, when he used my past as a way to increase his own popularity, it was very hurtful. Things I told him in confidence he had no issue telling others and hurting me in the process." Zane put her pictures on Facebook, maligned her name, taunted her behind her back and it took time to figure everything out. He had stopped being kind to her, ignoring her, didn't even want to touch her. She blamed herself, though she wasn't sure what she'd done to lose his love. Regardless, she didn't deserve the shoddy treatment he gave her. When she finally confronted him after discovering all the things he wrote about her on social media, his attacks increased instead of subsided. He used everything he knew against her.

Again, Bart would know nothing of social media or Facebook or how such things could make life unbearable.

Yes, she needed a vacation desperately just to get away from the horrors of her so-called life. How could she give in to trust again and so easily? Yet, here she was laying almost everything out to a man she'd only met a few weeks ago. A man she was angry with just minutes ago. True, she was infatuated with him, had a slight crush on him like some teenager getting all giddy and nervous at the thought of being with him. Sierra didn't want to be a person who believed the worst in people. She knew letting people close and not pushing them away would be rewarding, and maybe she could find a bit of happiness while she was stuck here. She took a chance and told him the truth. Well, as much as she could. She knew Bart couldn't betray her here like those others had in her past.

"I'm sorry that happened to you. I can see why you're nervous to trust in people when those you relied on betrayed you. Personally, I have always detested gossips. They rarely have any idea of how spreading stories of others affects those around them. But, thieves are worse, taking what you have worked hard for and achieved. I'm not a gossip and I don't steal. Thank you for telling me."

Immediately she felt awkward and self-conscious. They sat quietly for a moment before Sierra stood up. "I should get back to work."

Bart stood and grabbed her hand before she could escape. "I apologize if my behavior the other day upset you. I'd like to make it up to you. I believe you are off this evening after the last train at 6:10? May I have the pleasure of your company for dinner?"

Hesitating slightly, she smiled. "That'd be wonderful. Thank you."

"I'll be here at eight for you."

"I'll see you then." Quickly, she dashed back to the Eating House.

Chapter 11

Anna knocked on Sierra's door before she peeked in. Stepping in quickly, she shut the door behind her. "I heard you're going to dinner with Mr. Higgins." It was a statement, not a question.

Sierra stepped into the blue dress, pulling it up to slip her arms into the sleeves before smoothing it out. She was grateful the women in the West didn't wear petticoats or corsets. She didn't think she'd manage to dress herself if they did. "Yes. He asked me earlier today." She looked over at her friend who seemed a bit agitated. "Is everything alright?"

Sitting on the edge of the bed, Anna wrung her hands before clasping them tightly in her lap. "I don't know. Maybe it's Sophie and Louise both departing the premises the way they did. Maybe it's the feeling we aren't being told everything by Mistress DeVoe. Maybe it's lack of sleep and working so hard lately. Or maybe I'm just being foolish."

Sierra had picked up her brush to run it through her hair while Anna spoke, but now she put it down and moved over to her, taking her hands to hold between her own. "Granted, I've not known you a long time, but I can't believe you're distressed over nothing. Talk to me."

Anna sighed, looking down at their clasped hands. "I'm probably just being silly. I just feel like DeVoe isn't telling us everything about Sophie and Louise. I can't believe the two of them would just up and leave without any word to any of us here. And Sophie leaving her things behind? It doesn't make sense. Not to me, at least."

"It doesn't to me either. I don't know DeVoe well enough to know if she is hiding anything or not. But..." Sierra stopped as she started thinking. Okay, she has watched way too many Charlie Chan and Sherlock Holmes movies, which had been her inspiration to become a reporter. Them and Lois Lane.

Anna looked up from her hands, tilting her head slightly. "But what?"

"But, maybe we should look around her office. See if we find anything. If you can keep her occupied for a bit, I can check it out. It should be done in a day or two. Work things out and all."

"That's a wonderful idea. I can figure out a reason to get her out of her office. I just need to think about it. Oh, this is wonderful. Thank you. I just knew you'd help me feel better." Anna pulled her hands away and stood. "I have a comb for your hair that would look lovely with your dress. Let me get it."

Before Sierra could even comment, Anna dashed out of the room, leaving the door open. Moments later, Anna returned, comb in hand. It was made of abalone shell, and the blues mixed in with the other hues of the shell picked up the color of the dress beautifully. Anna helped Sierra put her hair up with the comb. Sierra realized it was time and grabbed a light wrap.

"Enjoy your supper and have a good evening."

Giving her a hug, Sierra headed downstairs at just a couple of minutes past eight. Bart was pacing in front of the Eating House and stopped when he saw her. "You're late. I don't like to be kept waiting," he growled when she appeared.

"I'm sorry. It took a bit longer to get ready than I anticipated."

He grabbed her arm forcefully and pulled her close, ignoring her yelp of pain because of his tight grip. "I don't like to be kept waiting," he snarled at her again, gripping her other arm just as tightly, shaking her. "No one keeps me waiting."

Sierra kicked him in the shin so he'd let her go. Her foot produced the desired effect, and he released her. "And no one touches me like that." She turned about to head back into the house when he gripped her again, this time more lightly.

"My apologies. I don't know my own strength sometimes. Please. Let us enjoy an evening repast."

Thinking about it a minute, she turned and moved to him. "Don't ever touch me like that again." Jerking her arm free, she moved past him and towards the saloon where they would get dinner.

It was a good thing she couldn't see the darkness that came into his eyes as she headed without him towards the building. He rubbed his jaw as thoughts ran through his head, then he took some long strides to quickly catch up to her.

She thought everything was good again, especially when she removed her wrap. Bart stopped to stare at her. His eyes devoured her figure, going up and down the length of her. She grinned. She'd caught him off guard with the dress, and knowing she looked good in it, was glad he thought so as well.

"Where?" His voice was deep and filled with emotion. He cleared it and started again on a lighter note. "Where did you get that? It's not yours. Where did you get that?" His jaw was working as he waited for her answer.

She tilted her head slightly in confusion but realized considering what she'd been wearing the past couple of weeks, he knew she hadn't purchased it or any material to make it.

"It belonged to Sophie. Since all of her things were left behind, Anna distributed some items to the other girls. She thought this dress would look good on me."

He helped her be seated, pushing in her chair, then moved around to his own before speaking again. "It does. Did you get anything from Louise?"

"No. She took all of her stuff with her. I'm glad she found happiness. Are you disappointed she's gone?"

"No. Not in the least. I told you, I wasn't interested in her."

"You didn't need to be interested in her to miss her."

"Well, I don't miss her." He stood and moved to the bar to put in their order. He'd been with her enough times he knew what she preferred and what wasn't rancid.

He kept glancing back towards Sierra, and after the fourth time, she was beginning to feel a bit self-conscious. His eyes were too dark under his hat for her to see his expression, but it was still unnerving, even though she wasn't absolutely sure why. She tried to brush the uneasiness aside when he returned so they could have a nice dinner.

"That was kind of Mrs. DeVoe to take over, so we could talk earlier. Have you known her long?"

Giving her a wary look, he shrugged. "Not really. She came to Colorado Springs last year when the house opened."

"When did Sophie or Louise come?"

"I've never paid much attention to the comings and goings of the girls."

"I'm surprised. I really thought you liked Louise at least. And you seem to like Sophie's dress. I got the impression you'd seen it before."

"This again? Louise was just being friendly, and the dress looks nice on you. I hadn't realized you owned something as pretty as you."

"How sweet. Thank you. Do you know who Louise might have left with? Have you noticed any miners not around?"

"Miners are hard to keep track of, unless they are working for one of the established mines. Most are transients who come and go without little notice. As for Louise, it was my understanding she left on her own. I believe she didn't like the long hours and extra work. She was going out West. Maybe California or Oregon."

"I suppose she told you all of this at lunch?"

"We didn't speak about anything personal at lunch. Why do you keep bringing it up?"

"I'm just trying to find out what happened to Louise or any of the other girls that are missing."

"I'm not the one to ask. I don't know any of them."

The conversation ended when their food arrived. As their meal progressed, the tense situation didn't seem to abate and Sierra was grateful when it was finally concluded so she could return to the house. Bart walked her back silently. When they arrived at the Eating House, he stopped just outside the door.

"I know tonight has not been our best time together, but I'd like to make it up to you."

"You don't have to do that."

"Actually, yes I do. The next full day you are off, I'd like to take you to a favorite place of mine and have a picnic. Would that be alright?"

Sierra should just say no, but somehow, she couldn't do that. He was trying to be sweet, planning something nice for both of them. Maybe he was more bothered by Louise's departure than he cared to let on. It would explain his outbursts and stern behavior. "Sure. That would be lovely. A day outside in the fresh air would be a welcomed relief."

"I'll take care of everything. I'll pick you up at 11:30." With a low bow, he left.

Chapter 12

Two days later and plans were in place. Anna and Sierra agreed no one else should know what they were about to do. This way no one would accidently spill the beans and ruin their chances of success. Anna felt it would be best to get into DeVoe's offices just after she had gotten the other girls rousted from their sleep.

Sierra planned on being up and ready for work before Florence knocked on all the doors. Then as soon as the other girls were awake, Sierra would sneak out of her room and head down the hall to the office. Anna would get Florence away to handle a concern with the coffee urn, enabling her to evaluate the problem. Once Florence was hastened out of her office, Sierra would slip in and search it, then join the rest of the girls heading downstairs. Sierra hoped nothing would go wrong. The hardest part would be getting up even earlier than she was used to, or so she thought.

As it turned out, Sierra was nervous about sneaking around and lay awake almost the entire night. She was antsy, her nerves on edge. She was up and dressed, sitting on the edge of her bed, when Mistress DeVoe knocked on the door to awaken her.

"Awake." Sierra hoped she still sounded groggy. Waiting a few moments until she knew Florence had knocked on all the rooms, she slipped out. Anna met her in the hallway, waiting until Sierra got into position within the shadows.

Once Sierra was hidden, Anna knocked on the office entry and ushered Florence out quickly. Before the door could fully close, Sierra slipped inside. She took a deep breath to try and calm her nerves. Her heart was racing, her palms sweaty. Thank goodness fingerprinting wasn't in existence yet, or she'd be leaving prints everywhere. Why did she think to do this? This was so out of her comfort zone, but she wanted to help Anna settle her concerns and she wanted answers to appease her own curiosity. Sierra needed to move quickly, there wouldn't be a whole lot of time.

Looking around, the desk seemed to be the

most logical place to begin searching. Opening the center drawer, she rummaged around. Nothing. She remembered hearing once that thieves started at the bottom drawer and work their way up because they didn't have to waste time shutting them to gain access to the next drawer. Seemed logical, so she started with the last drawer, opening it. There were so many papers there. Most were copies of the contracts, applications for future employment, correspondence between the training facility and the Eating Houses. The next drawer contained supplies of paper, envelopes and such. The top drawer contained ordering manifests for the food and beverages served in the dining room as well as Louise's letter.

Mistress Flo.

I can't handle such long hours anymore or how the girls are always disappearing. I'm headed west to California.

Louise.

Bart was right, although something nagged at her about the letter. Stuffing the letter back into the drawer, she continued searching the desk.

Well, this turned out to be a wasted effort.

Looking around the room, she tried to think of where else something important might be kept. She noticed Sophie's guitar sitting in the corner and a wave of sadness swept through her. Maybe Anna was just letting the situation get the better of her and there really wasn't anything untoward going on.

About to leave, Sierra stopped when she noticed a small chest in the corner of the room, partially hidden by the couch. Moving quickly, she tried to open it, hoping it wasn't locked or required a key. She was fortuitous. It was unlocked. Rifling through trying not to disturb its contents too much, she found a packet of letters at the bottom. Probably some personal, private correspondence that she shouldn't be reading, but she had to be sure.

Taking out the letters, she discovered several were from Bartholomew Higgins about some business prospects. Bart and Florence were business partners? She scanned the letter and it discussed keeping their partnership private. Something about

Bart's letters also made her Spidey senses tingle. On a hunch, she retrieved Louise's letter. The penmanship was the same! So, Bart lied? If he took Louise, where was he keeping her? Why did he write that letter found under DeVoe's door? And that was what bothered her with Louise's letter. No one called her Mistress Flo. It was either Mistress Florence or Mistress DeVoe, not Flo.

Looking over the letters Bart wrote, she noticed something else. He said he met DeVoe when she came to work at the Harvey House, but one letter indicated he'd invited her here. Were they a couple before she came? Is that why she's so unhappy with her? Does DeVoe think Sierra is trying to steal her man?

About to pull another letter from the pile, Sierra heard the other girls start to head downstairs. Shit. There wasn't enough time to read more. Quickly putting the rest away, she shut the lid of the chest. Reaching for the door knob, it turned under her hand and the door was pulled open by Mistress DeVoe who was shocked at seeing someone in her office.

Rapidly recovering, she scowled at Sierra. "What are you doing here?"

"I'm sorry. I came to ask you when you thought we might get more help?" It was the first thing that came to mind, hoping it sounded a plausible enough excuse.

"We're expecting two once the new class graduates, but that's three weeks away."

"That long? Okay. I was just wondering."

"You do realize, your own contract isn't up for almost a year."

"I'm aware. I just know we're really shorthanded and I was wondering when the load would get a bit lighter."

"Not for a while yet. In the meantime, don't you have work to do?"

"Yes, ma'am. I'm sure it'll be another busy day."

"Miss Hanley?"

"Yes?" Sierra stopped, turning again to face Florence.

"I know you've been seeing a lot of Mr. Higgins, and I'd suggest you find someone else."

Sierra wasn't sure what to say. Again, she wondered if Florence wanted Bart for herself. Was Florence jealous of her? Sierra didn't think DeVoe would be Bart's type, but then she didn't think they'd be business partners either. "Why?"

"I just don't think you're right for him. Heed my warning. Stop spending time with him. It'll come to no good."

"Okay, I'll give it some consideration. That's the best I can do at this time. I enjoy being in his company and he seems to like being in mine. But, I'll take your warning under advisement." Turning, Sierra headed downstairs.

Anna caught her eye the moment Sierra walked into the dining room to make sure her section was prepped for service. Florence was right on Sierra's heels, so Anna looked away. It'd be a while before they could talk about what, if anything, Sierra found.

The girls had their first break well after the

lunch crowd departed. Each grabbing a bowl of soup, they headed over to the counter to sit and eat. Anna didn't even ask, but her look said everything. Sierra looked around and nodded briefly, then whispered, "Not here."

Knowing they needed a viable excuse, Anna spoke up. "Sierra? I was thinking about getting some fresh air after we eat. Want to join me for a walk?"

"That sounds wonderful, Anna. I miss the fresh air on a day like today. It looks so pretty outside."

Once they finished, the women headed towards the doors. Florence stopped them.

"Where are you two going?"

"Just to get some fresh air. We won't be long," Anna replied calmly.

Anna makes a good actress, Sierra thought.

"Don't be too long. You only have three-quarters of an hour before the next train comes in."

"We won't. Just a brief encounter with nature." Anna grabbed Sierra's arm and led her outside. She began giggling slightly. "I thought we were caught for sure."

"We almost were. Actually, I was caught in her office. Well, sort of. I was just about to leave when she came in."

"Oh no! I'm sorry I couldn't keep her downstairs longer, but you know her. No time wasted."

"I think she suspects something, but because the other girls were heading downstairs, and I had put everything away in time, she has no proof, but I'm sure she thinks something is going on since I was actually in her office."

"True. Normally, we knock, and if no answer, just search for her elsewhere. What did you say?"

"I told her I was wondering when we were going to get more help. She didn't ask why I was actually *in* her office, so I didn't bring it up either."

"Did you find anything?"

Sierra walked quietly for a moment before she answered. "Actually, I'm not entirely sure. I did learn Florence and Bart are in some sort of business partnership, though what it entails, I don't know.

Only that they want to keep their alliance secret. What do you know of Bart's holdings, if anything?"

Anna shook her head. "Not much. I know he found a gold vein about three years ago and has been cashing in on it almost daily. He also holds investments in banking and a couple of businesses in town, but I'm not positive. It's just talk I've heard every now and again."

"Which do you think he shares with Ms. DeVoe?" Without thinking, she let slip a moniker used in the future.

"Mrs., actually. She was widowed several years ago. I don't know of anything they could be involved in together. Most of the men around here don't see the women as anything more than distractions, wives, servants and baby makers. They don't believe we can think or are aware of how to handle a business. Although Mistress DeVoe has proven herself competent, I was unaware Mr. Higgins paired up with her for any business venture."

"He lied to me about meeting DeVoe here. Not

that those were his exact words, but he indicated he only knew her since she came to Colorado to manage the Harvey House. I saw a letter where he asked her to come. And, Anna? His letters match the writing in Louise's post left for DeVoe. I think he wrote it, and if he did, then he lied about not knowing where Louise is. In addition, DeVoe had a number of letters from him. I can't believe she wouldn't have recognized his writing style with Louise's letter when it was obvious to me. Which means she's hiding something as well. It's all so mysterious. There wasn't enough time to get much else. I want to get in there again and look around some more. I found Bart's letters in a chest."

"I don't know if we can devise another plan to get you in her office again. She's going to be wary since you were almost caught this time."

"I know, but I'm going to try." Sierra noticed DeVoe watching them. "We'd best head back."

"Yes. I noticed her too. Thank you, for going to look and trying to set my mind at ease."

"I fear I've failed in easing your mind any. If

anything, I've made more questions, questions I myself am curious about."

"At least I don't feel like I'm going insane."

"No, Anna. There's definitely something going on and I'm going to find out what it is."

"Just be careful," Anna whispered as they neared the Eating House to return to work.

Chapter 13

Sierra was anxious, waiting for the next opportunity to sneak into DeVoe's office and check out the rest of those papers in the chest, but every time she had the chance, DeVoe made a serious effort to ensure the door was locked. It was impossible to get the key since Florence wore it around her neck, and she wasn't about to try sneaking into the woman's room in the middle of the night attempting to find it.

However, Sierra did ask around about Mistress DeVoe's relationship with Mr. Higgins, but other than the occasional public engagements, there seemed to be little between them. Alice did mention, however, that she heard Sophie state she saw Higgins go into DeVoe's office one day. There had been some sort of argument between them and both were in a foul mood afterwards, but she really didn't know much else.

"Sadly, Sophie isn't here to ask her for more details and I can only vaguely remember what she originally said. We just thought it odd since Mr.

Higgins didn't seem to have any business with Mistress DeVoe that we were aware of."

"Then you don't know of the two of them being in business together?"

Alice scoffed. "Business? The two of *them*? No. I can't even imagine. They barely seem to tolerate each other as it is, I can't conceive of them wanting to go into business together. Besides, although Mistress DeVoe is a fantastic house mistress, I don't believe she has the ability to help finance such an endeavor."

"Her husband didn't leave her anything?"

"Her husband?"

"Yes. I heard she was widowed. I had thought it was common knowledge."

Alice shrugged her shoulders. "First I've heard of it, but even if she was, she has been a Harvey Girl for quite a while. She was first employed at the original Harvey Eating House in Topeka, Kansas in 1880. She was transferred here as House Mistress after working for fourteen years in Kansas. If she is widowed, she might have lost her husband in the

Civil War. A lot of men were lost then."

"That's very true. I hadn't realized she was with Fred Harvey for as long as she's been. Kansas." Sierra had an errant question come into her head. She wondered if Bart knew her when he was in Kansas or if he'd known her longer. She knew it was only since the gold rush of 1890 that the men really began coming out west to Colorado. Is that how he knew Florence before they both arrived in Colorado Springs? He was too young to be part of the Civil War, but then she remembered boys as early as nine and ten served in the military. Even if they weren't soldiers, they were drummer boys and flag bearers. She'd have to remember to ask Bart these questions the next time she had the chance. Maybe on their picnic date. She was expected to have a day off very soon, the first in over a week, and knew Bart had been planning on the excursion. She had a lot of questions for him now.

Sierra asked others what they might know of Bart Higgins. What kind of businesses did he own?

Did he spend time with Louise, Sophie or the other Harvey Girls currently gone? Did they know how Higgins and DeVoe knew each other? Was he in the Civil War? Did he know DeVoe's husband? But, the visitors didn't know anything, and the locals weren't talking much. Sierra was aware of DeVoe watching her closely and giving her stern looks. Even Anna noticed, causing her to worry they'd been found out.

The women decided to start taking walks during their break or after their last service of the evening. The outside excursions would give the two women an opportunity to discuss things privately, as well as get some fresh air.

"Mistress DeVoe is getting suspicious, I think." Anna glanced over her shoulder to see if they were being watched.

"I think you're right. I've noticed how she's been watching me closely the last couple of days. I'm unsure if she knows I've been trying to get back into her office or not, but she's kept it locked up tight. I also have the feeling she either locked the chest or removed all the letters I originally discovered. Although, she warned me away from Bart, so she could just be watching me because I told her I'd consider it but doubted I would. No one seems to know anything about Bart's businesses or else isn't talking about them. It's becoming a stalemate. I'm not sure I'm going to find out anything else about Sophie or Louise's disappearances."

"You tried, Sierra. Better yet, you believed me. Alice and the other girls thought I was off my rocker for even suggesting something untoward might've happened. I appreciate you believing in me and trying to help me discover the truth of what's been going on around here."

"Honestly? I wasn't entirely sure Mistress DeVoe had any involvement, but after finding those letters, I'm left to wonder."

"What about Higgins?"

Sierra had to think before she answered, walking silently for a few moments. "I don't know, Anna. I really don't. He's been very kind and helpful to me. He saved my life when a robber on the train almost took it. I find it hard to believe someone who can be so kind to a stranger would be involved in something so…I don't even know what. Sinister? Malevolent? Malicious?"

"Do you love him?"

"No." Sierra didn't hesitate in her answer, and a part of her was surprised by that. "I like him, but I don't love him. Maybe I don't know him well enough, or maybe it's something more, but I'm not ready to stop seeing him."

"Maybe you sense the evil I believe resides within him. I don't trust him and I'm glad you don't either."

"It's not that I don't trust him. I have a hard time trusting a lot of people in general, but it's more than that. I just am not in love with him. I'm not even sure I can be in love. I've closed my heart off to it. I don't think it's possible."

"Don't say that, Sierra. You've got to believe in it."

Sierra shook her head. "I don't think love exists

for me. Maybe for others, but not for me. I don't believe in anything for me."

Anna sighed softly. "Then, I feel very sorry for you and hope one day someone will help you to change your mind."

Chapter 14

Sierra sat in the train station lobby as she waited for Bart. He was actually late, which was unlike him, especially knowing how much he hated to be kept waiting and endeavored to be prompt. What had happened to cause him to be this late? Reminded again of how much she missed her cell phone to get a text or call or check-up on him, she still wasn't used to being unplugged from the electronic world, even after all this time. She kept a look out for him as she waited, finally moving to stand by the window. The first window's view was blocked by a horse and carriage, so she moved a bit further down.

A door slammed within the house overhead and made her jump. She was about to investigate when she saw Bart storm downstairs and into the station. When he saw her, he stopped short, almost guiltily. He forced a smile on his face and headed over to her.

"I went upstairs to see if you were ready. I didn't realize you were down here waiting for me. I hope I didn't keep you long."

"No. Only a moment or two," she lied. She never saw him go up and she'd been there for close to twenty minutes. He'd never gone after her before, either, always lingering patiently at the foot of the stairs. And although he was smiling, his light attitude didn't reach his eyes. They were dark, almost foreboding. A cold chill ran down her spine at the look he gave her. She almost considered canceling, but she had too many questions she wanted answered that she hadn't gotten from other sources in town; the picnic was the perfect opportunity to get elucidations from him.

Grabbing her elbow, he steered her outside to the carriage she'd seen since she'd come downstairs. He helped her climb in, all the while she was trying to figure out the timeline in her head. If she'd been standing around for approximately twenty minutes, and the carriage was here prior to that, then where has he been for the past half-hour? He must've been the one to slam the door upstairs that she heard, and since Mistress DeVoe was very strict about letting men into the apartments, he could only have been in her office. Were they discussing business? Or the missing girls? Was Florence also warning him to stay away from her? The house mistress didn't seem to like her much, or was the woman hiding something from both of them?

Sierra's mind raced as he climbed in the other side of the carriage.

"Ready?" He gathered the reins in his hand and released the breaking lever.

"Yes."

Maneuvering the carriage towards the mountains, he headed out of town. She looked around, enjoying the quiet beauty of the area. It was far less hectic than in the 21st century with the multitudes of people hustling and bustling about, honking their horns being impatient to get from one place to another. The crisp, clean fresh air also felt good after so many days in the warm dining room. A number of people in this era didn't have the facilities or the inclination to bathe, and sometimes the body odor was a bit much in the enclosed dining hall, especially if they'd been on the train for many days prior.

The ride was quiet as they drove out of town. Sierra assumed he was still stewing over whatever argument he'd been involved in. Although she had many questions, she knew as a reporter that he'd be more responsive if he were feeling comfortable before she started to pepper him with her queries.

"You mentioned this is one of your favorite spots that you're taking me to. What about it makes it special?"

"Not sure. I just like it."

That was helpful. Not. "Where I grew up, there wasn't a lot of cities either. More country than anything, but I liked it. The greenery, the sounds of the animals on the farm. Here it's a bit different. The snow-capped mountains, the slight crispness in the air in the morning or evening. There's a cleanness to the air that has surprised me. How long have you lived here?"

"I came in 1891 as part of the early gold rush a

year after Bob Womack found the rich vein in Cripple Creek."

"Did many come then?"

"Yes. The towns went from a few hundred to thousands in just a couple of years. The trains helped bring the gold out and the people in."

"I know Mistress DeVoe is from Kansas. Is that how you knew her before you came here?" She knew she'd asked some of these questions before, but like any good investigator, queries were often repeated to see if answers would change slightly, thereby giving more information away freely.

Bart threw her a strange sideways glance before turning back to concentrating on controlling the horse. "Kansas is a big state."

"What about Sophie or Louise? Did you know them before you arrived?"

"No. Neither."

"Is gold the only holding you have? Or do you have other business adventures?"

Bart had been starting to veer to the right, which appeared more heavily traveled, but after she asked that last question, he jerked the horses to the left. "Sorry. Lost my train of thought. What's up with all the questions? Are you going to want a bank statement to make sure I can afford you?"

"I didn't mean it like that. Of course not. I was just curious and wanted to know more about you."

"I don't like being interrogated. That's all you need to know."

"I'm sorry. I just heard you had other business dealings and partners. I was curious about your partnership with Mistress DeVoe. I assumed something between your collaboration wasn't going well since you two were having an argument earlier."

He pulled the steed to a stop and leaned over her menacingly. "My businesses have nothing to do with you. For your own good, I suggest you drop any further discussion on this subject, including asking around about my affairs."

When he noticed her visibly cower, he started the horse back up. This time he headed for a line of trees and a bubbling brook. It appeared remote, and isolated. For the first time since meeting Bart, she was nervous in his company.

The ride to the area where he parked the carriage and let the horse go to graze was bumpy and affected her kidneys. Once he helped her to alight from the carriage, he moved to the back to grab a blanket and a basket.

"If you'll excuse me, the ride was very bumpy." Sierra quickly scanned the bushes, wondering which would offer her the most privacy.

He moved to a location under a tree and by the brook and spread out the blanket as she ventured into the woods.

She cast a glance back at him. He wasn't following her, though why he would, she didn't know. His change in moods, his predatory fierceness was something she couldn't quite get used to, and it was the first time she'd ever been scared to be alone with him. Worse, he never did answer her questions about knowing Florence before Colorado Springs or what his business dealings with her were about. It also bothered her that the two of them had been arguing this morning and Sierra couldn't help but wonder what the disagreement entailed.

She found a spot she was comfortable with and removed her vestments in order complete her business. As she finished up, she saw a glinting reflection off to her right. She tossed a look over her shoulder to make sure Bart wasn't paying her too much attention to where she'd ventured off. She could barely see him, but noticed his hat was close to the water. Feeling safe enough and overtly curious, she headed to where she saw the glimmer sparkling with the sun's rays.

The object was further than she originally thought and took her longer to approach. She was worried Bart would miss her and begin to search for her, though why that concerned her, she wasn't entirely sure. The whole conversation left her on edge. The hair at the back of her neck was standing up, sending chills down her spine. Yet, there was nothing in particular she could point to as to what was causing her apprehension.

Then she saw it. Someone must've lost their necklace. She moved to retrieve it and barely had it in hand when she heard Bart calling for her. "I'm here. I'm coming." A quick glance at the necklace in hand caused her to hesitate. She recognized the medallion hanging from the broken chain and her mind instantly filled with more questions as the mystery of Bart deepened. Slipping the necklace into her dress pocket, she headed back towards him.

He turned to face her as she returned. A dead weight filled her stomach as she couldn't see his face from the shadow of the hat. It bothered her for some reason, a sense of dread going right through her. Obtaining information was her goal, so she didn't run, but forge on. Instead, she put a smile on her face. "I can't believe what a gorgeous day this is. It's so good to get away from the house, even for just a few hours. And this picnic looks lovely. You said you've been to this spot before?"

"Yes. Often. I like the remoteness and solitude this place offers."

And no one can hear you scream, she added

silently.

He moved to sit down after she did, taking out some sandwiches, cheese and a bottle of wine, as well as a couple of glasses. "I know you don't care for ale, but I thought you might enjoy some wine?"

"I like wine. That sounds wonderful. Thank you."

"I also know you prefer tea, but it's hard to boil water on a picnic."

She laughed. If he only knew what the future would bring and the invention of iced tea from the St. Louis World's Fair in 1904. He had nine years to go. Funny that she remembered learning that fact from her sightseeing tour a few years back while on her vacation to St. Louis. She could almost hear the guide now as they drove around land originally set aside for that fair and now contained many museums and beautiful park areas. "The 1904 World's Fair gave us our first hot dogs, ice cream cones and iced tea, among so many other wonderful inventions and innovations," the guide had said.

"Yes. Maybe one day in the future it will be

possible to have tea at a picnic, but for now, the wine is perfect. This all looks really good." Sierra helped to spread out the items while he opened the bottle, then held out the glasses while he poured.

Setting the bottle aside, he took a glass from her, taking a sip.

"However did you find this location?"

"As you're aware, I came out here as a prospector. I had the opportunity to visit several locations looking for gold. This was one of them. I now own a good portion of this valley."

"Do you have problems with poachers or other prospectors coming on your land?"

"No. Only the Injuns seem to know about this place. The road isn't well known nor traveled. The few who find it don't stay long. There is no gold in the valley, and a little further away, I've a private area sign. As for the Injuns, most of the Utes have been relocated to the other side of Pikes Peak, and the Arapaho and Cheyenne are mostly gone. A few stragglers who didn't get pushed onto rez lands still mingle about, but for the most part, they keep to themselves."

"Have you ever brought someone else up here?" She took a bite of her sandwich.

"No. You're the first."

"Not even Sophie or...Louise?"

His eyes darkened. "No."

"That's odd. Because," she pulled out the necklace from her pocket, "this is Louise's necklace. I found it over in the bushes back yonder. How did it get here, I wonder?"

"What are you insinuating?" he asked through clenched teeth, his mood rapidly darkening. "You've been very inquisitive today. That could be anyone's."

"No. It's Louise's. I commented on its uniqueness when I first met her. Notice the medallion? She told me it was a medal her father got from the War and she had it made special, so she'd be able to have something of his close to her heart always. As far as I know, she never took it off. If you didn't bring her here and, as you said, it's fairly remote, then how did her necklace get here?

How had it come off? I can't imagine anyone else bringing her here." Sierra began to take a slightly defensive position, getting on her knees so she could get up quickly if she needed to run. She also picked up her glass of wine, holding it. It wouldn't be a good weapon, but the liquid in his face might blind him for a few seconds to allow her to get away, should she need to. The horse had been taken off the carriage tongue and left to wander the pasture. She knew how to ride, but she was used to a saddle and not sure if she could get up on the horse without stirrups. Her mind was working on an escape plan. She wasn't about to take any chances with her life, and his current demeanor made her feel she suddenly had a reason to be concerned.

He moved to snatch it from her open palm, but she quickly moved it out of the way and stuffed it back into her skirt pocket. Grabbing her wrist, he jerked her closer. "Why did you have to be an interfering female? Don't you know you're nothing more than objects to excite a man's fancy?" He lunged, pushing her backwards to land on top of her.

Her wine spilled, and she struggled to get her legs out from under her own body. She needed their leverage, but he was heavy and fighting her. He slapped her face with his free hand, still clutching her wrist with the other. If he thought the slap would deter her struggles, he was sadly mistaken. She increased them, a panic seeping into her very soul. He tore at her blouse and she cringed as she heard it rip. Despite his pushing her back and climbing on top of her, she managed to hold onto the wine glass. It wasn't a lot, but in desperation, something was better than nothing.

She smashed it on his forehead with all the strength she could muster. It broke and, in surprise, he let her wrist go as his hand went up to his head. It was enough for the moment. She twisted her hip up, tossing him to one side. Using her now-free leg, she kicked him in the middle of his chest. With him off her entirely, she was able to twist around and get to her feet, pushing off like a professional sprinter. She didn't look back. She couldn't afford to.

Running as fast as she could, she headed for the bushes where she'd found the locket. The area was unknown to her, but at least this was somewhat familiar. She had to hide and hope he'd give up. Or he'd kill her and she'd just be another Harvey Girl who mysteriously disappeared. How would he account for her absence? Others knew he was taking her on a picnic. Or did he have the law in these parts under his employment and no one would question it?

She could feel the ground shake as he pounded behind her. She threw a glance over her shoulder to see him. There was blood dripping down his face as a result of the cut above his eyebrow from the glass she broke against his head. He was gaining on her. She had to run faster. Sierra ducked around some bushes and focused on running. If he shot her, she doubted he would miss. She could almost feel his breath against the back of her neck, but she knew it was only her imagination as she turned to see how close he was.

He'd stumbled on some loose rock and she

scrambled to put more distance between them. There was a part of her that knew she wasn't going to get out of this alive, but she wasn't about to just give up.

"Sierra, you bitch. I'm going to kill you, you whore."

A gunshot rang out. It surprised her, but it missed. Running in a zigzag pattern, she hoped if he tried to shoot her again he'd find it more difficult to hit her if she wasn't running in a straight line. Maybe that only worked with alligators. She didn't know, but she wasn't really thinking clearly either. Only the need to live was uppermost in her thoughts.

Another shot, and she heard the wood of the tree beside her splinter. Gods. She shouldn't have asked so many questions in such a remote place. What the hell was she thinking? Truth was, she hadn't thought he would physically harm her. Maybe yell, or growl or something, but not actually attempt to kill her. He'd been so kind when she first met him, she didn't think it was feasible. But then, she wasn't in the 21st century either. The laws and rules in 1895 were vastly different. Killing in this era, out in a West that hadn't been civilized yet, wasn't considered anything more than survival. People died easily and often. In a place like this, death was almost a daily occurrence and she could understand how it'd be meaningless as people became immune to dying. What was one more deceased person?

Another shot, then another, and still he missed her. Maybe she was smart to not run in a straight line. Sierra tripped on something and as she started to fall; she felt a searing pain pierce into her thigh. She cried out, then turned to see why her leg hurt when she hadn't heard the gun and didn't think she was shot. Blinking in utter surprise, she saw an arrow protruding from her flesh, blood dripping down her leg. She couldn't deal with the injury at the moment. Bart was catching up and she couldn't just lie here like some sheep waiting to be slaughtered.

Pushing herself up, she felt something odd

against her hand. It must be what tripped her to begin with. Looking at the cold object, she fell back screaming. It was a human hand peeking out from the soil. The hidden grave wasn't deep enough, and the animals had dug against the dirt of the burial site, exposing the hand. The fingers were partially gnawed upon, and she was sure she was going to be sick as a result. Sierra's head pounded as she tried to keep the bile that swiftly rose to her throat from being expunged.

She couldn't think about any of this now. The need to survive was what she focused on. Her heart racing, she felt sick, but in extreme fear, one didn't think about things like vomiting but about making it through the next few minutes.

Dragging her injured leg, her hand around the arrow shaft, she limped as quickly as she was able away from Bart. As she passed a tree, someone reached out and grabbed her. She screamed, but when she realized it wasn't Bart, she stopped.

The man was dressed in buckskin leggings and a loose buckskin shirt with a geometric design made from beads. His hair was long, parted in the middle with yellow paint on the part. A long thin braid was also decorated with beads and a single feather, while the rest of his hair was in two thicker braids.

Feeling safe, she was relieved. Someone was there to help her. It didn't register that *he* was probably the one to shoot her with the arrow currently protruding from her leg. She didn't care. There was someone who could stop Bart and give her aid, at least until she looked into the face of the man who grabbed her, his amber gold eyes cold and distant. Her eyes widened. "No. It can't be! NO!" She started to struggle to pull away, her head spinning, though whether from loss of blood or from pure disbelief, it didn't matter. Her whole world was crazy, having been sent back in time, but now, it was totally turning upside down and inverted. How could this be? *He* was the man who stalked her in the 21st century.

Chapter 15

Sierra heard an ear-piercing scream. She couldn't comprehend at first that she was the one creating the cacophony until his hand covered her mouth and he pulled her down.

"Quiet or I'll punch you unconscious."

Tears streamed down her face, Sierra was so terrified. However, she did stop screaming. She had no idea what was going on, or where Bart was, but she heard horses and several whooping cries. Suddenly, there were several Natives on horseback. Arrows whooshed past, a couple of rifles shot, and she realized they were going after Bart. Bart fired a couple of rounds at the men, then beat a hasty retreat.

Only after Bart left did the male who had grabbed her pull his hand away from her mouth. He moved down to the arrow still sticking out of her thigh. Pulling his shirt off, he moved it to the wound. Without another word, he broke the stem of the arrow, then gave a solid push so it would go through and out the back of her thigh.

Sierra cried out in utter agony, then everything went black as she passed out.

"What do we do with her?" One of the men on horseback looked down at her unconscious form.

"Can't leave her. Bring her back to camp. Novava'e can care for her."

"Why? She is Ve'ho'a'e'. She is white woman. Leave her to fend off the animals."

"No. She might know something. She was running from him too. We aren't in lands of our own anymore. White man's land, white man's laws. Sadly, we have to live by both."

"She bad blood, but your call Stone. Just don't say I no warn you." He jerked the reins, turning the horse around. The others followed him.

Stone Red Tree looked down at the unconscious woman. She was pretty, even if she was white. Wrapping her leg in his shirt, he flung her over his shoulder and headed back to his own horse. Throwing her across the back, he took the reins, walking back in the direction the couple originated from. He wasn't sure what he'd find, but he had to check it out before he returned to camp.

His hope was Higgins left his horse and he'd be able to steal it. It was a way to count coup against enemies. To the Cheyenne, everything they did was considered a game, especially if they were able to count coup.

Counting coup was the ability of winning prestige for acts of bravery in the face of an enemy. Risking injury or even death was required in order for the act to be added to their reputation. Exploring alone and taking the woman would both be considered coup acts. If he could gain anything else from Higgins, he would add even more notches to his coup stick. Of course, it'd be better if Higgins was still around to fight, but then, the man was probably too smart to be caught alone with the Cheyenne. After all, they were notorious for their fighting skills and have earned reputations that made many quiver at the thought of facing them in battle.

Stone found the picnic site and a wagon, but the horse and Higgins were both nowhere to be found. He moved to the carriage and peered in the flat back area, finding a shovel hidden under a blanket.

Looking back at the picnic setting, then at the wagon, he found the whole set up very peculiar. Why would one need digging equipment if one is planning a romantic interlude? Or vice versa. Who would one plan a romantic outing only to kill them? It seemed very odd.

Taking the woman off his horse, he hitched his steed to the carriage, then laid the woman on the blankets in the back part of the open wagon section. He gathered up the basket items and put everything in the back of the wagon with her, except the open bottle of wine. That he dumped out. White man's fire water caused enough problems. He didn't need to bring it back to the tribe.

Stone noticed a necklace by the picnic blanket and scooped it up to hang on a set of beads he wore on his pants, tying it to them so it wouldn't fall off. Removing a small pouch off his buckskin pants, he mixed it with some water from the creek to create a paste. He then moved to the woman and tore her dress more, putting the muddy mixture on the wound. Its caking properties would stop the bleeding until a medicine woman could help her.

Climbing onto the carriage, he checked to make sure the female was still breathing, then slapped the reins on the animal, turning to head to the Cheyenne village.

"I can't believe you brought her back after all." Black Snake stared at the unconscious woman lying serenely in the wagon's rear.

"Higgins took his horse. I'm counting coup, with her as my prize. Her and this contraption."

"The contraption has use. Her? Not so much."

"We injured her. I wasn't about to leave her behind for the beasts or him. Besides, he was hunting her. She might be able to tell us something useful."

"She will stand by him. They are the same. Whether or not he tried to kill her, she will side against us."

Another man walked up and peered over the edge of the wagon. "She's human and alive. She will expose us."

"Standing Elk, I have those same fears. It was on my mind the entire journey as I returned here, but something about her prevented me from just leaving her behind. We can keep her in the tipi until she is well. Then we can decide what to do with her."

"It's not wise, Stone. In fact, it's very dangerous."

"I understand, Black Snake, but I feel it's a risk worth taking."

"You are responsible for her. If she finds out what we really are, it is you who will be dealt with." Standing Elk shook his head as he looked down at the woman.

"I accept the responsibility." Stone moved around to the back of the wagon, reaching in to scoop her up and carry her to the brightly colored tipi of River Bend. "Novava'e?" he called out as he approached.

"I've been expecting you both, Stone. Bring her in and set her on the skins."

Stone shook his head. True, his people had a lot of powers and gifts from the Great Spirit, but there were times some of those gifts surprised him. River's gifts were such an example.

One of the few Novava'e, or Medicine People of the tribe, she had the gift of sight as well as the ability to speak with the spirits. Like all females who became able to be more politically involved with the tribe, whether to smoke a pipe or serve as a medicine woman, they were older and post-menstrual. It's the Cheyenne, and in some regards most of the Plains Indians, who believe a woman is at their highest spiritual essence when they have the ability to produce offspring. Once that ability is no longer an option, they become revered in other ways. River went on a vision quest and saw her gifts as a healer. The quest also gave her many other abilities, such as those previously mentioned.

He followed the elder woman's instructions

and gently laid the female in his arms down. Taking a couple of the hides by her feet, he covered her up.

River put her hand on his arm as he straightened. "The others worry if you did the right thing by bringing her here, but you did. Don't concern yourself with wrongs when you feel you are right. She will not betray us. She is our hope against him and has traveled quite a distance to aid us in our cause, even though she doesn't know it yet."

Stone leaned over and kissed the woman's cheek. "I appreciate your telling me that. I was beginning to second guess myself, fearful I chose unwisely." He turned back to gaze upon the unconscious woman. "Let me know when she awakens." Without another word or glance, he headed out of the tipi. There was much to be discussed with the others of the tribe.

Chapter 16

Bart knew Sierra told several girls about going on a picnic. Returning without her would be suspicious, but he had a plan and it worked better than he could've hoped since the Cheyenne were so unwittingly helpful.

He'd seen Sierra get hit by one of their arrows, and though he failed to reach her to make sure the job was done, he knew the Cheyenne were ruthless enough to kill her for him. Bart was aware that past excuses wouldn't work for Sierra, so he devised a slightly altered plan.

He had really liked Sierra and thought his addiction would be nullified with her, but she turned out like all the rest. His skin crawled with the thought of her not being as different as he first thought. When he'd originally met her, she was a strong, independent woman facing the barrel of a pistol with bravado he'd seldom seen. She had a slightly fuller figure than most women of the era, indicating she had been well fed and therefore came from a well-to-do family who could afford the comforts of a rich diet.

As a man who'd been raised without parents, scavenging for food had been a daily necessity. He envied and yet admired those who didn't have to struggle. He swore he'd be one of them when he got older, and he did. Now he was the one to be envied. He was making a name for himself. No one would ever make him feel worthless, nor would he ever be hungry again.

Bart knew he had to have a plausible explanation as to why Sierra left with him and didn't return. He also realized his pistol wouldn't work for his excuse, since the Cheyenne's used long-distance rifles, but an arrow would work. He pulled one of the extras he had hidden earlier and had been able to retrieve from the carriage before he got on the steed, leaving the fight behind. Looking at the weapon closely, coldness in his eyes, he braced himself, then jammed the arrow into his shoulder with all the force he could muster.

He grunted from the sharp pain. It took him several minutes to let his body adjust to the sensation. Once it did, he broke the arrow so the long shaft wouldn't be quite so bothersome. Making sure he was appropriately disheveled, he allowed himself to slump over his horse, letting the steed amble into town.

As anticipated, as soon as he as he was spotted, men came running over to help him.

The townsmen brought him home and called for Doctor Whalen to attend his wound. Sheriff Cosco waited in the foyer until the doctor indicated it was okay to enter the bed-chamber. As Doctor Whalen came out, drying his hands with a towel, Sheriff Cosco approached him.

"How is he, Doc?"

"The wound missed anything important. He'll be extremely sore and unable to move his arm until his shoulder heals, but he'll live. Just need to watch for any fever that might develop."

"Is it okay to talk to him?"

"He's exhausted, but you can try. Just don't force it. Let him sleep if he does. He needs rest more than your questions. That can wait."

"Thanks, Doc. However, there is a missing woman involved. I need to find out where she might be, so talking to him really can't wait."

"Cosco. You should know it was a Cheyenne arrow, and he did say he was attacked by them. They probably ain't none too happy with the proposed mass production gold mining operation he has planned. By the way, how's that coming?"

"Just waiting for the men and equipment now. Everything else is in place. Higgins got the last of the deeds just yesterday, so ain't no one else can claim it's theirs."

"Good. Don't need to deal with that among everything else going on. Any more word 'bout them missing Harvey Girls?"

Sheriff Cosco shook his head. "Nah. Doubt we'll ever see 'em again. Just ain't figured out which miners they left with. I mean, I know they come and go pretty fast, but ain't none new that's gone."

"Ya gonna put any effort in finding 'em?"

"Higgins pays me not to look too deeply into

whatever the Harvey Girls do, or the miners, unless they're trespassing. Says it's a waste when both are so nomadic. I just do what I'm told."

"You mean what he pays you to."

"He pays you too, Doc. You got just as good of a reason to make sure he lives. Ain't no chance y'all are going to find a job where ya spend most of your days just lounging about."

"That's not an issue, Sheriff. He ain't hurt that badly. He's just tired. Most likely from the exertion and the loss of blood."

"I think the last thing Higgins wants is to have Fred Harvey and the AT&KC authority snooping about his business because of another woman gone. With all the girls missing, Harvey's gonna want to know what's happening to them all. Especially Sierra. After all, he left with her and came back alone and wounded. There are going to be questions, and someone is going to have to answer to them. Higgins ain't one to be sharing all his business with everyone, but she ain't one of them girls that just up and disappears. She's gonna have to be accounted for. If she's alive but hurt, we'll need to fetch her, but we need to know where to look and asking him is the only way to find out that information."

"Doubt you'll get many answers until he's more awake, and that could be hours." The doctor grabbed his medicine bag and headed towards the door.

"I just hope Miss Hanley has time to wait for him to come to his senses." Cosco watched the door close behind the doctor and braced himself for facing his boss. He hesitated as he wavered between remaining in the foyer or going into the bedroom. Truth was, he wasn't a very brave man, which is why Higgins probably hired him to begin with. Higgins probably knew he'd do anything for a lazy life of leisure, turning his head to ignore most of what went on around him. Doing the bare minimum was fine with him, as long as he got paid. However, the sheriff was keenly aware Fred Harvey was not one to just let all of his help disappear without following up as to why. Most of the girls who left departed with miners and were rather expected, but Miss Hanley was a different story. The problems with the Cheyenne had mostly been resolved when the majority had been moved to a reservation off Colorado land. There were a few die-hards who remained behind, hoping to continue to find buffalo or work the trade routes. They mostly stayed by themselves, although recently their activities and interactions in town have been increasing.

Making up his mind, Cosco entered the bedroom, keeping his eye on Higgins, who lay on his bed. The usually robust man looked pale and, well, almost, dare he say…frail? The fact he was still kicking after a Cheyenne attack was astounding, but it must've taken everything the man had to get away alive. The Cheyenne were known to chase after their enemies and fight to the death. They were considered one of the most fearsome tribes on the Plaines.

Maybe they were concerned with only obtaining a coup. But if that were the case, where's the female?

"I can feel your eyes on me. What do you want?" Bart's voice was raspy, his eyes still closed.

"Sorry, sir. I need to know what happened, especially with the girl you were with."

"Sierra. Her name is Sierra. She's a Harvey Girl, but she has a name."

"Sorry. I need to know what happened."

Bart opened his eyes and stared at the sheriff. A cold feeling coursed through Cosco and he shifted from one foot to the other uncomfortably. No one wanted to confront their employer for any reason, and the circumstances for this situation was not conducive to making the position Cosco found himself in any easier.

"We were enjoying a picnic on some of my land for privacy. She needed a moment for personal reasons. The next thing I know, I heard her scream. I pulled out my six-shooter and checked out the area to make sure she was okay. I thought maybe a rattler or something similar scared her. Then I saw arrows flying and her going down. More gun fire was exchanged, and more arrows now started flying towards me. Since she wasn't making any sound or answering me, I hightailed it outta there. Just before I got on my horse, I got hit. I had hoped to get some help, but I also don't believe there's any hurry. I'm pretty sure she's dead. She told me once she ain't got any family here. If we find her body, I'll pay for her burial. Now go. I want to rest."

The sheriff took mental notes as he talked, but he found it peculiar Bart seemed as unconcerned about her as he appeared to be. Even though Cosco was on Bart's payroll, and he probably wasn't as good of a lawman as he should be, he still had to wonder about the laissez-faire attitude Bart seemed to have with regards to a woman he appeared to show personal interest in enough to plan a private picnic.

Maybe the Cheyenne had heard about the special project that would be starting soon and that was why they went after Higgins, and the girl, Sierra, just got caught in the crossfire. If they had thought she was his, it would've been a major coup to capture or kill her. Cosco knew he'd have to form a posse, comb the area and see if they could find the girl, but he knew that could take a couple of days. Most of the men in the area owned mules, not horses, and if any of them were in town, they'd be here because they found gold and turned it in to buy supplies or entertainment or both. If they were sober, they'd be busy, and if they were drunk, then they were useless anyways.

There were times Sheriff Cosco really hated his job. Good thing Higgins paid him well.

Chapter 17

Sierra's mind became alert before she could even contemplate opening her eyes. She felt weighted down but was still able to move under the heaviness. Moving an arm from under the warmth, she realized the density was the wraps covering her. Still, her eyes were shut, weighing as heavily as the blanket over her. She heard some talking, although it was distant and unintelligible. It almost sounded like she was in a camp or something. Trying to remember what happened, it finally all came rushing back to her. She'd asked questions and Bart seemed to panic with her inquiries. As a result, Bart tried to kill her. She was then shot with an arrow to her leg, found a gnawed-off hand in the dirt and Louise's necklace. And, she ran into *him*. The most impossible thing yet. The man who stalked her in Colorado Springs was here in 1895. Had he followed her through time? Or had he just lived without changing until 2018? Neither seemed possible, yet one of them had to be. After all, *she* traveled through time, why couldn't he?

Scuffle footsteps sounded. "How is she, Novava'e?"

A raspy, older woman responded. "She is awake, though she isn't willing to admit it to herself yet, much less the world. Do you wish to wait until she is ready?"

"Our first encounter didn't go so well. I'm afraid I might cause her fear until she feels safe enough."

"Safe is a relative term, Stone. Go then. I'll call for you when she is ready to face all the challenges of the day."

Sierra heard a soft thud and still didn't move. She felt a presence near her.

"Sometimes, the darkness of sleep is better than the light of day, but the light is important too. It helps truth shine. You have questions. The light will show you the answers."

Struggling, Sierra rubbed her eyes to get them to open. She took in her surroundings. A small fire was in a dirt pit. The tipi she was laying in had the bottom edges rolled up to let in some air. Two large flaps were also pulled back. A pole in the center contained several hides draped over it. The weight she felt on her body was skins, most likely of buffalo.

The elderly woman sat beside her, staring. "Ah. You have decided to come back to the land of the living after all."

"How?" Sierra's voice cracked, and she cleared it a few times to get it to work again.

The woman held out a ladle of water. Sierra sat up enough to ingest the cool liquid.

"How long have I been asleep?"

"Fourteen rises of the sun."

"No. That can't be right?"

"I'm old, child, not stupid. I do know how to count."

"I'm sorry. I didn't mean to say you... I mean, I'm just surprised. I can't believe I slept so long."

"Your wound became infected. You became feverish. The heat of your body finally unwrapped its arms around you yesterday, the wound healing better."

"Who were you talking to?"

"Stone. He's the one who brought you back here."

Stone. So now she could put a name to the face that haunted and terrified her at the same time. "Where is here?"

"Our camp."

That didn't get her far. "Who are you?"

"Tsitsistas."

"What? I don't understand."

"Tsitsistas. It's what we call ourselves. Your people call us Cheyenne. It means people of strange speech. Personally, I think that's a silly name. Our speech is clear enough for us."

The older woman stood, moving over to the fire. Stirring a pot slightly offset from the center of the flame, she put some in a hollowed-out gourd. "Now that you are acknowledging the living, I will call for Ho'honaa'e. Eat and gain strength."

Sierra took the gourd, sipping slightly at the hot stew-like concoction within. Looking past the opening of the tipi, she saw young children running around attired in adorable deerskin outfits with geometric beads as designs or different colored cloths woven in-between the skins. The work was absolutely beautiful. One of the young boys stopped and listened to the old woman, then dashed off. Sierra realized the reason why she couldn't make out their words earlier was because they were speaking their own language. It was unlike anything she'd ever heard before.

Bringing the gourd up, blocking her vision, Sierra tipped it back for more of the stew mixture. As she pulled the container away, she looked up at the hulking man in the center of the opening. Her eyes widened. The gourd fell from her numb hands as she scrambled to her feet looking for an escape. Had she thought logically instead of out of fear, she realized she would've been better off rolling under the tipi's opening, but she was too panicked to think straight. A piercing scream erupted from her lips as she put weight on her injured leg for the first time, but it wasn't the pain that was causing her to scream. She was wigging out, frantic and frightened at the man before her.

Both the old woman and he looked at each other as if Sierra had just lost her mind. She realized she was trapped. He stood unmoving at the entrance, waiting for her hysterics to subside. It took several minutes before she realized she was making a fool of herself and quieted. Panting slightly, her heart racing, she stopped screaming but stayed vigilant. Logically, Sierra knew there was no place to run even if she did get past the two of them. After all, there was still a whole Cheyenne village she'd have to get through as well, all on an injured leg.

"Are you finished? Or do you need more time for your tantrum?"

Lifting her chin, she didn't answer. She wouldn't give them the satisfaction.

"Good. I don't need a Ve'ho'a'e who's causing a problem."

"Ho'honaa'e, why is she scared of you?"

"Novava'e, I've no idea why."

"Because he tried to kill me," She told

Novava'e, then turned to him. "Don't try to kill me again, please."

"He saved your life, child. Why do you think he would take it now?"

"I…. Because he… He tried strangling me in Colorado Springs," she blurted, unable to stop herself.

Perplexed, he looked at the old woman. "I've not been to the Springs in many, many moons. And I certainly didn't try to strangle her even when I was there." He turned to Sierra. "I've never seen you until you ran into me a couple of moons ago."

"No. I…" She was confused and skeptical. Everything was confusing. She was dizzy from trying to put her past with her present. She'd thought he'd come back in time to finish the job he'd started, but he didn't seem to remember or even know her. Had it not happened for him yet?

"Maybe it was someone else? After all, I've heard your people say we all look alike. Half the time you seem unsure which tribe we even belong to." Stone crossed his arms. He didn't know she was not right in the mind when he considered bringing her here.

Those words made Sierra angry. "I don't judge people by race or culture. I know it's you. You attacked me and said I'd never leave you again. Or…maybe it was 'don't leave me again.' But either way, it *was* you just before you attacked me. If the cops didn't pull you off and arrest you, I'd probably be dead."

"I told you I saw something about her. She is Saeota'e," the woman exclaimed almost excitedly.

"I'm sorry. I don't understand these words you are saying. Are they your names? What is Saeota'e? And who are you? I don't get any of this. Please, tell me what's going on."

The old woman seemed happy to explain. "Ho'honaa'e is his name. It means Rock, but we call him Stone. He is alpha."

"Stone is easier to pronounce. That's what most call me."

"I'm Novava'e. Medicine Woman, but my given name is River Bend, though you may call me

River. Most do. Seota'e means Ghost Woman. You see ghosts of things past and yet to come."

Sierra knew as soon as she'd said he tried to kill her she'd made a mistake. She wasn't thinking. She was so astounded she didn't give thought to anything that had come out of her mouth. "I'm not a ghost. What do you mean by alpha?"

"The leader of the tribe. What some would call chief, I guess. But we don't have just one chief. We have many. He is but one of many." River spoke since the Cheyenne leaders would never speak of their status as it'd be considered prideful. "There are 44 chiefs, but since this band was special, having been granted gifts from Ma'heo'o, the Great Spirit, there were some who have alpha status."

Stone moved farther into the tipi. "She didn't mean like ghost of someone who is deceased. Not all ghosts are dead, some haven't been born yet."

"Yes. Yes. You're a ghost, out of time."

Sierra was relieved. She didn't understand how they guessed, how they knew, but they understood. At least River did. She was out of her own time.

"Yes. Can you help me get back?"

"There is no going back, child. You'd be dead and nothing more than the dust from which you came. You were brought here to do something. You have a destiny here, in this time. In this place. You have to fulfill your destiny before the universe would even contemplate on returning you." River moved to collect the dropped gourd.

Sitting back onto the furs, Sierra shook her head in disbelief. "No. I can't stay here. I don't know what I'm supposed to do."

River gave her a knowing smile but didn't say anything. It wasn't time for her to know everything yet.

Sierra had the feeling River knew more than she was saying. The fact River knew what she did was bothersome to Sierra but that she wouldn't tell her was even more so.

Stone moved opposite the fire and sat down. "He tried to kill you. In the woods. The white man tried to kill you, not me."

"Yes. He did."

"Do you know who he is?"

"Yes. I met him several of weeks ago. He saved my life from a thief trying to rob the train and who murdered one of the other passengers."

"Tell me more." Although Stone was aware of who Higgins was, he was fishing to see what she'd be willing to divulge.

"His name is Bartholomew Higgins. I didn't know much about him. I tried to learn a few things recently." Sierra didn't know why she was inclined to tell him everything, but she was. Maybe it was because they seemed to know and accept she didn't belong here, or that she needed someone she could confide in. They both exuded a feeling of security she felt confident about in order to tell them more than she normally would. Or maybe she missed having the opportunity to write down her observations and needed to be able to spread the news, so to speak. "I've been working for the Harvey Santa Fe Eating House in Colorado Springs. There have been a couple of girls who have disappeared recently. Although, now I seem to be a missing one as well, I'm sure. I highly doubt if he told them the truth. I can't even imagine what he told them. Anyways, he's been acting strange lately and one of the other girls in the house, Anna, felt something was off, and so have I. She's been really nice to me. I've come to consider her a dear friend. Anyway, she's also been concerned over the last couple of girls who have just disappeared. I understand there have been others too, before I arrived."

"But something he has done recently has made you and Anna concerned over his behavior, or their disappearance or both?"

"Both. Though it started with the disappearances. I'd been told when I arrived there were three girls who left in as many months. The first I was personally aware of was Sophie. We woke up one morning and she was just gone. She left everything behind, including her guitar, which she had told me earlier belonged to her mother. It was her most precious item and yet, she just left it. The house mother, Mistress DeVoe said some of the girls do that when they are in love and the miners want to take them away quickly. Though, to me and Anna, it didn't make any sense."

"Why?"

"The girls are hired for a year contract, but if they leave early, their base pay is cut in half, but it's not like they would go to prison or something if they wanted to walk away sooner. So, there's no reason for them to sneak away and leave everything behind. If they did, there has to be another reason. And Louise, the second girl who left, she took everything, but she wasn't the kind of person who'd leave without saying goodbye. Neither girl talked about meeting anyone they were even contemplating running away with. Add to Sophie and Louise, the three who left before I arrived, and it just seems too coincidental to be random."

"Please continue." Stone waved his hand, indicating he didn't want the stew Medicine Woman was offering.

On the other hand, Sierra was grateful for taking another gourd-full of the hearty stew. After a few sips, she held the gourd between her hands as she continued.

"Anna and I tried to snoop around some, to try and figure out what was going on. Bart offered to take me on a picnic and I thought it was the perfect opportunity to ask him some questions. In the process of poking around beforehand, Anna and I discovered some disturbing things. Seems Mr. Higgins and our house mistress are in business together, but we couldn't tell what kind of business. When I questioned him on this, as well as more information on Sophie and Louise's disappearances, he became rather irate. But it wasn't until I showed him Louise's necklace that I found in the area that he flipped."

"Flipped? I've never heard that term. What do you mean?" River flittered about while the two of them talked, stopping only to ask her question.

"I just meant, when I showed him Louise's necklace, Bart became extremely upset and antagonistic towards me. That's when he tried to kill me. I ran. In trying to get away, I got shot. By an arrow. How did I get shot by an arrow? He was armed with a gun."

"Black Snake shot you. It was an accident, though. He was aiming for Higgins, but you ran in his line of fire with all the crisscrossing you did."

"It was probably silly to run that way, but I thought I'd make a more difficult target for him if I did."

"It is a clever tactic. Most run in a straight line, so it's easier to hit them, but the strange way you were running, it was certainly more difficult. Black Snake does regret hurting you. It is never our intent to injure a woman."

"That's good to know." Sierra set the gourd down, giving her head a slight negative shake when River went to give her more. "Thank you. It's delicious, but I've had enough for now." She turned back to Stone who was studying her carefully.

"So, what happens to me now?"

"What do you mean?"

"I mean, when do I get to leave."

"You're not being kept prisoner here. You were

not well enough to travel, even to bring you back to your own people."

"But, I'm better now."

River spoke up. "Child, you just woke up from a very long illness. Stay and regain your strength. You are going to need it for what you are about to face."

"What about Bart? Can he come here looking for me?"

Stone shook his head, his hair braid with feather almost slapping him in the face as he did so. "He wouldn't dare. He may be powerful in his world, but he has no power here with my people."

"Why were you there? He said he owned that land."

"Sadly, that is true." Stone cocked his head to River who nodded in understanding and left the tipi. They both watched her depart before Stone turned back to Sierra. "I know you have questions and I'm not going to be able to answer them all, but I will tell you this much. Most of my people have signed over the lands to the government. A few of us, this group in particular, have avoided moving onto the reservations. The Great Spirit gave us this land and we are not quite ready to leave it just yet. We know who Higgins is and what he plans. We are just unsure how he is going to proceed. Regardless, we need to protect the land and those who live upon it. It is our sacred duty and we will not dishonor it by leaving."

"What are his plans? Is this part of the business I was mentioning earlier? How are you going to stop him?"

Stone turned to the opening of the tipi as if the answer to her question lay beyond the buffalo hides. It was several minutes before he turned back to her. "It most likely is, but we have no proof. No one to inform us of the evil he is about to bring to our lands specifically. He has paid off many with the golden wealth he has found here."

"Then how do you know he is about to bring evil here? How do you know that he plans to ruin the lands? Have you taken any prisoners and asked them? Or gone into town to investigate?"

"It's not our way to take prisoners and question them. We either count coup against them or kill them. As for how we know, we do. Just as River knows you are a ghost woman, out of place. Out of time. Yet, you do not question her."

Sierra frowned, rubbing her injured leg in almost an afterthought. Deciding it was best to let them think what they did without confirmation, she didn't respond to his last comment. "What about the body that is buried there? Louise isn't part of your tribe. Are there other bodies there?"

Now Stone frowned. "Bodies? That is not our burial place. You say there are bodies there?"

"Yes, but she wasn't properly buried. I tripped on an exposed hand. It had been gnawed upon by some animal, but the rest of the arm was still under the ground. I was running and didn't realize it was sticking up. I didn't realize what it was at first. Some of the fingers had been chewed down to the bone."

"Possibly it was just an animal bone?"

"Look. I may not know a lot of things, but a

human hand I'm well aware of."

"You're sure it wasn't just lying there on its own? Dragged there by an animal?"

Sierra had to think about it for a moment. "Maybe. I'm pretty sure the main part of it was still underground, and when I tripped on it, surely it would've been kicked further away, but it wasn't. It just flopped a bit, but still remained secured to the dirt under it. However, I was pretty startled, and I was already scared because of Mr. Higgins' attempt to kill me, so I could be mistaken. It all really happened so fast and my main concern was trying to get out of there, not investigating who it was or how they were buried."

"When you're feeling better, would you be willing to go back to see if we can find it again? As a culture, we find it extremely disrespectful to disturb one's grave, but if, in fact, they're hidden there, then their souls are probably not at rest."

"Yes. Let's go now. I don't want to wait a moment longer. Bart said he was the only one who went there. If that's the case, then how did that body get there, unless he buried it? And if not him, then who placed the body there? How did they die? And if he did do it, then he must be turned over to the police."

"The sheriff won't do anything. Higgins owns him and many others. As for leaving now, no. You've not even fully recovered. This is the first day in weeks you are awake. If you relapse, River will have my hide to decorate her tipi with, or worse, to wear on her body. Your muscles ain't strong enough to handle a journey back to the area. It can wait another day or two for you to be healthier."

"No! It can't. If he's the reason there's a body there, and if I became another one, then he has to be stopped. There's no telling how many he might've killed. How many will go missing if we don't stop him now? There are already five people missing that I'm aware of."

Stone stood and leaned over menacingly. "I said not today. I'll be back later with more questions. Rest, and when I return we'll see how you're feeling and go from there."

Sierra waited until he left, then stood and cringed as she put weight on the leg. If River hadn't come in when she had, Sierra was sure she would've fallen back down. As much as she hated to admit it, Stone was right. There was no way she had enough strength in her legs, or lack of pain from the injury, to make such a journey. However, she really detested he was correct about anything. She knew part of it was what he'd put her through just a while ago. Or rather, was it *would* put her through? This time travel stuff gave her a headache, when her past was his future and her present was all mixed up.

River helped her to sit back down. "We need to work your muscles to being active again. Can't rush these things. As much as you dislike it, he is right in making you wait before you go away from this camp. Right now, it's the safest place for you. The evil man can't touch you here."

"I know. I just hate that he's right, though. Something about him just wants me to do the opposite of what he demands. However, I'm sore and even this little bit of energy has worn me out greatly."

"You've been ill for many moons, child. You need to give your body time to readjust to being alive."

"I know. Doesn't make it easy, though, but I'm aware that you're right."

Chapter 18

River took very good care of Sierra, but after two days of being stuck in the tipi, Sierra was anxious to get out and go back to the Santa Fe Eating House. At least to let them know what happened to her. Bart should be arrested, the area he had taken her to for the picnic should be investigated. As far as she was aware, there was still a hand sticking out of the ground and she had to assume there was still a body attached to it.

She worried the body was Louise. After all, it was her medallion she'd discovered in the area. It dawned on Sierra she wasn't sure where the necklace was now. The last she remembered, she was showing it to Bart, and that was when he went bat-shit crazy as easily as if someone had flipped a switch. Sierra had always heard about people doing that, one minute being fine and the next just totally gone like they were instantly inhabited by something evil, but she'd never experienced it firsthand. Until recently, Bart had gone from caring and sweet, even a bit romantic, to dark, cold and sinister.

She'd have to ask Stone when he came to visit her today if he knew anything about Louise's necklace. She seemed to have lost it and it broke her heart. It wasn't in the dress pocket where she thought she put it when Bart tried to grab it.

Stone had come multiple times since she had awakened. According to River, he had checked on her when she was unconscious as well. His behavior was perplexing to her, considering she was sure he was the exact same person who attacked her when she first came to Colorado. Although Stone had been in to see her, he refused to answer many specific questions she had about Higgins.

She was sure he was getting aggravated, She'd become more reserved in her responses because of his increasingly harsh attitude at times. She was no longer scared of him. At least there was some benefit to his gruffness. No matter how irritated he got, Stone hadn't touched her in any way, respecting her space. When they weren't talking about Higgins, their conversations were pleasant and enjoyable. Each of them talked about their culture, their childhood, familial bonds and growing up as they had. Minus, of course, the modern conveniences and experiences Sierra encountered as a child.

Today, with permission from River, Stone stepped into the tipi with gifts. He gave them to River, then stepped out, closing the flap to give them a few minutes of privacy. He'd brought Sierra a Cheyenne beaded dress and a pair of high-fringed boots, also beaded to match the dress. The workmanship was impeccable, and Sierra was immensely humbled by the beading she knew had been done by hand. Helping her wash and change, River then opened the flap, ushering Stone to come in for his visit. When he saw Sierra, he stopped, his eyes drinking in every aspect of her. He was stunned. How had he not noticed how beautiful she was until this moment? Even his inner beast sat up, curling his tail around his front legs in a regal pose, giving her his full attention.

Sitting down, Sierra couldn't help but inwardly

smile at his stunned reaction. "Thank you for such a lovely gift. Did you make it?"

"No." He chuckled as he moved in to sit opposite her. "I'm sorry I ruined your dress when I brought you in. I figured it was time you had something nicer and clean to wear. I didn't make it, though. One of our women, named Sage, made it for me as a gift for you. I hoped you would like it."

"I love it. I can tell there's been a lot of hard work that went into this outfit. It's absolutely stunning. I'm very honored by your gift." It was the first time he'd been particularly nice to her. Seeing him smile and laugh warmed her heart. Without fearing him, she found him gentle and sweet. And very handsome, as the smile transformed his features to become softer. She often found herself staring into his gorgeous eyes. They were so unique, a rich amber with flecks of gold, making them almost glimmer. She had to admit she found herself almost drowning in them. She realized during the past couple of days how much she'd come to look forward to his visits, almost giddy with anticipation.

Thoughts of Bart quickly left her mind. What she had with Bart was an infatuation, a crush, but when he started becoming harsh and cruel, she quickly backed away. She realized she only continued to see him to appease her own journalistic curiosity in uncovering the mysteries that seemed to surround him.

Admittedly, Stone was also enigmatic, but not in a creepy psycho-killer way. She knew he was hiding something from her, that they all were, but she assumed it had to do with tribal issues. She was the outsider after all, and she couldn't blame them for being cautious around her.

"Why are you the only one who visits me?"

"What do you mean?"

"I assumed I'd see others, considering I'm a stranger here. Does your village not see me as any kind of threat? Or are you generally unconcerned of foreigners in your village?"

"I brought you here. I claimed you as coup. You're mine. My responsibility, so others do not concern themselves with that which doesn't belong to them." If he was honest with himself, she was more than just his coup. Their talks over the past couple of days told him how intelligent she was, which intrigued him. Once she got over screaming in terror every time he neared her, he found himself actually enjoying being in her company. It didn't seem to matter to her that she was with his people, nor was she overtly concerned with their differences. Instead, she was curious about the Cheyenne way, interested in learning and showing respect. That impressed him greatly, which wasn't an easy thing to accomplish. He didn't trust whites, male or female. He assumed they were all the same until Sierra. She had an inner spirit she wasn't even aware of, but his lion was very titillated. The cougar inside of him wiggled his rear every time he neared River's tipi, and once Stone entered, he had to reign in the pounce his lion wanted to do.

Somehow, she affected him in ways he hadn't thought himself capable of until she fell into his arms. His cat licked his whiskers, waiting, wanting to use his tongue on her, yet prevented by the man.

"Is Sage your wife?"

Again he chuckled. "No. She is berdache. She was married once, but her husband and sister-wife have both passed. Now she helps those who don't have another to care for them."

"Why don't you have someone to care for you?" Although she didn't know what a berdache was, Sierra found him being single to be great news and her focus was more on his availability than on berdaches. However, after what she'd learned of Cheyenne way, she found this also unusual.

"I was engaged once. I would rather not talk about it. It was long ago. Why did you come out West? To find a husband?"

This time Sierra laughed. "Goodness, no." Letting out her sigh, she gave him a weak smile. "I guess you could say it was an adventure to come out here. I had a premonition my destiny lay in Colorado."

"Do you think you found it with Higgins?"

"God, no. I admit I was infatuated with him, but I think part of that stemmed from the fact he saved my life on the train and guided me to Colorado Springs. The more I got to know him, the less I liked him. He was a hard, cold man and that's not my type. I didn't come out looking for a husband, or someone to be with."

"What do you think he's going to do to the land?"

"Actually, I wish I knew. I'd tell you in an instant, if I did. I have no loyalties to Higgins. Not anymore. He lost any respect and obligation I had when he tried to kill me. Speaking of which, when can we go search for that body. I really think it's Louise, and if it is, I'll have proof she didn't just run away."

"Soon. Very soon. I know I'm asking you to be patient a lot, but there are things you are unaware of that need to be dealt with before we can go."

"Okay. I'm trusting you to handle whatever is going on, but I'm also hoping it will be soon. Too much time has passed as it is, and it concerns me. If I can find something on Higgins legally, we can prevent whatever he has planned for the land you are trying to protect. It's a win-win, but time is of the essence."

"I'll speak to the others again." Stone stood but waved her to remain seated. Stopping just before he walked through the flap, he turned to gaze longingly at her. "I apologize if I'm out of line, but you look beautiful in that dress."

Blushing, Sierra demurely lowered her eyes. "No apology needed. Thank you for your compliment."

He lingered a moment longer, needing those few minutes to reign in his beast and calm his manhood down, wondering what got into him all of a sudden. He waved River back to the tipi as he departed.

Chapter 19

Anna entered the kitchen. She was somewhat surprised to see Florence packing up some soup and sandwiches. "May I be of assistance?"

Florence shook her head. "No. Thank you. I'm almost done."

"Where are you going? Got a hot date?"

"Hot?" Florence gave her a quizzical look.

"It's something Sierra would say."

Florence scowled, returning her concentration to packing the basket with the last of the items she planned on bringing. "I'm headed over to Mr. Higgins. I, too, want to know what happened to Miss Hanley. I hope to discuss the subject with him."

Anna perked up. "May I accompany you?"

Florence didn't even look up. "No." When she did, she noticed the utter sadness in the younger woman. "I understand your desire to come with me, but you're too excitable at the moment. Mr. Higgins won't be as cooperative if there is a hysterical woman in his presence. Calmer heads must prevail, and I can't take the chance of you becoming temperamental."

Anna sniffled. Florence was right. Anna was far too emotional on this subject. It was bad enough Louise and Sophie were gone, but losing Sierra when she should've been safe with Mr. Higgins, enjoying a beautiful sunshiny day on a romantic picnic, was too much for her to contemplate.

Anna had family back east, and though she'd loved them dearly, she felt the need to go west and make her own way in life. She admitted it was hard at times to be without her kin, but the girls of the house made it so much better to get through those rough patches. Especially Sierra. Something about Sierra gave Anna a sense of comfort and familiarity that was reassuring to her. Knowing she was killed by the Cheyenne, her body not even retrieved so she could even be given a proper burial, left Anna depressed and lost. She didn't know how to accept such a senseless death. She didn't have a chance for any type of closure to say goodbye to her dear friend.

"Please, please let me know if you find anything. I miss her so much. This shouldn't have happened. She should've been safe. He should've protected her, or at least brought her body back for a proper funeral."

"I agree. Too much has been happening of late. Too many have gone missing, and Miss Hanley is the last straw which will go unanswered. We'll talk when I return." Florence went over to Anna and gave her a very uncharacteristic, comforting hug. It surprised Anna, but she was also grateful the normally hard woman showed such compassion in her time of need. Maybe she'd misjudged the woman all along.

Florence pulled back, patting Anna's arm before she grabbed her shawl and moved it around her shoulders. Snatching up the basket, she left the Eating House kitchen without a backwards glance.

Of course, Florence knew where Bart lived. She headed right for the elaborate building located only a couple of roads away, knocking on the door to notify him, or anyone else, she was there. With no answer, she entered and called out, "Bartholomew? It's Florence."

"In the library," he called back.

She turned left and headed to where she knew the library was situated. He opened the door just as she approached. His arm was in a sling to prevent him from moving his shoulder and making the injury he sustained worse. "What are you doing here?"

She lifted the basket to show him. "Thought you might appreciate a good couple of meals without having to go out for them. I'll set up the meal in the dining room?"

"Fine." It really wasn't, but he didn't want to start an argument over his preference to be alone. He followed her into the dining room and sat down. "Hope it's stuff I can eat one handed."

"I brought some soup and sandwiches. Both easy to maneuver with one hand." She set the food before him, then took the chair beside him.

"You're not eating?"

"I'd prefer you gain your strength. Anything

left over I can wrap and store for you for a later time."

"What do you really want, Flo?" He grabbed a sandwich and took a bite, watching her closely while he chewed.

"I need to know, Bart. What really happened with Sierra?"

"Just what I told the sheriff. I took her on the picnic and we were attacked by the Cheyenne. She was hit and went down. I barely escaped with my own life."

"And you're sure she's dead? You didn't just leave her without trying to save her?"

"No. She wasn't moving and we're talking about the Cheyenne. They don't leave anyone alive."

"Except you."

"You sound disappointed, Flo."

"Surprised. Why didn't they hunt you down? Finish the job? That's more their style. Suicide Warriors. Dog Warriors. Fight to the death. It's all a game to them. It's all about counting their coup. So why let you live?"

"Maybe taking her and just hitting me was coup enough."

"Why did you go to that spot? I know you own the land now, so why did they go?"

Bart took another bite of his sandwich, chewing thoughtfully. "I wanted her to see my land. As for the Indians, you know how they are about what they still think of as theirs."

"Were you falling for her? I saw the way you looked at her."

"Yes. I liked her."

"She was dangerous."

"I know. I told you I would take care of it."

"I expected you to be more discreet."

He pounded his fist on the table, making all the dishes bounce and clatter. "It was never my intention to have it go down that way. The Cheyenne appeared out of nowhere. They should've all been removed to the reservation. I own that land legally. I've got the crews coming in two weeks. You think I need this shitstorm? I hoped to convince her to drop her nosy ways. Instead all she did was ask more questions. She was worse than my mother. I hadn't planned on it happening this way, but I take advantages when I see them. I saw an opportunity and I took it. End of story."

Florence watched him closely. "You've gotten good, Bart. I used to be able to tell when you were lying, but now I'm not so sure."

"You need to start minding your own business and stay out of my affairs too."

"No. This is my affair. When you asked me to get those introductions for you for that mining, you made me a part of this. When you wanted me to get the land deals and oust the Cheyenne with my contacts with the government and Harvey, you made me a part of this. When you asked me to be your partner, *you* made me a part of this. But, I want to know exactly what I'm now a part of. First my girls go missing, and then Miss Hanley is Cheyenne bait. This has got to stop. Tell me the truth. Are you back to your old habits again?"

"Now why would you ask such a question?"

Florence leaned forward. "I know you. I know you and your tendencies. I thought once you got the gold you'd be better. You were doing so good, but recently things have been changing back to your old heinous ways. First Edith mysteriously vanishes, then Stella, Nancy and Sophie disappear. Then Louise, and I know you were in the house the night *she* supposedly departed, and *you* left the note. You and I have a little discussion about Sierra, and suddenly Miss Hanley is attacked. How many more? How much longer is this going to continue? You can't keep doing this."

"I'll do as I please, when I please. I own this town. I own the law here. Hell, I *am* the law. What I say goes. Don't make me add you to my list of problems to be handled as well."

"I'm not afraid of you."

"Sure you are. I've always taken care of you and I know when you're trying to put on a brave front. I scare you just as I scare all the yellow-bellied cowards I employ. You know I would break your scrawny neck as easily as if it were a twig and not give it another thought."

"You can't be that cold and heartless. You're better than this. I know it."

"A better, more efficient man, yes. Even better at not wasting opportunity and money. But I'm as cold and heartless as my parents were. Maybe more so."

"Did you kill them, then? Sophie, Louise, Nancy, Stella and Edith? Did you kill Sierra too? I thought you left those horrible habits behind in Pennsylvania, along with the other dozen women that mysteriously disappeared. Why are you so cruel and callous? It's wrong. You've got to know how pernicious you're being."

Bart stood so rapidly his chair fell backwards, hitting the floor with a loud thud. He grabbed Florence by the neck, lifting her off her seat as he squeezed. Snarling into her face, his eyes cold and dark, he whispered harshly, "Don't test me. I'd have no hesitation to do the same to you."

He flung her back into the chair and stormed away from the table. "I suggest you don't visit me again. As for our business deal, I will make sure you get paid, but if you step in my home again without my invitation, I'll kill you as an intruder."

As he headed upstairs, Florence sat there stunned, knowing she couldn't stay in that house any longer. She couldn't protect him any longer. This was a smaller town than where they were raised in Pennsylvania. It was there she could help cover for him when girls he seemed interested in turned up missing or dead. When he decided to go west, she was glad. Fewer women meant fewer chances of his continuing his macabre, unholy tendencies.

As she started to leave the residence, she saw a stack of papers on his desk opposite the dining room. She looked around to see if he was nearby, then quickly entered his study, curiosity getting the better of her. The papers were about the mining project, which was what she expected. What she wasn't expecting was how he planned to work the mines. No wonder the Cheyenne were up in arms. If they had any inkling of what was about to befall this area, they'd do anything and everything to stop him. Maybe the Cheyenne really did go after Bart and Sierra was just an innocent who got caught in the crossfire.

She heard a door open upstairs. She knew she had to get out of there as fast as possible. Taking one more glance at the papers, she returned them the way she found them. Cautiously, she made her way out of the house, slipping out the front door as quietly as she could. He was wrong. Florence wasn't scared of him, she was terrified.

Chapter 20

River was out of the tipi getting more supplies. Left alone, Sierra stood to test the weight on her injured limb. It was still sore, tender, and although it was painful, it was manageable.

Moving to open the flap to peer outside, she was thrilled no one was near the tipi. Cautiously, she stepped out. Immediately, the sun warmed her skin and she tilted her head up, her eyes closed. The fresh air caressed her and the sun on her face felt glorious. It seemed like forever since she felt fresh air, not just what managed to come in from either the open flap or the rolled-up bottom.

Children's laughter and the sounds of dogs yelping seemed more pronounced outside. She most likely looked like a complete idiot as she stood with her face raised to the sun. She hadn't moved when a few minutes later, a strange chuffing sound made her open her eyes and discover the source.

Gasping in fear, she watched as a couple of bears came close to the playing children. And the dogs? They were wolves. She was astounded, watching such wild and dangerous animals romping around the children and the adults paying no attention to such a perilous circumstance. Until a bug flew into her mouth, she hadn't realized she was standing there agape. She coughed to spit it out before her eyes widened as a bear started to chase an eight-year-old boy. Sierra barely registered the fact of no one else being worried about the situation. However, her own concern for them overrode all other thoughts. Sierra screamed for the others to help prevent the impending attack, but instead of leaping into action and protecting the child, they all stopped to stare at her as if she just grew antennae out of her head.

They probably didn't speak or understand English, but she was also frantically gesturing to indicate the child was in danger. Couldn't they see the animals within the circle of tipis?

A mountain lion began to approach her, and she looked around desperately for a weapon since no one else seemed to care she was about to be attacked. Surely these wild animals weren't considered pets!?

She felt a tug on her dress, then her arm being taken to pull her away. When she resisted, River shoved her back into the tipi, pulling the flap closed before turning on Sierra.

"What do you think you're doing?"

"What is *wrong* with you people!? That boy was about to be attacked and none of you were doing anything!"

Stone burst through the flap. "Just what do you think you were doing out there?"

Hackles going up as soon as he came in, Sierra lifted her chin in utter defiance. "I was getting fresh air and warning you people about your children almost being injured! How could you all stand by and watch while such ferocious animals kill your young? Do you just sacrifice them or something?" Sierra knew she was yelling at him, but she didn't care. The whole idea was just insane to her as to how they could just ignore the whole situation going on around them as if it were an everyday event.

"They're safe. It's *you* I'm going to be lucky to save!" He turned on River. "Why didn't you stop her from going out?"

Moving to stand between Stone and River, Sierra glared at him. "Hey! Don't attack her. I left on my own! You can't keep me locked up here! You told me I wasn't a prisoner here and I could leave any time."

River's softer, calmer voice came from behind Sierra. "I have other work to do and you won't let me have her help. I can't be with her all day. Besides, she was bound to find out."

"Find out? Find out what?" Sierra's temper changed to being confused.

They both ignored her. Stone moved slightly around Sierra so he could talk directly to River. He switched to speaking Cheyenne. Sierra noticed how his jaw worked, but he kept his tone soft and respectful. *"The others don't want her to know. They already aren't pleased she's here to begin with. You know the terms of allowing her to remain."*

"I know she's important for you to learn what she knows so you can fight the ve'hoe. She's more than that, my son. You've no idea what she will be to you and this tribe. If you can't make them understand, then I will speak to them on her behalf."

"Regardless of her importance, she can't go beyond this tent. She can't learn what we are or how different we are. She will turn on us like others have in the past. Remember Sand Creek? We can't go through that again. We lost too much."

"There are worse things than death, Stone. Each of us carries out own burdens. She is no different. If we can't trust her, then we lose her faith to trust us. She needs to know what we are in order to protect us from them. She will stand witness for us."

"She's a white woman. They don't respect their women any more than they respect this land. What makes you think they will listen to her?"

"Because it's why she came to us."

"She came to us because I counted coup. But

the others would just as soon see her dead or ransom her."

"You can't let that happen. You are going to need her. She is why you and the others will continue to exist. Without her, we're all doomed."

Stone frowned. River spoke in riddles, but he learned, as they all had, that River's predictions usually came true. If she said Sierra was important to them, then he couldn't argue.

He turned back to Sierra, giving her an appraising glare from head to toe. Switching back to English, he commanded. "Stay in here until I see what damage has been done."

"And if I don't?"

"Woman! You try my patience. Your throat may be slit as easily as you breathe air if you disobey me."

"I'm not one to take orders well."

River stepped up and put her hand on Sierra's arm. "Just this once, child, listen and obey. We're trying to help you. It's for your safety we ask you to remain inside. Let Stone speak to the others. He will make them understand the need to be in the living air. Now that you're healing well and building strength, you can help with communal duties. Give you purpose while you convalesce."

"Why can't you just let me go back to Colorado Springs?"

"Because it's not safe. Not until we know what Higgins is up to. He already tried to kill you once. He will do so again if he suspects you are still alive." Stone moved towards the entrance, his hand on the flap. "I understand why you want to go out. Let me talk to the others, but until then, stay here." He slipped out of the tipi, standing still a moment to gather his wits about him. She infuriated him to no end, but she also set his blood afire. She was in his thoughts almost every moment of every day. He looked forward to checking in on her, even when she was being obstinate. He didn't care. Stone wasn't sure what it was about her that captured his imagination, but she was all he could think about.

Sierra grumbled. It wasn't a request. It was a command, and it set her teeth to grinding. The man was infuriating, but she did respect River and everything the woman has done for her with great appreciation. It was only because of her that Sierra decided to not argue any further, nor be rebellious and just walk out the tent.

Stone sat in the circle, listening to all those around him. He knew it was going to be difficult, and he wasn't wrong. With her causing the commotion she had, discussions increased on what to do with her. Selling Sierra to another tribe, holding her for ransom or just killing her outright were the ones in the lead. It had been many years since the Cheyenne had a captive, and usually when this band did, they would give them away to a human tribe quickly. What happened to them after that wasn't any of their concern, but Sierra was different. River insisted she was needed with this group, that she'd somehow be important for their future.

As they continued to discuss her outcome, one

of the young boys came and stood, waiting to be acknowledged. Stone held up his hand as he nodded towards the boy to speak.

"Seven men are approaching."

Everyone rose to their feet and headed out. Anyone approaching their village was rarely a good sign, especially over the past couple of decades. Since most of the Cheyenne had been relocated to Indian Territory in Oklahoma or Montana, they've been able to remain here undetected and unbothered. Had their group gotten too big? Had they stayed here too long? Had the ve'hoe, the white man, told the soldiers they were nearby and their camp was now discovered? Maybe they heard about Sierra and came to buy her freedom?

Speculation was rampant, but they all knew until they met with them, none would know the true meaning of their visit. Stone, Black Mountain and Sitting Fox made their way to the forefront while the others headed to various points around the village, making sure the women, elders and children were protected.

The three men moved out of the protective circle, waiting as the soldiers approached them. They knew once the other men made sure the others were safe at the opposite end they would join the three. Stone had long ago given up any trust of white soldiers. The Cheyenne suffered greatly at the hands of soldiers, and unlike humans, this village endured much personally. Their life spans were vastly increased over those of the human world, but that didn't mean they were invincible. They could still die with a mortal injury. It just took more of an effort to kill them. As such, this group became the first of the Dog Soldiers in order to protect the humans.

In a way, Stone regretted that the human Cheyenne's were unaware of their true natures. Being a part of the Dog Soldiers or Suicide Boys was an honor they chose, even if it included giving up their lives to protect others. It was ingrained in their soul and a major part of what made them Cheyenne.

In the 1860s, the settlers and miners who came

to Colorado for the gold in the hills couldn't care less about trading with the Indians or respecting their culture and territory. They wanted the land and instant wealth. It didn't matter how they obtained it. The white man felt entitled to take the land as they desired. To them, a good Indian was a dead one, or one removed from the area and thrust onto reservations. Whites killed the buffalo, not for meat or hides but for leverage in pushing the red man out. The Cheyenne and other Plains Indians pushed back.

The Dog Soldiers became a group of Cheyenne militants who started within the tribe before becoming an independent faction. They got their name from the ropes originally used for dog travois before horses were used to pull the sleds, hooked up to the back of them as the nomadic tribe would move from one location to another. The sleds enabled each horse to pull between 600 to 800 pounds. When horses took over, the Dog Soldiers held onto the dog ropes and gained notoriety when they would sing their death songs as they rode out to meet the enemy. They would then jump off their horses and drive stakes into the ground so they had a line of maybe twenty men out in front. These men vowed that once the stake was driven in, they wouldn't pull it up. One end of their sash was tied to the buried post and the other would be looped around their shoulder. To the enemy, the Dog Soldiers would look like easy prey, but that was far from the truth. The dog men were close enough together so they'd be able to help each other, forcing only one horse to pass between them. Standing, they could shoot their guns or arrows with greater accuracy. Some of the Dog Soldiers would have a lance or even a club, the latter used to knock out a horse so they could attack the rider more easily. If a horse made it through, the others behind the line would chase them down to be killed.

The Cheyenne were relentless. If the enemy turned to retreat, the young boys would bring up fresh horses for the warriors to chase them down. It was a blood fest, which seemed to only increase to the point it culminated in 1864. The Sand Creek

Massacre.

When Colonel John Chivington organized an expedition from Denver to retaliate against the Indians, he attacked a peaceful faction along the Sand Creek in southeast Colorado, where the Cheyenne had been told to camp by an Indian agent at Fort Lyons.

Most of the warriors were out hunting, so the camp consisted of women, children and elders. Before the attack was finished, over 250 were killed, many of them tortured, murdered and then dismembered in a heinous fashion. Some of the regular U.S. soldiers refused to participate in the butchery, and even testified against the offenders at an official inquiry, but that did nothing to assuage the Cheyenne of their mistrust of the white man, who seemed intent on exterminating them all.

Stone's band avoided the site after the massacre and realized it would be safer if they weren't with their human brethren. Ma'heo'o, the Great Spirit, allowed one band in each of the various tribes that roamed the Earth to have the ability to channel the spirit guides that led them throughout their lives, taking on the special attributes of each animal belonging to their personal totem. Along with the abilities to shift into their spirit animal, they also enjoyed longevity. An average life span for one blessed by Ma'heo'o consisted of hundreds of years.

His reverie broken, Stone brought himself back to the situation at hand. The lead soldier got off his horse and walked with the reins in hand to stand in front of Stone and his men.

"Anyone speak English?" He was short, stocky with a small, trimmed mustache.

"I do." Stone took a couple of steps towards him. "What do you want?"

"I'm Sergeant Rover from the fort. We have a witness who states that you have a white woman being held hostage here. We've come to pay the ransom on her."

"We do have a ve'ho'keva'e here, but she was wounded and we took her under our care. She is not being held hostage."

"I'm not sure what a ve'ho'keva'e is. Are you saying you have no white women here?"

"None that are not here of their own volition. Ve'ho'keva'e is white woman."

"Bring her out, then, and let her tell me she's here of her own free will."

Stone turned and nodded to Sitting Fox to bring Sierra to them.

"What's this about?" Stone was well acquainted with the soldier's tactics. They would look for something small to approach them on and then hit them with a bigger complaint to incite something worse. Stone had the soldiers outnumbered, but that didn't mean there weren't some in reserve close by.

"As we stated, we had a source say you kidnapped a woman."

"How do you know we kidnapped anyone? We're caring for an injured person. Nothing more."

"And how did she become injured? If you didn't kidnap her, then how do you explain our witness saying you did?" Rover gestured for one of the mounted men to bring forth an arrow broken in two, the tip and part of the rod bloody.

Stone recognized it as the one he took out of Sierra's thigh. Were they being set up? How did they find the arrow, unless Higgins went back or sent someone to look for it or Sierra? It wouldn't be out of the realm of possibility, but to what end? To get them onto a reservation like their brethren? To establish a reason for a retaliation so they could kill them all with cause?

Sierra, dressed in the Cheyenne way, with beautiful needlework, porcupine needles and fringe, limped alongside of River, the latter allowing Sierra to use her as a type of crutch. The gathered men parted for the two women.

The disgust on Rover's face was readily apparent. Sierra knew from his contempt he assumed she was a traitor and chose to live with the Cheyenne. If it weren't for the fact they wouldn't let her leave the tipi, she would've found the whole experience intriguing and educational.

River had asked her not to mention anything

negative and Sierra understood her concern. She wasn't great at history, but she was well aware the Native Americans never really got the best deal out of a government confrontation. It was only in the last few of her decades that the Native American plight was coming to the forefront of being addressed. Previously, the past was written by the victors, who skewed the information to their benefit, forgetting the fact horrendous attempts at cultural, social and heritage genocide for the Natives was how they became the winners. Any time the Native Americans stood up for themselves, or tried to get justice for their wrongs, they were ignored and overlooked.

It had taken a long time for native tribes to get the government and American citizens to recognize them for who and what the native people were. Although they were still going through struggles before she left, they were doing far better in 2018 than they were in 1895.

The sergeant took off his hat as he approached the women. "Ma'am. I'm Sergeant Rover. May I ask your name?"

Sierra wasn't sure what was going on, but worried Bart might have sent them to see if she was still alive, and therefore a viable threat. She decided to be safe in her answers. "Yes. I'm Miss Hall."

"We'd gotten word there was a white woman here who might be in danger. I notice you're limping. How did you get hurt, if you don't mind me asking? Did they hurt you? Are you here against your will?"

Sierra couldn't help but notice the soldiers seemed antsy, as if itching for a reason to draw their weapons. She didn't appreciate the Sergeant's pompous attitude. Their whole demeanor set her nerves on fire, which was reflected in her response.

"Actually, I do. But since you asked, I was bitten by a snake while taking a shit. They didn't hurt me. I'm not here against my will. Is that good enough for you? However, I can't imagine the fact that I got bit by a snake to be of such concern that so many of you came out all this way to check up on li'l ole me. So, what's this really about?"

"Are you the only white female here?"

Sierra hesitated a moment, then responded truthfully. "I'm the only one I'm aware of."

"Are you here under coercion?"

"No. I'm here by choice. Now, unless you tell me what this is all about, I'm not answering anything else."

"We were just riding through, ma'am, on our way back to the fort. Just wanted to check on the welfare of any white women who might have been in distress."

"I'm not in distress, Sergeant, but thank you for your concern."

Chapter 21

After meeting with the sergeant and his soldiers, Sierra watched the men leave. When she knew they were out of earshot, she turned to Stone, her chin lifted. "I lied for you. I don't lie, not ever."

"I know you did. Why?"

"It seemed the right thing to do. Until we take care of Bart, I'm safer with you and your people. But I want to be outside. I want to know everything. You can't hide me or keep things from me. Not if you want me to trust you."

"I can't agree to that condition."

River moved up to the two of them. "Bring it to the others. I will speak on her behalf."

Stone gave her an odd look. "You should know better than that. Everyone knows we can't let outsiders know about us."

River switched to Cheyenne. *"Then make her one of us."*

Stone stepped back, aghast at the suggestion. *"No! Are you out of your mind?"* He was shocked at the proposal, and yet the idea of taking Sierra as his own also excited him. The lion inside roared with pleasure at the thought, almost clawing his insides to claim her.

If he were honest with himself, he'd been captivated since she ran into him in the forest. He'd spent every minute he could to be with her, even under the pretense of questioning her. Even though he might know the answers, he would ask her the same things, so he wouldn't have to leave her presence. He'd thought he was clever and no one would be the wiser, but he should've known he couldn't hide anything from River, even if he'd hidden it from himself.

Sierra was feisty and had a spirit worthy of a lion such as him. Other than those first few moments when she seemed terrified of him for some unknown reason, she hadn't seemed afraid of much else. She didn't cower. Often she stood her ground, meeting him toe to toe. He'd resigned himself to letting her go soon, but he'd never considered an alternative. Suddenly it was all he could think about. Stone realized he hadn't allowed himself to think of her as anything but an outsider. He was keenly aware of his desire to spend copious amounts of time in her presence getting to know her, but he'd lied to himself as to the real yearning of being with the human woman. He didn't even contemplate it as a possibility, so he never entertained such a notion.

However, River saw through his own charade. She alone realized his lion's hunger to make her his own, to ravish her body, to taste her sweetness. His mouth watered at the idea of her honey nectar under his tongue, and he felt the blood rush to his cock at the thought of it all.

The three stared at each other. Sierra tried to gauge what the two were saying. Whatever they were discussing, it'd caught Stone unprepared and she blushed at his close appraisal of her, wondering if whatever they were talking about would affect her positively or negatively.

"She won't do it. Look at her. She'll be repulsed at the idea of what we are."

River clucked her tongue at him. *"I don't*

believe that. Besides, she's already seen some of us in our spirit form."

"Precisely, and look how she responded."

"Only because she didn't know we weren't going to harm the children. She cares about us and cares about protecting us or she wouldn't have made such a fuss, nor would she have lied to the soldiers."

Sierra wasn't sure what was being said, as they both spoke their native language, but she knew from the looks they both gave her it was about her demand to have more freedom in the village. "I can still scream for the sergeant to come back. I'll tell him I lied out of fear if you'd rather I go, but I won't be kept locked away any longer. I'm getting better and stronger. I'll face whatever it is you're hiding from me."

"You don't know what you're asking," Stone snarled, leaning over her. The idea she'd leave and go back where she belonged frightened him almost as much as if she stayed and spurned him as her mate.

"I don't care. I agree to it." And she meant it. Then something dawned on her. With the soldiers coming, what happened to all the wild animals? She quickly looked around, then asked the question now on her mind. "Hey! You didn't kill the animals, did you? I don't see them anymore."

"Why would it matter? They were about to hurt our young. You said so yourself."

"True. I was concerned for the children, but that didn't mean I wanted the animals hurt. Please tell me you didn't kill them," she pleaded.

"We didn't, child," River reassured her, patting Sierra's arm.

"Then where did they all go?"

River gazed over at Stone, who returned her look with a glare. "They're safe."

"Are they your pets?"

"Goodness, no!" Stone sighed. "Let's go for a walk. We need to talk." He nodded at River. It was obvious this wasn't something he wanted to do, but felt resigned to this course of action. He knew River would inform the rest of the village of their impending conversation.

He realized Sierra was still limping, so he offered his arm for support. Gingerly, she took it and they walked out of the protective circle of the nomadic village. It was only when they were far enough away did Stone look for a large boulder or stump so she could sit.

They'd been in silence for the entire walk. Sierra knew he had a secret to tell, something that affected all of them. It was the only thing that made sense as to why they were so protective and refused to let her out of River's sight.

Once a fallen tree trunk was located, Stone helped her to sit, then paced in front of her. She knew he needed time to deal with finding the right words for something so vitally important—a secret the whole village bore. She was honored they believed in her and trusted her enough to share it. Her lying to the soldiers was probably what proved she was willing to protect them.

Not many would put such faith in a virtual stranger with such intimate knowledge, and she was impressed they would extend this arm to her.

After several minutes of only the sound of shuffling back and forth, Sierra spoke up. "Listen. I won't tell anyone whatever you're about to confide to me. I'm very good at keeping secrets and even better at not judging people. So, just know you can tell me anything and it'll be okay."

Stone curled his lip at her little speech. "It's our code I'm breaking. And know that if you betray us, there's nowhere on this Earth you can hide. We *will* kill you in order to protect ourselves. Are you sure you're really ready to learn our truth, knowing that it could cost you your very life? Are you willing to die for this knowledge and never share it with any other? Because that's the price for this information."

Sierra gave it some serious thought. Was whatever this secret was, which a village was willing to kill for, worth her knowing? In her heart, she knew it was, and her journalistic curiosity needed to be appeased. She wasn't sure why it was so important for them to trust her, believe in her, but she knew it was something she desired greatly. Her instincts told her she needed to know everything about the as it had something to do with why she'd come here, why her dreams had insisted her destiny lay in Colorado. She realized she hadn't known her destiny also lay in the past, but considering how bizarre her intuition was in general, she shouldn't have been very surprised. Unexpectedly, Sierra became cognizant that she had just the thing to prove her sincerity, an incident in which she protected her source, but she altered the story, so he wouldn't suspect she was from the future where women were able to work any job they desired.

Tugging her collar, she pulled it aside, exposing her collarbone and a bit of shoulder where a very long scar ran. "I got this from my friend's boyfriend. She was cheating on him and I promised I wouldn't tell anyone. When he learned I knew all along and hadn't told him anything, he slashed me with a knife. I had promised her I wouldn't, and I kept my word even though I almost died in the process." She released her collar and pointed at her injured leg. "I could've told the sergeant and his men I was shot by an arrow, and I didn't. I promised River I wouldn't say anything to incriminate anyone here in the village. I know I threatened to call them back, but I wouldn't have said anything or actually done so. I bluffed. I lied to get you to trust me which, now that I say it out loud, sounds totally ludicrous, even to me. Look, all I'm saying is, I understand the risk, and when I give my word about something, I swear it." Sierra didn't mention that as a news reporter she'd been willing to do as much to protect her sources. This was an easy choice for her to make.

The feathers in his hair flapped softly from the gentle breeze. She didn't know when or how this man she'd once feared was stalking her suddenly meant so much to her, but during her time here, she'd come to know him—his wisdom, his honor, his loyalty and his respect for his people. He'd checked on her daily and, admittedly, she looked forward to his visits. At first, she wondered if it was because it broke up the monotony of the day sitting and doing basically nothing, but then she realized it was more than that. She had come to talk to him. More than just answering questions that he asked her over and over again, but about him and life in the village; what the Cheyenne people had suffered in the hands of the Europeans who had invaded their lands, eventually forcing them out and onto reservations or killing their buffalo, which was not only their source for food, but their tipis, their clothes and much more. Their entire way of life had been disrupted and corrupted as a result, and though she knew some of it from the history books, she'd never been so keenly aware until she was actually living with them. It was an eye-opening experience with regards to the fortitude of these people.

She found herself craving more details. She wanted to know everything about the tribe Stone was from, and in a moment of clarity, she was aware she wanted to know more because she wanted to be closer to him. The fear of him dissipated and changed into something else, something more meaningful but scary none-the-less.

Was she actually falling for him?

She realized that even when he visited her, he was still holding something back. She assumed it wasn't anything she really needed to know: daily tribal issues that needed to be handled and resolved. She was aware he was one of their chiefs and alphas, though what the latter meant, she wasn't quite sure. There were 44 chiefs in the Cheyenne culture; she wondered how many were also alphas.

"No one outside of our band of Tsitsistas, not even others of our ilk, know what I'm about to share with you. That's how sacred we take this gift we have."

"I'm extremely honored and humbled by your confiding in me. I won't betray this trust."

"Should you do so, you'll put us all in danger, even the children."

"I understand. I'll protect all of you with this secret."

He stared at her as if wondering if he could really believe her. White men had always promised things, then betrayed them when their word didn't suit their needs. He didn't want to believe that of her. He wanted to have faith she wouldn't use the knowledge he was about to impart for her own gain. So often, they'd been told one thing and would lose everything because of the white father, just as Sweet Medicine had foretold long ago.

Sweet Medicine had gifted the Cheyenne four special arrows: two with the power over man and two with the power over the buffalo. He also warned them against the light-skinned people with such powerful ways who would appear, and many things would change when they came. Sweet Medicine urged them to keep their ways, even though he predicted the Tsitsistas wouldn't listen, but instead pick up the strangers' behaviors and forget all the good things in life. In the end, the Tsitsistas would be crazy.

Now Stone wondered if he were the crazy one, about to tell something so important to one such woman. "The animals you saw? They're us."

She raised an eyebrow in questioning consternation at him as she waited for more explanation. His statement hadn't made any sense. When no further information seemed forthcoming, she rolled her hand in a small circle. "And? I don't fully understand what you're trying to say."

"Have you ever heard of spirit guides?"

"Yes. They're your people's belief that an animal totem will be beside you all your life and assist you through difficult times guiding and helping. I'm sure I'm not exactly correct, but I hope I'm understanding the essentials. I believe the spirit of an animal or element guides your path in life."

Stone nodded. "Essentially, yes. That's correct. We go through a vision quest to locate each other. However, for one band in each tribe, we are given an additional blessing. Ma'heo'o, the creator of all things, what other tribes call a Great Manitou or Great Spirit, has given us special abilities. What you might call...special gifts."

"Why? Why did he choose only one band? What are these gifts?"

"In a time long since passed, Ma'heo'o was saddened. He saw his people suffering and weak while others prospered. So, he held a decree that each tribe had to forfeit one band in sacrifice for all the others. Some refused, and they no longer exist, but the rest of us selected or volunteered to sacrifice ourselves for the good of the rest of our people. For the Cheyenne, we are that band. We are the Dog Soldiers willing to die for our people's protection."

Sierra was totally engrossed in his story, leaning forward slightly as she listened intently.

"He wasn't as cruel as it might sound. It's like that bible story of the Catholics. How Abraham had to sacrifice his only son, but at the last moment an angel stopped him. At the last moment, Ma'heo'o stopped all of us; every one of us from every tribe was spared. But, because we were willing to sacrifice ourselves for the good of our people, he rewarded us instead. We were given some very special gifts."

"What does this have to do with your spirit guides?"

"Ma'heo'o bestowed upon us the ability to become our spirit animals and use those attributes.

The animals you saw earlier were us."

Laughing slightly, Sierra wasn't sure what she was expecting him to say, but that certainly wasn't it. "What do you mean you're the animals? That doesn't make any sense."

Stone looked around. "I wish our word meant something more to you, but since it doesn't, I'll show you."

One moment he was a man standing before her, and in the next he'd shifted in front of her eyes, transforming from a human into a mountain lion. When he roared, she screamed.

Chapter 22

Startled, Sierra unconsciously pushed back out of fear and fell on her ass, her legs sticking straight up in a V. She rolled to her side and got up, peeking over the log to see him in his lion form. If she didn't know better, she'd swear the beast was laughing, his mouth open, his head bobbing up and down. Standing slowly, she looked around, searching before focusing on the cougar standing in front of her. Now the animal was just watching her, sitting down in a dignified cat pose, his tail swishing behind him.

"Stone?"

The lion nodded once and did nothing more other than twitch his tail.

Cautiously, she moved back around the log and approached him. Sticking her hand out slowly, he jerked his head under her outstretched palm. The motion reminded her of a tabby she had years ago who would nose her hand when he wanted attention from her or his ears scratched.

Knowing this was Stone just felt strange to her.

The whole situation seemed bizarre. She pulled her hand away and stepped back. As soon as she did, he shifted back into a man, standing so close he towered over her. She should be intimated but found him more intriguing than fearsome.

"Are all of you cougars?"

"No. Our spirit guides are what lives inside of us and share with us their powers and abilities. As a result, we are all different. Each of us are as individual in our animal form as we are in our human one. This is just one of the many gifts bestowed upon us."

"Bear? Wolf?" These were the animals she'd seen around the children. Why the others hadn't worried about the kids being in peril from all the different dangerous predators romping around the village.

"Yes. And more." He watched her closely. Stone wasn't sure what he expected, but he was glad she wasn't being irrational or emotional. He'd had enough of that twice already. Once when she ran into him by Harper's Creek, and then again in

River's tipi when she first awoke.

She reached out and poked his bare chest. It was warm and hard and human.

Capturing her hand in his, he pressed it against his beating heart. He'd not been this close to her since he carried her into River's tipi all those moons ago. She'd fascinated him. She was intelligent, strong and spirited. These were all qualities he greatly admired but didn't think any woman, white or otherwise, capable of.

His warm breath caressed her face. His unique eyes seemed to hold something more than just wariness. Something unfathomable. He leaned down to press his lips against hers. There was no reason to kiss her, but he couldn't resist her rosy lips. He'd been fighting the feline within almost daily over the past couple of weeks, but seeing her accept him in his animal form, as well as having gotten to know her over the past couple of weeks, he just needed to claim a part of her, or at least try.

He'd never thought of light-skinned women as particularly beautiful, and though many might consider her so, it was her inner beauty and strength that impressed him the most. Although at first he seemed to terrify her, she adapted quickly and even had a spunk of her own.

She was surprised and even hesitant as their lips met. It wasn't until that moment that she realized how much she'd desired him over the past few days, only to culminate in this kiss. It was as if they were meant to be, and she realized another piece had clicked in place. She melted in his embrace, a euphoria draping over her. If a single kiss could be perfect, she was sure this was it.

Eyes snapping open, she pushed him away. "You said changing into your spirit guide was one of many gifts. What are some of the others? Were you the one watching me at the shack in Cripple Creek? Have you been hunting me here like you did in…before?"

Stone's eyes narrowed as he became instantly wary. "I was the one at the cabin, but I wasn't hunting you. I was keeping an eye on Higgins. Why do you think I've been hunting you? Why would you ask?"

"I need to know. I remember the lion in the tree and he didn't attack. It's nice to know that was you, but I need to understand something. Is longevity without aging one of your gifts? Or time travel? What else can you do?"

"As I mentioned, each of us has a different guide, and as such, we have different powers. However, a common one is longevity without aging as rapidly as humans do. For some, even time travel is possible under the right conditions. All of us also share increased strength and agility."

Rubbing her wounded thigh unconsciously, she moved to sit down. Her head was racing with the thoughts of her arrival in Colorado, especially of a man who looked exactly like him stalking her. More important were the words he called back to her as he was being arrested and dragged out of the hotel. Could it be possible? *'Don't leave me again'* suddenly made so much more sense if they'd been together here. Now. How could she do that? How could she give into him and then leave? "How old?

How long can you live?"

"If the conditions are favorable and we're not killed, then we can live for hundreds of years."

"Who is your oldest?"

"These are strange questions."

"Please. I need to know."

"Black Mountain would be our eldest member."

"How old is he?"

"1,248 years."

She paled at the thought. "How old are you?"

Working his jaw, he couldn't help but wonder where this line of questioning was going. "201."

His answer was what she needed for her theory. It really was Stone she'd seen in the photos at the Cripple Creek Jail and again at the museum. It was truly him that had followed her in Colorado Springs. If only she had known then what she knew now, she'd have run to him with open arms. But the question remained, why had she gone back to her time and left him? Maybe she died of old age and he saw it as a chance to be with her younger self again? Or she didn't really have a choice, just as she hadn't a choice in coming? Certainly her love life wasn't the only reason why she was here. There was something more important going on. Something, for whatever reason, she was involved in and crucial to. Maybe she should've paid more attention to those photos, and to the museum exhibits. Everything was so confusing.

"I'd like to go back, if I may. I need to think about things."

Feeling hurt and disappointed was a complete surprise to him. Maybe he shouldn't have kissed her, but her sudden change confused him. And if he were truthful with himself, it also upset him. His mountain lion was clawing at him, but for a different reason now. Stone could feel his spirit animal pacing within and he had to keep a tight grip on the beast. Despite his spirit clawing at him, he bit back his ache for her and held out his hand to assist her back to River's tipi.

They were as silent upon their return as they were on their way to the spot where they'd talked, only this time the reason was entirely different. When they entered the village circle, all of the Cheyenne were standing in a group. River was at the head of them, and once Stone gave a grim nod, she stepped up to take over helping Sierra back towards her accommodations.

"How are you doing, child?"

"I don't want to talk about it, River. What you and your people can do is amazing, but it's also confusing for me. I've a lot to think about, a lot to digest. I'll keep your secret, so you don't have to worry about that."

"The consensus is that you start earning your keep. We'll teach you to cook or bead or something to be of use to the other members of our band. You have a place here now."

"Because I know the truth? That was all it took to have a place here?"

"Yes. And the freedom to be an integral part of our band."

"It's so much, River. I just need some time." Sierra couldn't tell any of them what mattered the most. This secret was easy to keep because it rivaled a secret she'd been carrying around for weeks. With all they have entrusted to her, all they've done for her, how could she tell them the truth—that she wouldn't be remaining here. Not here in this camp, not here in this time.

She was brought here for a mission, a job she alone had to accomplish, and her love life wasn't part of it. She knew Stone felt rebuffed and hurt, but better to hurt him now than destroy his future too.

"Not too much. There are too many forces around us that are pulling one way or the other. We'll have to face them head on sooner than we'd like."

"I understand. Kind of. I'm not sure about these forces you're talking about, but I need to think things through. I'll keep my promise, though. I won't tell another living soul about how special all of you are. I just have to sort it all in my own head."

"Then rest. We will start your training tomorrow." River held the tipi flap open for Sierra.

Just as she entered to lie down, Sierra turned

back. "How old are you?"

River smiled. "734."

The woman barely looked 55, but she was hundreds of years old. A feeling of dread crept in and she worried what her gut was warning her about now. Sierra moved to lie down. Her head was throbbing with everything she'd learned in the past few minutes. Worse, her heart was in just as much pain.

Chapter 23

Sierra awoke. At first, she was sure what she'd learned the previous day was all a nightmare. People don't change into animals. People don't travel in time. Yet, she knew when she looked up at the inside of the buffalo-skinned tipi that it wasn't a dream. Everything had happened, even though she wasn't sure how or why. Nothing made sense, and yet, as her memory came flooding back, she knew it had all occurred.

Turning her head as River entered, Sierra sat up.

"Are you ready, child?"

"Ready?" She wasn't sure how much more she could deal with when she hadn't adjusted to what she'd learned thus far.

"To become an active part of the band. You know our secrets now. You knew this was a condition of that knowledge."

"Yes. Sorry. I'm still a bit sleepy. I remember, though. What do you want me to start with?"

"I thought I'd introduce you to Sage. She will

teach you how to do beadwork. Later, she will have you work with the plants, and then have you help her make the evening meal."

"Sounds like a busy day. I'll be ready in a few minutes."

River nodded as she waited for Sierra to prepare herself. Leading her across the field surrounded by tipis, Sierra watched those she passed carefully. The young children were playing, ignoring them as they walked by, but the older children and adults stopped whatever they were doing as they watched the two of them move across the field. Sierra had to keep her feet moving, but she was astounded as she saw the incredible strength of the villagers. One man was carrying an entire tree trunk on his shoulder as if it weighed as much as a sack of grain. Another was walking with an entire buffalo carcass. She was absolutely amazed and wished she had her camera to record it all.

River ignored them, concentrating solely on her destination. However, Sierra was keenly aware of the dozens of eyes upon her. She knew she was the interloper, the intruder. They didn't know her, and she was sure they felt they couldn't trust her. After all the times they'd been lied to, cheated and abused by the U.S. Government, she couldn't blame them for their wariness towards her, especially with a much bigger secret at stake.

Many different animals meandered about as well. Some wouldn't have made her think twice, but a bobcat and opossum playing together certainly caught her attention. Seeing the animals among the human population definitely stood out now that she understood the dynamics of their presence. "What are you, River?"

River stopped, turning back to face Sierra. "Lynx. I'm the keeper of knowledge and wisdom."

"And Sage? What is she?"

"A beaver. She is the hard worker of our group and the perfect one to teach you our ways. You'll be staying with her from now on."

Stopping dead in her tracks, Sierra was stunned. "Have I done something to offend you? I'm sorry."

River took her arm to continue walking. "No, child. It's time for you to move into a tipi that can take care of you better. Although you should, by rights, go to Stone's tipi, we didn't think it appropriate. Mine is a place of healing and you no longer need my services. Sage's is a place of learning. The time has come for you to move forward in your journey. Nothing stands still for eternity. Life is more like the river. It's not stone."

Sierra bit her lower lip nervously and River could sense how apprehensive she was feeling. What she hadn't realized was not going to Stone's tipi was what had upset her.

"I'll still be nearby should you need me. You're not being abandoned, child."

"I know. I guess I'm just nervous. Having only really been with you and Stone the past few days, I'm concerned I might be disrespectful without meaning to. I've learned that much from being with you both, that respecting other members of your band is very important, and I worry I might make mistakes."

"Mistakes are a human condition. You'll be okay. Sage has quite a bit of patience. She'll be good for you to learn from."

"I'm sure you're right. Forgive my timid behavior. This is all so new to me."

River looked up at the sky where an eagle was flying by. "Do you think an eagle takes flight each day worried where the winds will take them? No. They have faith that the winds will lead them where they need to be in order to survive." Lowering her head from the view of the sky, she smiled at Sierra. "You're no different, my child. Each day is for learning something new and trusting the winds to lead you down the correct path, especially when you have Ma'heo'o guiding your journey. Come. Sage is waiting."

Sierra followed River to an elaborately decorated tipi. The designs were amazing and, though she was no artist herself, she appreciated those who could create such beauty.

Remembering Sage made the beautiful outfit she was wearing, she needed to make sure she commented on it to her.

A woman was sitting on a hide in front of the opening to her tipi, bent over, her long, cascading hair covering her face. Her hands were working the material with beads. Her dress was also richly decorated with beautiful artwork. River pointed to an empty place next to the woman, indicating for her to sit.

"Sage. This is Sierra, whom we've discussed. Sierra? Sage has accepted the responsibility of training and caring for you." From beneath the shawl she was wearing around her shoulders, she placed a bowl with berries and a bone knife beautifully carved.

Sierra realized these were offerings of thanks for the undertaking Sage had agreed to. Sage lifted her head and Sierra was momentarily taken aback. Sage was a him, not a her. Not entirely. She was a transvestite. Sierra had no clue people with this proclivity were so accepted as a part of this society. Although she wasn't prejudiced, she was surprised and happy to know they weren't ostracized as they were by some in her time.

"Sage is a berdache." River seemed to understand her stunned reaction and quickly reassured her. "Her husband, Little Crow, entered death many moons ago, as did her sister-wife. Sage teaches our young now. She is a gift to our band."

"I'm very sorry for your loss and very grateful for your willingness to train me and let me stay with you. Stone told me you made the dress and boots I'm wearing. The work is stunning, and I'm honored you'll be my teacher."

"Thank you, Sierra. We have much to do today, so let us begin." Sage lowered her head to River who departed, leaving the two women alone.

Sierra was educated on much more than just beadwork, sewing and cooking from Sage over the next three days. She also learned about the ways they respected each other and protected all within their band. She was informed some men had multiple wives, while most only had one. Some, like Stone, never had any and didn't seem interested in taking on a wife.

"Has he no interest in women at all?"

Sage let the corner of her lips twitch upwards in a wistful smile. Her eyes scanned the field for him. He was always one of the easiest to spot, being a head taller than most in the camp, which was saying a lot since none of them were small in stature. She often found Sierra watching him, but quickly looking away whenever he turned in her direction. Sage caught him doing the same; a visual cat and mouse game. A part of Sage wondered what happened between the two of them. Stone had rallied for her to remain, pushed to have her know what they really were, urged to have her learn about them. It was the first time in a very long time Sage had ever seen him so intrigued by a female. However, once he found Sierra in the crowd, all his attention would cease, and Stone was once again aloof.

"He hasn't shown interest in anyone, male or female, in over a hundred years."

"What happened then?"

"The woman he cared about was killed."

"How awful! If I'm not considered prying, I'd like to know how."

Sage moved her hands over to Sierra and gently instructed her again on the needlework for the beading she was doing. Frustrated, Sierra dropped the material in her lap. "I'm just not going to get this."

"You have so little patience. Time and practice will always prevail. Maybe if you know that shirt is for Stone to replace the one he ruined on your leg, you'll be more focused." Pulling back, Sage looked up to find Stone gazing at them before quickly turning away. "You know, he cares for you."

Sierra's head popped up and she immediately roamed the area trying to find him. Once she did, she turned away, not wanting to let Sage know Stone affected her as well. Silly, when it was obvious to any who watched her that Sierra's eyes kept searching him out.

"A woman's chastity is highly regarded by our

people. It's an extreme offense to even attempt to take from a woman who is not giving of herself willingly." That explained why she hadn't gone to Stone's tipi even though she knew he claimed her as his coup. "Starving Deer had another who was jealous of Stone and her relationship with him. One night, Dull Axe followed Starving Deer when she went to relieve herself and attacked her. She fought and escaped, able to call for assistance. Dull Axe was beaten to death, but one of her family members who set out to destroy his property and kill Dull Axe's horses accidentally tripped and fell. The gun went off and killed Starving Deer by mistake. Stone has never been the same since. At least, until you. He's captivated by you. You like him as well. I can tell." Sage pointed again to the piece she was working on. "Finish that up. We need to sew it to the main piece and it must be done before we can start the evening repast."

"May I ask a question?"

"Yes."

"I've noticed when the evening meal is

prepared, and you call that it's ready, no one rushes to get the food. Why?" One thing that stood out the most for Sierra was the amount of respect the Cheyenne gave each other in almost everything they did. Each time one of the elders walked by, or one of the chiefs, Sierra would notice the deferential treatment they were given. It was impressive and something her world lacked. Sure, there were those who respected their parents, grandparents, and other relatives, but overall, the reverent dignity given to on older person didn't entirely exist to outsiders.

"We don't like to be first. It's arrogant to put ourselves above others. Our elders have earned respect and should be the first taken care of, then our helpless babes. The rest takes care of itself in time. We should never be considered selfish or putting our needs and wants above the other members of our band."

Those simple words clarified many things for Sierra. Stone may want her, but by going after her, he would consider himself selfish and going against his Cheyenne character. He also wouldn't force her, because of their strong belief in the chastity of the woman. Sierra had witnessed a courting from a nearby Arapaho tribe. The prospect would visit the girl, sitting outside of her tipi during the evening, and the two would talk. The first time she'd seen him enter the camp, he carried part of a buffalo, which he left for her and her family outside the tipi, indicating to her family he could provide for his prospective wife.

Sage informed her that was how courtships were done. "If the girl wasn't interested, she'd inform her family and they'd prevent any further interaction. This one seems to be going well. Marriage seems imminent as the girl's family has been preparing a tipi for them, which needs to be completed and furnished before the ceremony occurs. Thankfully, the Arapaho male is also blessed by Ma'heo'o and he's a Spirit Walker, a name chosen for those of us who have the ability to shift into our animal totem."

"Is it always the man who will court the woman? Do any of the women let their interest for a man be known first?"

"It can happen, but it's rare. Are you thinking of courting a particular male of our tribe?"

Sierra's cheeks reddened as she cast her eyes downwards. She could feel the blood rush to her face, the heat almost searing her skin. She knew she didn't have a right to want to be with Stone. She knew from their short interaction in the future she would leave him, and she didn't want to hurt him that way. "No. I was just wondering."

Sage reached over and took Sierra's hand. "You'd be good for him. I think he'd be good for you. Don't let your mind be the obstacle that prevents your happiness together."

"It's not, Sage. You don't understand. There's a lot more going on than just what I want. Besides, there's still the issue of whatever Higgins is up to and the body I found while on our picnic. I need to solve those mysteries."

"Speaking of which…" Stone's voice rumbled above her.

Her cheeks reddened even more. How much

had he heard? She looked up at him from her seated position, hoping her face wouldn't give too much of her emotional state away.

"Your leg seems to be doing better. If you're feeling up to it, I'd like to go back and see if you can locate that body."

"I feel up to it. It's been a while, do you think it will still be there?"

He held out his hand to help her up, then took her elbow to guide her to his horse.

"You stated only a hand was sticking out of the ground. Although other animals might have found it and pulled on it more, I doubt it would've come away from its shallow grave so easily."

"Why does it matter to you whether or not we find this body?"

He swung himself up on his steed's back, then reached down for her. Easily pulling her up to sit sideways in front of him, he nudged his horse to begin walking. Stone remained silent until they were out of earshot of the village.

"I have my suspicions. I don't believe the body

you found is the only one."

"What are you thinking? That he's a serial killer?"

"A what? What is that?"

"Sorry. A murderer of several people?"

"Yes. I've been aware of several women disappearing from the Harvey Eating House, Cripple Creek and Victor. Some were suspected of leaving on their own, but others were said to have been taken or even killed by the Cheyenne. We've had a hard time remaining in the area, with most of the Cheyenne and Arapaho being moved onto reservations. You know what we are. We wouldn't survive under such close scrutiny. It would be dangerous for all of us."

"Why do I have the feeling that's not the entire reason?"

He looked at her closely, and for a brief moment, she wondered if he were going to kiss her again. She wanted that kiss, and yet part of her realized it would cause complications, confusion and entanglements that neither of them needed nor could afford the luxury of.

Stone must've realized it too, for he quickly put his eyes back on the road in front of them. "I asked you before what you knew about the mining operations Higgins had planned."

"Yes. I'll tell you the same as I did then. I don't know anything other than he has a business plan to increase his mining operation and it involves the Harvey Girls' House Mother as part of it. And I only learned the last part because I found a letter indicating they were partners and they were arguing just before we departed on our picnic. It was something I was asking him about. What is it you suspect him of planning?"

"He's preparing to destroy the land and all the living creatures around it. I just can't prove it. But if I can somehow stop it by uncovering bodies in the area, I'll have more time to find a way to stop him permanently."

"Do you mean kill him?"

"Not unless it's necessary."

"I don't condone his plans, especially if he's

going to damage the land and everything around it, but I also don't condone his death either. Surely you can get help from the law? Maybe if you speak to the sheriff?"

"He owns the law in these parts. The only ones he doesn't own are the Rangers."

"The Rangers? Who are they and how can we get in touch with them?"

"The Colorado Rangers. They were established in 1861 and are sent to handle disputes of land and miners, or anything else the local sheriffs can't handle. I don't know how to ask for them to come here without going to the sheriff, which would defeat the purpose, since I doubt he'd notify the Rangers. Instead, the sheriff most likely would alert Higgins, preventing anything that could really be done."

"Is there no way to stop Bart?"

"I'm hoping if there *is* a body on his land, we can appeal to the governor. He might listen and send a Ranger to investigate."

Stone felt like his hands were tied when it came

to guarding the land from being exploited by Higgins. He thought he might be able to use Sierra in some way to stop him, but she wasn't much of a benefit in that regard. He had to wonder why River suggested he get close to her, why River felt Sierra was a key in protecting their future. It was confusing, and bringing in an outsider didn't seem like it would help. He was keenly aware of the way white women were treated and he didn't see how Sierra could do anything noteworthy.

After what seemed like hours of riding, her ass fell asleep, but she started to recognize the surroundings from the events of that fateful day. Like Stone, her mind had been occupied on Higgins and trying to figure out a way to stop him, though from what, she was still unsure.

Stone stopped the horse by the tree where Bart had originally set up the picnic. He hopped off, then grabbed her by the waist to lift her to the ground. "Which way?"

It took her a moment to get her bearings. Her head was heady from his closeness and touch. She needed to get oxygen to focus. "This way." She moved towards the bushes she used as cover while she needed to relieve herself. From there, she looked around before heading towards the area she'd run into Stone and his party. "I was scared. He'd just tried to strangle me and I was trying to get away. I knew he had a gun, so I ran in a zigzag formation in hopes I'd make a more difficult target. It's been weeks. I don't see how we're going to succeed."

When she turned back, Stone was in his cougar form, his nose on the ground. "Well, I guess there's that." She wasn't sure she was ever going to get used to his being able to turn into an animal at will. They walked side by side. Every now and again he would move in an erratic way and she realized he was picking up her movements from when she ran. It was several minutes before she saw it.

Bleached by the sun, the now-bare bones of what once was a human hand extended to the elbow and lay on the ground. Using his claws, he dug around the arm, then shifted when he felt he was going to disturb the body lying there. Kneeling down, he brushed the dirt away. A bit of cloth could now be seen. Sierra gasped and turned away, though whether from the sight or the smell of death assaulting them, Stone wasn't quite sure.

He'd been around death often and, though he wasn't fond of the smell, he could tolerate it a bit better than she seemed to. Grabbing the arm, he pulled the body out of the dirt. "Do you recognize her?"

"Yes." She took a step back, her head still turned, her hand over her nose while the other was over her stomach. She felt sick, but she was also overwhelmed with sadness. No one should be left out here, buried and forgotten, even if they'd been dead over a hundred years before Sierra had even been born. The thought gave her an even bigger headache, which in turn made her stomach jump even more.

Sierra took another couple of steps to a nearby tree, leaned over and vomited. She felt him move beside her, pulling her hair back so she could throw up without getting any on herself. When she felt her stomach had vacated all of its contents, she looked over, eye level with his waist. Standing upright, she reached out and pulled on the necklace he had tied there. Why had she never noticed it before? She pulled at it while pushing him back at the same time. "Where did you get this?"

Puzzled, he had to see what she had taken from him. Then he remembered. "From the grass by the picnic area when you were shot. I'd forgotten about it. Is it yours?" He pulled a water skin from his wait and handed it to her, so she could rinse her mouth out.

"No. It's hers." She pointed to the torso pulled from the dirt. "It's Louise's."

"She was a friend?"

"Yes. You found it?"

"Yes. In the grass by the blanket."

"I had shown this to Bart. Asked him what had happened, and that's when he attacked me."

"He won't ever do that again, Sierra. Let me protect you." Stone raised his hand, gently caressing her cheek, his thumb rubbing against her lips. He wanted to kiss her again. He'd wanted it for days, but he purposely stayed away to let his feelings subside. Only they didn't. Instead, the cougar inside paced and growled, wanting out, wanting to claim her. The Cheyenne wouldn't force himself on her. It was against his code, his honor, and he wasn't one to disrespect another, especially one he'd a growing concern for.

Sierra almost gave in to him, to the unspoken words between them and the desire that was so thick it was almost palpable. He'd taken a step forward, so close his warm breath was on her cheek. The heat radiated from his bare chest and she wanted to reach up and touch him. His masculine scent was heady and a warmth spread down to her toes, centering on the pit of her stomach.

She jumped when she heard a shotgun blast. Stone pushed her behind him, the tree at her back as he searched for the direction of the blast. Then another blast and some hollering from the grove where Stone had released his horse to wander. He pointed to her. "Stay here." Then, shifting into his mountain lion form, he ran as fast as a cat to see what was going on.

Chapter 24

Sierra stood there, stunned, her hand still clutching at the necklace that once belonged to Louise and the water skin. Lifting her eyes, Louise's corpse lay slumped against the dirt as something inside Sierra turned cold and calculating. Deep down, she knew Bart was behind her death and he'd planned the same for her. What about Sophie? Or the other girls that went missing before she even arrived? She'd heard they had mysteriously left with some miners, which wasn't unusual for Harvey Girls, but that they were never seen again, some even leaving behind all their belongings, was a bit peculiar. Were they out here also?

Stone didn't know about serial killers. That term didn't come into place until the mid-1970s, even though the murderers have been around since Jack the Ripper, if not before. Sierra ran a shaky hand through her long locks. Was she supposed to be the next victim who just disappeared before Stone and his men serendipitously intervened? Was she supposed to be buried here as well? How would he have covered up the fact she was supposed to be on a date with him?

She looked around for anything out of the ordinary, even though she had no idea what she was looking for. *Think!* What was it that looked out of place when she tripped over Louise's hand? Was Louise grabbing her from beyond the grave? Asking for help? Catching Sierra's attention?

Sierra's eyes examined the soil closely. Were there any unusual patterns? Did anything look disturbed? Something recent maybe? For Sophie? If this was Bart's modus operandi, placing them here, on his land, which wouldn't be investigated or explored, were the others here as well? How many had Anna told her were missing before she arrived? Three? Four? Why hadn't she paid more attention? *Because the whole thing was overwhelming, and I was more concerned with getting back to the 21st century than figuring out what happened to people who had been dead for a century or more before I got here.*

She could hear shouting and more gunshots. She feared for Stone. What would happen if he got shot in his animal form? Would he change back to human in front of their very eyes? Would they understand? Did he just put his whole band in jeopardy? Heading to where Stone ran and the shots came from, she made her way back to the clearing. There were several men shooting at Stone's cougar form as if it were a game to them.

Furious, she stepped out of the cover of bushes. "What the hell do you think you're doing?"

They all stopped, stunned by her presence. The cougar took off while they were focused on her. Breathing a sigh of relief, she focused on the men who were there. Five men, most in jeans and shirts, with one in a brown suit, who seemed to be in charge, making his way to her.

"You're the wrong color to be wearing that Injun shit on your back. Maybe, I should know who you are to even be asking?"

"I'm a Harvey Girl. I was injured a few weeks back and the Cheyenne have been caring for me. I ask again, who are you? And why are you here? This is private land."

"I'm the foreman for Higgins Mining Conglomeration. Not that it's any of your business, but we're here getting ready to make Mr. Higgins' company operational."

"Do you mind if I ask what this operation entails?"

"Gold. Lots and lots of gold."

"Somehow, I don't see you panning for it. So, how do you plan to accomplish the mining?"

"Gold cyanidation."

Of course, that meant little to Sierra. It tickled a part of her mind. Why was it slightly familiar? "What is that?"

"Why are you bothering her with all this?"

"Shit! Where did that lion go?"

One of the men shot his rifle up in the air. "Here, kitty kitty. Look at the nice bullets I have for you."

The foreman stepped closer. "Why are you so interested? This isn't your concern or your land."

"Call me a nosy female." Sierra took a step closer to the foreman, showing him she wasn't afraid.

"It's where we take a hydrometallurgical technique for extracting gold from low-grade ore by converting the gold to a water-soluble coordination complex using sodium cyanide, which is mixed into the grinding machinery after it has created a slurry. Got all that?" He assumed she was a dumb female and none of it would make sense, but he was wrong.

When he explained to her the process, she'd remembered doing a story about this exact issue going on in Alaska and the multitude of concerns it raised if there were insufficient precautions in place or an accident occurred.

"Wait. Did you say sodium cyanide? That's poison! You can't do that!"

"Yes, we can, and we are. It's only poison for those that live here, and since Mr. Higgins owns everything, no one will get hurt."

"What about the animals? The Cheyenne?"

"Ain't no Injuns supposed to be 'round these

parts. And who cares about the animals? They're just target practice," the rifleman spoke up.

"I care about the animals and the Cheyenne." Sierra wasn't sure what she was going to do to back up those words, especially since Stone just up and left.

"You're in the wrong place for caring, missy. This here land is made for getting rich."

"That may be true, but you don't have to kill everything in the process. Sodium cyanide is a deadly poison. If it gets into the water, it'd get the people and the animals sick with chest and abdominal pains, headaches and vomiting. Eventually, they'd all die because their cells were being depleted of oxygen. It'll be a long and miserable death, and who knows how long the effects would last with the land." She knew this wasn't how it was supposed to be. If it were, she would've read about it at the museum.

"Again, girl: it isn't any of your business," the foreman said. "Take her."

Just as he said that, she realized the workers

weren't paying the foreman any attention. Both the foreman and Sierra looked up to see what caught their interest. Sierra couldn't help but smile.

There was a line of Cheyenne warriors on horseback facing the group of men down, and they knew they'd lose the battle should they even try. Dropping their tools, they ran to their horses and headed back towards town as fast as the steeds could carry them. It was only as they started to move away that Stone and the others approached her. She stood, watching the men retreat, her back to the Cheyenne.

Stone stopped beside her, climbing off. "I told you to stay away from here."

"You're welcome for saving your life." She turned and glared at him. "Or did you think getting shot in your cougar form would be entertaining for all of us? Aren't you supposed to keep shit like that secret?"

"I was. I'm also supposed to make sure you stay safe, and I can't do that if you keep disobeying orders."

"Be glad I did. Not only did I save you from being shot or discovered, I also found out what Higgins has planned for the land. And bucko, it ain't good."

Stone raised his eyebrow at 'bucko,' but his concern over what she found was more important. "Let's go. We can discuss this back in the village."

"No. I have a gut feeling about something here and I need to check it out. Actually, you and the others can help."

"Help do what?"

Sierra held up Louise's necklace. "Louise wasn't the first. Sophie disappeared before her, and before I arrived at the house there were several more who were missing. The townsfolk figured they just met a transient miner or someone else headed out west and joined them. But most left their belongings behind and departed without word to anyone else. It's not like they would've been stopped if they packed their things and said a proper goodbye. So where did they go? Why so many of them?" Sierra lowered her hand. "I'm thinking if

Louise is out here, then maybe others are too. You said you thought so too."

"The serial killer thing, whatever that means."

"Yes, the serial killer thing. I just think we should search and see if there are any other bodies hidden around here. Bart brought me out here and tried to kill me. He might be the one who buried Louise out here too. Since he owns the land, there probably isn't any cause for others to come out here and search. It'd be the perfect hiding place."

"What if he did? What difference would it make?"

"Don't you see, Stone? If he did and we can prove it, then the governor has to get involved. Rangers will have to come, and you'll get the true law that is not under Bart's thumb to go after him. If we can get him for murder, he won't have a chance to start the mining using cyanide poisoning. You, the land, your people, all of them will be safe."

Stone stared at her for a minute, then, in the Cheyenne language, told the others to start looking for more hidden graves. Several shifted, utilizing their spirit guides' instincts better. Two were birds, one a raven and one a hawk. Their aerial view would give them an advantage the others wouldn't have on the ground. A few others transformed as well. One a wolf, another a fox and the third a dog. Stone watched her as the others changed. "They have good abilities to sniff out things. Including the smell of death. If they're here, we'll find them."

Chapter 25

By the time they were finished searching the area, they found 22 bodies. From the clothing, Sierra was sure they were all women, and she was sickened by the thought of such atrocities. Higgins used the land as his private burial ground. Worse, he was arrogant enough to believe he could continue to work the land for gold, even if the mining killed everything else around it. The body count would rise, that was for sure, but how did he plan on making sure these stayed hidden and buried? They were all over the place, near where she had accidently discovered Louise.

She'd been sick with each of the first ones discovered, but as more and more were being unearthed, her queasiness turned to shock and she slowly became desensitized with the multitude of women killed and the different rates of decomposition they were discovered in.

The sun was starting to set when Stone returned to Sierra's side. "Come on. We need to get back to the village."

"What about them? All of them? We can't just leave them here. Not like this. Not out in the open. What about other predators coming in the middle of the night?"

Stone looked over his shoulder at the bodies lying neatly besides the holes they were buried in. "We'll take care of it. Some of the others are going to guard them while Silver Hawk is going to find a Ranger and bring him here. We have more than enough evidence of Higgins killing these women."

"Do you? Because the evidence I see are weapons with feathers, or bits of feathers near their bodies. That could implicate your tribe much worse, not make things better."

"That may be true, but any who know the Cheyenne know we'd never kill women. And even if we did, we don't leave our weapons behind. We take scalps."

"And what about the mining?"

"If Higgins is in jail, then we shouldn't have to worry about the mining operation. As far as I know, he is the only one who put everything together. He used the money he got from the gold he first found to finance this adventure. Without him, I assume the other investors will back out. Especially if they are associated with someone who has no honor but kills helpless women."

"You have a good point. I just hope you're right."

Sierra let him lead her to his horse, climb on and easily lift her to sit sideways in front of him.

As they started to ride back, Sierra couldn't help but notice how close they were. Instantly her mind went to that kiss from a few days ago. She was trapped between his arms, his silky hair brushing lightly against her skin. She had the chance to really see him up close, admiring his strong jaw, the color of his eyes and his body warmth. Unlike many of the other Cheyenne men, he preferred to be without a shirt unless it was colder or there were a lot of outside interactions he was going to be involved in.

"When we get back to the village, I would prefer you stay with me tonight."

Sierra pulled her mind away from the admiration of his body and gave him a quizzical look. "May I ask why?"

"Higgins is going to know from his men that we were there. I'm sure he's going to come out to investigate, and when he does, he's going to see what we found. He could come after all of us, but you especially. You survived his assault and he'll know you're alive. You're a liability to him. If we can get the Ranger here quickly, Higgins won't have a way to deny anything, but we've got to beat him to the law. If we don't, he could wipe us all out with a posse of his hired guns. You'll be safer in my tipi as it's more centralized and protected."

"What about River? Or Sage?"

"Sage can take care of herself. As can River. If it gets bad, they will shift and head into the surrounding woods. It's the larger animals that we'll have an issue with. Like me, as a cougar, or the bears, wolves, foxes, deer, elk. They will be harder to hide as easily. That's why we are more in the center. Our Dog Soldiers, like myself, will fight to the death and not think anything of it. We can protect you better if you're surrounded by all of us and not at the edge."

She wasn't sure how she was going to feel about spending the night with him in his tipi. He must've realized her concern, because he quickly added, "Besides, until this is over, I'll be keeping watch outside. You'll be safe. Even from me."

"I wasn't too worried about you attacking me."

"You don't have to say it like that. I can be rather menacing at times. I am a skilled warrior."

She chuckled softly. "I've no doubt of that either. I just meant, I know you wouldn't hurt me, because if you wanted to, you would've done it a long time ago."

"That's good. I thought you might think I wasn't man enough."

"For what?"

He looked at her, his gaze softening. "For you."

Amazed, she let her eyes roam his face, swallowing hard as she found her mouth suddenly very dry. Her heart became rapid and those warm tingles went straight into her stomach, like she swallowed a dozen butterflies who were now trying desperately to be released into the world. Alarm bells rang in her head. She wasn't from this time or place and she knew she couldn't remain here. She was sent for some greater purpose. She believed she was here to stop Bartholomew Higgins from his mining corporation and his killing of the Harvey Girls and every other woman who'd mysteriously disappeared. She couldn't stay here. She couldn't be with him, no matter how desperately she wanted to. Yet, despite her head, it was her heart that was screaming at the top of its lungs to be heard. Even if it was just one night, it could last her for the rest of hers.

"Don't leave me again." His words from the 21st century rang in her head, yet again. In order to come back to him, she had to be with him. Who was she to defy providence?

"Stay with me tonight. I don't want to be alone."

He pulled his steed up once in the village and

hopped down. He then grabbed her by the waist and lifted her off the horse, only this time he didn't set her down. Instead, he carried her into his tipi while a young boy collected his horse.

He laid her gently on his hides and peered down into her face searchingly. "Are you sure?"

"I don't expect marriage. I don't need forever. I only want this moment, this night. Please."

He answered her with a kiss before he pulled back enough to flip her to her stomach. As he undid his breeches, but she rolled back around. "No. Not like an animal. I want to make love, the intimate, human way."

He nodded and let her guide him to the way she wanted to be touched, caressed. It was a new experience for him. A different way he'd never experienced before. She helped him remove her clothes. He was anxious, ready, but she slowed him down, making their time together last. She would allow herself one night with him, but she'd be damned sure she'd make it last and give him a night to remember. This was what felt right. True, she was sent into the past for a higher purpose, but she also knew this had to happen or she'd go crazy wondering what being intimate with him felt like.

His hands slid over every inch of her pale skin, tracing her freckles. With the glowing embers of the nearby fire, her skin glowed with the flickering shadows. He hadn't been with a woman in so long, he almost forgot what a woman felt like beneath him. A warm body, soft and pliable against him, he hardened almost immediately. His cougar was tired of waiting. He wanted out. He wanted to claim her, mark her and make her his.

He held her down, his nose pressed against the crook of her neck. Breathing in her scent deeply, she became ingrained in his soul. She'd never escape him now. She belonged to him, even if, he reminded himself, it was only for one night.

His knees pushed her legs apart, his manhood pressed against her inner thigh. He continued to move down her body, gripping her arms to hold her as he sniffed her bare skin.

However, he stopped when he reached the

juncture of her legs. Releasing her hands, he pushed her wider, opening her up to unfold before his eyes.

Her sex glistened in the firelight and he leaned in to just breathe the smell of her. He grinned, noticing her nipples stiffen when he exhaled onto her moist bud. Her inner folds reminded him of pink petals, the scent sweeter than any flower he'd inhaled before.

Her hips twitched, silently begging him to do something more than see and smell. He wanted to give his body one sense at a time, respecting, almost worshipping the gift she was bestowing on him.

Sierra couldn't wait for him any longer. She needed to feel more than the gentle breathy caresses over her heated skin. Sitting up, she pushed him to an upright position, enabling her to reach down and grab his thick member. Using her finger, she spread the velvety liquid of his pre-cum onto the head of his cock. They were silent. Even their moans were barely audible. Sierra memorized everything around her: the sound of the crickets and owls, others talking as they walked by his tipi, the sound of the buffalo hide as the wind tickled against it. Nothing escaped her, but most of all, she was focused on Stone. A part of her wondered if he was ever going to actually take her. She knew she asked for slow, but damn…this was torturous.

She whimpered, her hands increasing as they moved over his hard body, feeling each muscle flex as he played with hers. When she thought she would go insane, he lowered himself to her sex, using his tongue to glide inside her slit, lapping up every bit of juice he could.

Sierra had to bite her tongue so she wouldn't cry out.

Stone must have sensed her body tighten in pleasure, for only then did he plunge his tongue repeatedly into her wet core. He ate her like a man starving for the nectar her body provided and he didn't stop until she came twice. Only then did he move up her body, his hard rod enflamed with his desire. Hovering over her, he searched her face, as if seeking that final bit of confirmation that she wanted this as much as he did.

Seeing the need within her eyes, he pulled back on his haunches, grabbing her hips. He could see her wetness at the tip of his elongated rod. Gripping her ass, he pressed his cock into her glorious hole, letting her sheath him with her velvety heat.

She arched to meet his thrust, her hands on his hips. After a couple of thrusts he stopped deep inside her, pulling her up so she could sit on top of him. Wrapping her arms around his neck, he pounded her like she was riding a steed instead of a stud. His hand was on her back as he guided her with each upward movement deeper into her core. One of his hands cupped her ass to guide her, but the other flicked against her nub. Sierra was sure she was going to go insane as her whole body tightened in response. When he was sure she was going to come again, he pressed his mouth against her to swallow any sound she might make in her ecstasy.

Stilling to let her regroup, Stone laid her gently back onto his buffalo hides. When her breathing started to return to some normalcy, he started to ride her again, this time harder and faster than before. She used her hands to move to his hips and she taught him to swirl slightly as he pulled out. Her soft cry of pleasure told him he needed to learn that move perfectly and do it more often.

He'd never made love to a woman where he faced her and could see every bit of enjoyment he gave her. It was incredible. Her body was so soft, he couldn't stop rubbing his hands against every inch of her, and he was fascinated with how her skin had a sheen of sweat, making it sparkle in the light of the gentle fire.

Though he was thrusting, she was guiding him, and he willingly gave her the lead to direct their enjoyment of each other. Her fingers raked his back and arms, her warm, slick sheath tightened around his thick member. Both were relatively silent since they knew they'd otherwise be heard.

She couldn't ever remember being so quiet, with nothing more than soft groans and hard breaths escaping from her lips. He was unbelievable. He brought her over the edge several times before he came himself. A part of her was actually glad when he sent his hot seed to flow deep within her tired channel, but he surprised her when he only gave her a few minutes to rest before starting all over again. She should've said she had enough, but damn, who would turn down a hot stud like this who was ready for more almost immediately. He turned her around when he started and took her like an animal would. This time, she said nothing. He made her female parts scream, partially in soreness and partially in pure ecstasy. She hadn't had such constant rubbing of her insides that lasted for hours in ages and she knew how sore she was going to be as a result in the morning. But, it was so very worth it.

The sun started to rise by the time he released for a third time and he finally lay beside her. He'd lost count of how many times he brought her to fruition. "I didn't know human women could keep up with the likes of us."

"I didn't know men like you existed, much less had so much stamina. You do realize I'm going to be dead to the world for a good portion of the day.

Sage won't be too happy with me for missing another chance to poke my fingers as I try and bead." She curled up next to him, ignoring the totally drenched apex of her legs. He gave her a lot of himself each time and no time to clean up in-between. However, she was far too exhausted to clean herself up, so she was surprised when Stone pulled away from her and gently washed her. When he was finished, he wiped himself, then crawled back under the hides to lie next to her.

"Sleep. I've a feeling it will be a long day."

Chapter 26

Sierra finally drifted off to sleep. She couldn't ever remember being so exhausted, and yet so content and sated as she did when she let the darkness of slumber cradle her in his arms. Sadly, it didn't last long. The sun was still rising when she was startled awake.

Stone was already up and attired as he tossed her clothes to her. "Get dressed and for once listen to me. Stay in here." He bolted out of the tipi, letting the flap fall back into place.

Scrambling to put her clothes on, she pulled her hair back, twisting it and making a bun, tucking the ends on the underside. Her hands were shaking as the cacophony on the other side of the buffalo skins continued to erupt in utter chaos. Screams, horses thundering by, children crying, and a variety of animal sounds could be heard with complete panic. Of course, Sierra wasn't going to blindly obey him, as if she were some pet to be commanded to sit and stay. Rushing for the opening to pull the flap aside, she was stunned by the carnage going on.

Although the tipis were in a circular position near the head of a river, their position was unable to prevent the group of men who came barging in on horseback. There was no prior warning Sierra could tell, but then she remembered from what she read on the walls of Cripple Creek Museum, often soldiers would disrupt tribal villages in fear of being attacked by them in the early mornings to get them off-guard. She'd heard of Wounded Knee and Sand Creek, two of the worst massacres in history. She was sure there were others as well, but those two were the more prominent ones discussed and the carnage among the worst.

But these weren't soldiers. They looked like the men she'd occasionally see in the town saloon or at the lunch counter. However, they were just as vicious and cruel as the soldiers she'd read about, some setting the tipis on fire, others shooting in the air, not caring who they frightened or hurt.

Some of the men jumped off horseback and pulled some of the women and children out, but Sierra was keenly aware a good number of them were missing. Sage and River were not among the group, nor were some of the children she had become accustomed to seeing around the camp.

One of the men grabbed her and pulled her to the center with the rest of them, throwing her in such a way she landed at the feet of a crying child. She should probably cower, or try to stay hidden, but that wasn't her way. Not anymore. Not since she was attacked in that parking garage and took self-defense classes. Not since she was thrown back in time to a place where death was as commonplace as eating, or so it seemed. Reassuring the little girl, she climbed to her feet. Pushing the youngster back towards who she assumed was her mother, she spun and literally pushed the man with both hands from behind. He was about to spin around and slug her when he stopped with his arm pulled back for the punch. He squinted at her. "Sierra?"

Her anger quickly dissipated. "Doctor. I thought you were supposed to heal folks, not hurt them?"

"If only. What are you doing here?"

"I was injured, and the Cheyenne saved and cared for me."

"We all thought you were dead. Higgins said he saw them kill you."

"Higgins was wrong. Regardless, what are you doing here? These people have done nothing to deserve what you are doing to them!"

"We're looking for a murderer. Once we find them—"

"Once you find them, what?" Sierra cut him off mid-sentence. "Are you going to kill him in front of his people? Without a trial? Without a jury?"

"That monster doesn't deserve either!" he snarled back.

Sheriff Cosco approached them, then stopped in shock as he realized the woman was Sierra. "What's going on?"

"You need to stop this, Sheriff. No matter who you're looking for, the entire village of innocent women, children, elderly and others don't deserve this. I thought you were better than such common bullying. You're the law. Uphold it."

"They're Indians!"

"So? You're an immigrant from Europe somewhere. Docs that mean all Europeans are assholes without a soul or conscience?"

Doctor Whalen stepped between the two of them. "Enough!" He turned to the sheriff. "We came here for one person, let's find him and take him back to jail to await his trial, which is what we all agreed to. Enough people are dead as it is."

The tone of reason calmed the sheriff down. Turning, he called for the others to stop. Although it took several attempts and him actually going over to a couple of them to push them aside before he shot his gun in the air twice to get everyone's attention, he managed to succeed. In silence, they watched him pace, looking over each of the warriors who were itching to get back into the fray of the fight.

"We're looking for the one who often goes out alone to the Higgins property."

"Why?" Black Mountain, the eldest member of the band, asked as he stepped forward.

"We believe he has killed a number of women

and will be arrested to await trial."

Stone stepped forward. "I'm the one you seek, but I didn't kill those women. I found them."

Sierra was shocked. She never expected Stone to give himself up, which wasn't the Cheyenne way, but then she realized why he did it. He was protecting his people. This wasn't a battlefield where the men could do as they pleased. This was their village, a place for their respected elders, cherished women and children. It was their home. Those men brought the fight to them, knowing protecting the others was more important than fighting, especially after Sand Creek or Wounded Knee.

"If you found them, they why didn't you come to me?" Cosco moved towards him.

"Because I didn't have proof of who did it, and I didn't think you'd believe me."

"You're right. I don't believe you."

"It's true. I actually found the first body before I was injured." Sierra stepped towards the men, ignoring Stone's look of fury at her disobeying him and getting involved.

Whalen grabbed her arm and jerked her back to his side. "You'll have a chance to tell your story later. For now, don't interfere. This is a stick of dynamite about to explode. Don't be the flint to start it."

"I'll come willingly. Don't hurt the others." Stone stepped forward, giving his head a shake when other members of the tribe tried to approach. "Check on Trout and the others at the sight," he ordered, then went quietly with the sheriff and other men.

Doctor Whalen kept Sierra's arm in his grasp, making sure she came along as well. She looked around again for River or Sage, the two she'd come to know the best, but they were nowhere to be seen.

She wanted to say goodbye, but without the women near, she let him lead her away from the Cheyenne village that she'd considered her home for the past few weeks.

During the ride back to Colorado Springs, she felt awful for Stone, who didn't even glance her way as he was forced to walk in front of them while they rode on horses. His hands were bound with a rope, which was also tied to the sheriff's saddle horn. She wanted to explain everything to Cosco, but she remembered that he and probably most, if not all, of these men were part of Bart's payroll, so they wouldn't listen to her, or care. Being female while he was Native American, she knew neither would be listened to. She had to find a way to get the Colorado Rangers to Colorado Springs. Without the law being under the influence of Bart and his cohorts, they might stand a chance in actually being heard.

Looking around at the other men that were part of the posse, she could tell from their grim looks and determined faces none of them could be trusted. She knew Mistress DeVoe was part of Bart's business adventure, and therefore under his thumb as well. She honestly didn't know who to turn to or who to trust.

"Don't put yourself in danger by trying to help me. They killed Trout and the other men I left at the

grave sites. I've also been informed Silver Hawk was stopped before he could get help. They'll kill you too if they're given a chance. Don't give them the opportunity to take your life." Stone's voice was in her head and she gasped.

"What's wrong?" Doc Whalen asked when he heard her intake of breath.

"Swallowed a bug." How was Stone talking to her in her head? Was this also one of his special gifts? Could she talk back to him? She wasn't sure how, or even if, she imagined it, but then, she wouldn't know the men he left there were dead if he didn't actually tell her. Unless she was imagining everything.

"Keep your mouth shut."

"Yes, Sierra. I'm in your head. Don't be afraid. Don't tell them anything and don't put yourself in danger. Higgins won't be happy that you're alive. You must do whatever it takes in order to stay that way. I won't be able to help you."

Gazing over at him, she watched as he walked alongside the sheriff's horse. He gave no indication that he was even talking to her. She tried to talk back to him, but he didn't respond any further. Maybe because she wasn't a Spirit Walker she couldn't speak to him mentally. She turned her focus back on the road, watching the town grow larger as they approached.

Chapter 27

"Sierra!" Anna burst through the doors and down the porch stairs as she ran towards Sierra, almost knocking her over in an embrace. "We thought you were dead!" Anna cried with relief as she refused to let her go.

Florence came outside, watching the two of them. "I'm glad you have returned without too much damage. We have a train coming in 45 minutes. I could use the help in service. Do you think you can wash, change and be ready by then?"

Anna giggled as she finally pulled back. "Ever the task master. I'll have your section set up so all you'll have to do is collect the vouchers, pour the drinks and put food out." She gave Sierra a quick hug again. "I can't believe you're alive. I never thought I'd see you again." Wiping her eyes, she released Sierra, grabbed her hand and pulled her into the house. She let go at the base of the stairs. Pulling out a handkerchief, she dabbed at her eyes again before using it to blow her nose.

"It's good to see you as well, Anna. After it

calms down and our shifts are over, we really need to talk. Let me go up and change. Where is my stuff?"

"Despite what they promised us, we didn't get any new girls in since you left. Mr. Harvey didn't like we were losing so many, so we're off the list for getting new recruits for a while. Mistress DeVoe packed up your things, but they're in boxes in my room. Your room is still empty. I'll help you move back in after this train leaves. It's the only one for today."

"That's unusual, but I'd appreciate the help. Thanks."

Running up the stairs, Sierra found the box of her items exactly where Anna said it would be. It was almost sad how her life, or anyone's life, could fit neatly away in a box. Taking the square container back to her room, she washed up and changed into her Harvey uniform, making her way downstairs. She was almost at the end of the staircase when the door opened and Bart walked in.

They stood and stared at each other for several

heartbeats. Just as she was about to take another step, he swiftly moved to block her forward movement, gripping her wrist tightly.

"Tell anyone and I'll kill you like a sacrificial lamb, as well as everyone you might have told, whether or not you actually did. Do you understand me?"

She could've kicked him in the balls, twisted her wrist free, but she knew what he was implying and she wouldn't risk Anna or the other girls, or Stone and the other Cheyenne. Besides, he didn't know what a spitfire she could be and she knew it was an ace up her sleeve to be saved for a later time.

"I understand. I have no desire to tell the others how you tried to kill me, or how I believe you killed Louise, Sophie, and god-only-knows how many others." She leaned forward to whisper in his ear. "You're sick and you're going to suffer for all eternity for the depravity of the existence you lead. I'll never again be alone, so you won't have the opportunity to try killing me."

He snarled at her as she pulled back, but he let her go. "We'll see about that, Miss Hanley. I have plenty of friends who have no qualms about taking you and others out, including the Indian." He spun on his heel and departed the Eating House.

Leaning on the balustrade, she tried to catch her breath. As much as she hated to admit it, he scared her. He could easily kill anyone here in the house, make more trouble for the Cheyenne village and influence the jury to hang Stone. She couldn't risk any of it.

Shaking slightly, she headed into the dining room. Florence had been watching her and most likely saw the confrontation between Bart and Sierra, yet she said nothing. Her look was cold, almost hard. Sierra didn't know what to make of it, but the train was rolling in and there was no time to give it any further consideration. If one wanted to forget about anything, work would certainly take care of it. Mindless moving around, bringing food, pouring coffee or tea, collecting the vouchers, one certainly didn't need to think in order to do this job.

Paste a smile on her face, ignore the questions from those who knew she was considered dead, focus on a pleasant, delicious and speedy service. Thankfully, it was done before she knew it and soon the whistle blew, getting everyone back on board the train before it departed the station.

Sierra started to clean up when Florence moved next to her. "I'm sure you've had a rough couple of weeks. This is the last train for the day. Why don't you go upstairs, unpack your things and relax? Take your time to get reacquainted with civilized life."

Clenching her jaw, she let the civilized life comment go by. She didn't need to be starting issues after just returning. She already had enough to deal with in regard to Bart's threat and Stone's incarceration. "Thank you." Taking off her apron, she headed to her room.

Looking around, she wasn't sure where to start, but unpacking wasn't it. She needed to get word to a Ranger. Needed to find help that wasn't on Bart's payroll. And most of all, she needed to save Stone while putting Bart into the prison system. Her head throbbed with all of the things she needed to get done, which gave her a good case of anxiety, along with feeling overwhelmed, when she wasn't even sure how she'd accomplish any of her tasks.

Moving to her window, she opened it, needing the fresh air. Wagons were coming in from the direction of Bart's mining company. Tarps lay over the open backs, but she still saw a hand in one and a woman's shoe peeking out of another. They were the bodies found yesterday. "Trout and his men were killed," Stone informed her in her mind. Were they with the bodies of the women? Were they brought in or left to lie like trash where they fell?

Sierra wasn't one who gave in to breaking down. At least not often, but everything finally added up to the point she'd held herself together for as long as she could and couldn't deal with any more. Seeing the bodies of those women, or at least parts of them, was the final straw. She sank to her knees and wept.

Anna finished cleaning downstairs, and as soon as she was able, headed to Sierra's room. Still not able to believe Sierra was alive, she was going to spend as much time as possible with her friend. Stories of her being killed by the Cheyenne and knowing how ruthless they were, she'd been saddened by such loss. Yet, Sierra was back at the Eating House, safe.

Raising her hand to knock, she hesitated. She could hear Sierra weeping and it broke her heart. Why was she so sad? Instead of knocking, she gently opened the door and peeked in. Closing the door behind her, she moved over to Sierra on the floor and knelt beside her, gathering her in her arms for comfort. She wanted to know everything, but Anna was also aware there'd be time. Sierra needed to adjust, and she'd speak about her experiences when she was ready.

Cradling Sierra, Anna noticed the wagons outside as well. She'd been so excited over Sierra being alive, she'd almost forgotten the almost two dozen women who weren't so lucky.

"I'm sorry. I shouldn't be blubbering like some baby. It's just everything added up and I couldn't deal with it all anymore."

"It's okay. I can't imagine what you've gone through the past couple of weeks. Or being with the people who killed so many of our friends."

Sierra pushed her back, wiping her eyes. "No. The Cheyenne didn't kill those women. B-b-b-bad men did, but not the Cheyenne." She was about to say Bart, but she wasn't sure she could trust anyone, not even Anna. At least not yet.

"Their weapons were all over the place. They're known for being murderous and ruthless. It only makes sense."

"No, Anna. They were framed to take the blame for someone else's deeds. The Cheyenne don't bury those they kill. They scalp them, so they can add the coup to their coup sticks. These were kills by a person who was cowardly. He hid the bodies. Tried to bury them. I found one by mistake. The Cheyenne helped me find the others. There are 22 women. *22!* All killed at different times. The Cheyenne don't pick one at a time, they do massive attacks. They don't go after women or children, or even the elderly. It'd be against their honor system. They arrested one of the Cheyenne chiefs, but he's innocent."

Anna looked doubtful at first, but Sierra made sense. "Do you know who killed them then?"

Standing, Sierra moved to the door and peeked out, making sure no one was around.

"Can I trust you, Anna? I really need your help and I don't know who I can trust."

"You can. You can trust me. Tell me how I can be of assistance."

Sierra rushed to her and hugged her tight. "Thank you. You have no idea how relieved I am to hear you say that. I need a really big favor and I need you to be sneaky."

"You're beginning to scare me. What's going on? What do you need me to do?"

Chapter 28

Galloping as fast as the horse would take her, Anna headed north to Denver. The State Capitol would be the perfect place to find a Colorado Ranger, and she might even be able to talk to the governor on behalf of the Cheyenne people as well.

Her mind still reeled with everything Sierra told her. She had a hard time coping with all of the information, but some of it made sense. Now she had to convince others enough to help set right what could be a disaster if left alone. The poisoning of the water and land would damage more than just the Cheyenne and animals. That river was also the town's water supply. They'd be making hundreds of people sick, maybe even thousands since that was also the water they used to make the tea and coffee they served to their clients on the train. Was gold so important to Higgins that he'd risk killing so many people? Or at least make them seriously ill?

The mountains were pristine, beautiful. The thought of them being turned into a slush field to mine gold faster was appalling. Even if Anna didn't believe Sierra at first, she realized the woman was too distraught to be saying anything *but* the truth. The concern she had for the land, the Cheyenne and the town made Anna realize she couldn't stand by and do nothing either. She'd given Sierra her word she could be trusted, and she'd help. Now she was racing through the afternoon to get to Denver in time to prove it.

She had to slow the horse down, walk him for a while, even stop and rest him for a few minutes. Thankful they had the rest of the day off, if she wasn't back in time tomorrow, Sierra would say she was ill in order to cover for her not being there.

"Just tell Mistress DeVoe. She'll let me get help and you won't have to pretend I'm ill."

"I can't do that, Anna. I don't trust her either. Remember she and Bart are business partners."

"I know you found that letter, but DeVoe doesn't seem to have much of a head for business. She was trained to run the house, but that's not difficult."

"It's probably more difficult than you think.

The woman is smart. Savvy. Conniving. I know they've been talking about business. Arguing, actually. I don't know the exact cause of the verbal spats, but I know Bart wasn't too happy afterwards. Regardless, I can't trust her."

"And you really think it's Mr. Higgins who killed all them girls?"

"I don't think it, Anna. I know it. He tried to kill me when I asked him about Louise. She's who I found first and by accident. Her hand was sticking out of the grave he dug for her. I think an animal discovered it and pulled it out enough to cause me to trip. And it was her necklace I also recovered. Her father's medallion he'd gotten in the war that she had made to wear around her neck. When I questioned him about it? Well, he went ballistic and tried to kill me. I barely escaped and only did so because Black Snake accidently shot me with an arrow. That seemed to cause Bart to slow his pace when he saw how many Cheyenne were in the area. I ran into Stone, who then protected me from Bart, brought me to the village and had their medicine woman care for me. I guess I got infected by the arrow, because they say I was unconscious for a couple of weeks with a high fever."

"You're lucky you didn't die. Who knows what they use for medicine. Probably why you got infected to begin with."

"Don't, Anna. You don't know what you're talking about. Those people are good and honorable, and they shared what little they had. Helped me when I needed it and saved my life."

Anna peered at her closely. "You're in love with one of them, aren't you? Which one? That Stone you mentioned?"

Sierra gasped. "What makes you say that?"

"The way you talk about them, particularly Stone. Your cheeks flush when I say his name. Admit it."

Looking away, Sierra's lips twitched upward slightly. "I guess I do." Slightly panicked, she turned back to Anna. "Don't say anything to anyone though. It doesn't make a difference. I know I can't be with him. He can't be with me. He probably doesn't feel the same anyways. I'm…different from him and his people. They… He'd never accept me." That was one secret she wouldn't share with anyone, not even Anna. Sierra had given her word to Stone and she'd keep it with her dying breath. No one would know they were Spirit Walkers. That they were special and blessed with unique gifts. Or that was the real reason they could never be together. She'd always be human with a miniscule lifespan compared to them. She was also from the future and couldn't stay here. Her purpose here was very clear. She was in 1895 to stop Bart, not to be with Stone. Stopping the destructive mining practices, stopping Bart from more killings and assuring Stone went free were the goals she needed to accomplish. She couldn't let herself get side tracked with Stone, no matter how much her heart ached to be with him.

Anna knew there was more to the story than Sierra was letting on. After all, it was 1895 and it wasn't unheard of for Indians and whites to be together, albeit, it wasn't the norm. So, what was the truth and why wouldn't Sierra share it with her?

Denver loomed up ahead. She'd been so busy thinking of their conversation, she hadn't realized how swiftly she'd gotten there. She'd never been to Denver before, so she'd have to ask others for assistance to find where to go.

As she approached the town, Anna started looking around for anything that might be impressive enough to be part of the State Capitol, but all she had to do was look up. On top of a hill sat a regal building and Anna knew instantly it was her destination. She was sure she'd find the help she desired. She knew her horse was exhausted, so she hopped off and tied him up by a trough. She'd need to properly care for the horse with food, washing and rest, but until she completed her mission in getting assistance, she couldn't take the time to do so.

Once she was sure her steed was secure and at least had water, she hiked up the hill only to find most everyone had gone home for the day and most of the doors were secured. She finally found one open, entering the building to look around, hoping to find anyone to assist her.

"What are you doing here? You can't be in here, you know."

She spun on her heel at the deep voice behind her to find a tall, light-haired man before her who took her breath away. "I...I'm looking for the governor or someone in charge. Even a...a Ranger. Please. I...I need help." Normally, not one to be flustered, she'd never met anyone who affected her in such a way. She'd always heard about love at first sight, knowing the person you were supposed to be with for the rest of your life could just appear and you'd instantly know, but until this moment, she'd thought it was all a hokey excuse. Even if it wasn't, she never believed it'd happen to her. Until she'd turned to see him. He had such a profound effect on her, she realized she stammered slightly.

"I'm a Colorado Ranger, ma'am. How can I be of assistance?" He'd taken his hat off when she turned around, twisting it around in his hands. She was so small in stature, he felt the immediate need to protect her. Whatever problem she had, he'd be the one to deal with it and keep her safe. He had the instant urge to take her under his wing and protect her, solve whatever problem she was having and hoped it wasn't about another man vying for her attention. His heart pounded in his chest, his breathing became shallower and his palms were suddenly sweaty. She was so beautiful and delicate, like a butterfly. He didn't want to let her out of his sight. "Please. Have a seat over here and you can tell me everything."

"Thank you." Following him to a bench, she sat down, her gloved hands clasped tightly together. Admittedly, she couldn't stop looking at him. He was dressed simply enough, and it was only as she dragged her eyes away from his face did she noticed the gleaming badge on his chest proclaiming the words 'Colorado Mounted Ranger' on a circle surrounding the star.

His head bent down to see what caught her attention. When he realized it was his badge, he gave her a dimpled smile. "What kind of help do you need?"

His dimples caught her unaware, her stomach flipping over as if a team of gymnasts were having a competition in her belly. She wanted to reach up and run her fingers along them, feeling them conclave against his stubbled cheek. Lowering her eyes further, she needed to be able to concentrate on what she had to say and not get flummoxed by his appearance. "I'm not sure where to begin."

"Take your time, miss. How about we start with something simple? What's your name and where are you from?"

Smiling, she raised her eyes. "Anna Meyers. I'm currently residing in Colorado Springs at the AT&KC Harvey Eating House."

"You're a Harvey Girl?"

"Yes. May I have the pleasure of knowing your name, sir?"

"My apologies. Ranger James Crandall, at your service. May I have the pleasure of your company for an evening meal, Miss Meyers? I have a feeling you've not eaten for a while and it'll give us a chance for you to tell me everything and take your time doing it."

"I'd be honored, Mr. Crandall. Thank you."

"James, please." He stood, holding his hand out to assist her.

"Only if you call me Anna." Slipping her dainty hand into his much bigger one, she stood.

He didn't let go of her, tucking her hand in his arm as he escorted her outside and down to a small hotel that had an elegant restaurant just off to the side. They were shown immediately to a table and he released her in order to pull out her chair, tucking her in once she sat.

"Would you mind terribly if I ordered for you?"

"No. That'd be very kind of you. May I please have some water and tea for my beverages?"

Calling the waiter over, he placed an order for a couple of steaks and their drinks, ordering coffee instead of tea. He didn't want to order an alcoholic beverage because he wanted his wits about him for whatever trouble she was in.

Once the waiter left to fetch their beverages, he turned his full attention on her. "How did you get here?"

"Horse. I left her tied up at the trough at the foot of Capitol Hill."

"What breed?"

"A paint. Why?"

He lifted his hand to call the server over, using his other to pull out some money. "Get Jesse to take care of Miss Meyers' paint tied up at the hill. Have him take good care of him."

"That's very thoughtful and kind. Thank you."

"It's getting too dark to head back to Colorado Springs tonight. It would be best to depart first thing in the morning. Do you have some place to stay?"

"No. I'd not given much thought to anything other than finding help."

The waiter returned with their drinks, setting them on the table. "Jesse has taken care of it, as you requested, Ranger," he stated simply before moving away, letting them return to their conversation. They'd been seated in the back corner of the restaurant, with no one near them, so their discussion was completely private. Anna felt more at ease by his care of her and now her steed.

"Mrs. Montgomery has a boarding house for young women. I'm sure we can get you a room there for the night. Now, please. Tell me your story as to why you need assistance from a Ranger and not utilize the sheriff already in town."

Anna drank some of her water as she thought about what to tell him first. Answering his question seemed as good a place as any to begin the story. "To be truthful, I'm here on behalf of a friend of mine, Miss Hanley, who was presumed killed by the Cheyenne. We only learned early this morning she was still alive and returning to the Eating House. It's her story I'm repeating. She didn't feel she could get away since she just returned, and she's too frightened to go off on her own. I volunteered to come, thinking I wouldn't be missed as much."

"They're fools if they wouldn't notice your absence immediately."

She felt her cheeks flame with heat, knowing

she was blushing. Folding her hands in her lap, she answered, "Sierra, Miss Hanley, was going to cover for me until I returned. We couldn't go to the local sheriff, because Mr. Higgins owns him. Mr. Higgins owns most of the people in town. He's doing awful things and getting away with it, because no one dares to oppose him. Sierra felt, and I agreed with her, we needed law from outside of Sheriff Cosco's jurisdiction and out from under the heavy arm of Mr. Higgins."

"Are you talking about Bartholomew Higgins, who found that vein of gold a few years back?"

Immediately, she was disappointed and worried. If he knew Mr. Higgins, he might be part of the buy off. She'd let herself become infatuated and forgot about the potential dangers. Cautiously, she continued. In for a penny, in for a pound. She hoped she was doing the right thing in continuing to confide in him.

"Yes. Since he became wealthy, he's bought up quite a bit of land and hired Cosco and many others to protect it and him."

"Not unheard of. He probably pays better than lawmen make otherwise."

"Which would be fine, if he were still living within the law, but he's not. Sierra is pretty sure he's a murderer."

"Does she have proof?"

"Not exactly."

"What evidence does she have? Why does she think it's him? What are we talking here, with the murders? How many? Who? Have they been found?"

"So many questions. Evidence? I'm not sure, but he tried to kill her. She ended up with the Cheyenne who saved her. When they went back to where she found the first body, a friend of ours named Louise, the Cheyenne looked around and found 21 others."

"22 women? Are you serious?"

"Very serious. Sierra knows if Mr. Higgins tried to kill her once, he'll try again, and she might not be so lucky the next time. Somehow, Mr. Higgins has managed to frame the Cheyenne for the murders. From what I've heard, they found some weapons with feathers attached, just like the Cheyenne use."

"Then how does she know they weren't the ones who killed them? They aren't known for being sympathetic to others."

"Because she lived with them for the past few weeks. And because the Cheyenne don't kill women over a period of time and bury them. That's not their way."

The waiter brought over their meals, setting them down and asking if they needed anything else. Crandall shook his head and waved him off.

"That's true. I've never heard of the Cheyenne burying any they've killed. They take their dead back to their village. They scalp and leave their enemies where they fall. But bury them? I've never heard of such a thing."

"Sierra also said the Cheyenne are very loyal and respectable. They wouldn't kill women just for no reason. They'd find such a practice dishonorable."

"The Cheyenne used to attack all the time."

"That was when we first started coming onto their land and destroying their food source. It was never the individual, single woman who hadn't ruthlessly invaded their territory."

"You do have a point, Anna. But why would Higgins even bother?"

"I'm not totally sure on that point. However, he might be trying to frame the last of the Cheyenne to get them away from the area. Most have been moved onto reservations in Montana and Oklahoma, but there are still a few around. Although they mostly keep to themselves, Mr. Higgins probably wants them gone entirely."

"Do you know why? Or does Miss Hanley?"

"Sierra believes it's because Higgins plans to bring in gold cyanidation. If that's true, he'll destroy the land and the water. The Cheyenne would be the first to get sick from animals that drink the poisoned water supply or from the water itself."

"What were you expecting to be done about all

of these presumptions?"

Anna set her knife and fork down. "I was hoping for someone to investigate the murders. I was hoping for the possibility of stopping Mr. Higgins from turning our beautiful land into a killing field. I was *hoping* for someone who wasn't under Mr. Higgins' financial thumb to assist the everyday people, even if that also includes Indians."

James pushed back his plate and wiped his mouth. "Higgins probably has contacts all the way up to the governor, if he got those land deals. I know I've heard of him and am sure it was from talk around here. Mr. McIntire is a good man, but he'll take money when offered and not think twice about it or look into the details from where it came."

"McIntire has only been in office for a few months. Do you think it might have been his predecessor, Mr. Waite, who had those dealings with Mr. Higgins?"

"I've no doubt about it. If Governor Waite started the proceedings with Mr. Higgins while he was still in term, I am sure Governor McIntire didn't do any background checks, assuming it'd already been done. As such, he would've just passed whatever was needed. It makes sense." Picking up his coffee cup, he held it between both hands while he was thinking.

"Can anything be done?"

"I'm not sure. Governor McIntire is determined to do what is right, regardless of who he might upset in the process. Don't get me wrong. Governor Waite did a lot of good things for our state, but he was also influenced by others to do the right thing as well, regardless of the consequences. For instance, when he sent in the militia last year to remove all the police and fire commissioners he thought were shielding crime in Denver, like gambling and prostitution. He stopped Harvey from bringing in the Harvey Girls and Eating Houses because he was sure it was just another way to get prostitution into the city."

"We *aren't* prostitutes. We serve food and beverages. Nothing more."

"I didn't mean to imply that's what *I* thought. I meant that's what Waite thought and why we don't have the AT&KC lines running through here with Eating Houses. I'm sure that'll change in the coming years." He set his cup down and reached over to take her hand. "I don't think you're a prostitute, Anna. I think you're a good woman and I'll do whatever I can to help you and your friend."

"Thank you, James. I'm much appreciative."

"Let me walk you over to Mrs. Montgomery's. I'll pick you up in the morning after I've had a chance to talk to a few people. We'll have you back by late afternoon, early evening at the latest, and go from there."

"James, I can't even begin to thank you for everything you've done. Just listening to me was special, but that you are helping and taking care of me, I've very grateful. I'm not sure I can repay your kindness."

"It's my pleasure, ma'am. Ain't one to let a woman be in distress when I can do something to help." He stood, threw some money on the table, and offered her his arm as they walked to the boarding house.

After seeing her settled in, James bid her goodnight and headed to his offices. He had some work to do.

Chapter 29

Florence checked all the doors and windows. Normally, she didn't bother with making sure they were locked, but with Sierra back, she wasn't about to take any chances. Bart couldn't be trusted as far as she was concerned, despite hating to admit that, even to herself. She thought he was better, that attaining wealth would buy him the happiness he so desperately craved. Although she was older than he was, he always managed to take care of her. That was probably why she turned her head away to what he did, the crimes he'd committed. Hoping a new place would be the beginning of a new world for him and he could leave his horrific past behind. She'd no idea he took it with him. How long? She'd only been missing five girls over the past few months, yet, they found a total of 22. Where had the other girls come from? Vagrants from the train who never got back on? Girls from the saloon or brothel? She didn't remember hearing about any other missing women from town, but she'd focused everything on the running of this house. Maybe she should've been more vigilant to what was going on. However, she knew Bart was very good at hiding things from others when he wanted. She also knew he had a small cabin at Cripple Creek. He might have taken some of them from that town as well, or even nearby Victor.

So why was Sierra still alive? How had she managed to escape his deadly grasp? How could he possibly let her live? She'd want to tell her story of what really happened and was sure it would implicate Bart. He wouldn't stand for that. He couldn't. Thing was, she wasn't sure she would or even could stop him.

Looking out the window before pulling the heavy drapes shut, she saw a group of men standing in front of the saloon talking. One of them turned towards her and she realized it was Bart. The look in his eyes, even from this distance, sent a coldness into her bones. It was menacing, vicious, ruthless. That wasn't her Bart; that was a monster. She pulled the drapes closed, turning her back on the men outside. God help her, what had she protected for so long?

Heading up the staircase, she stopped outside of Sierra's room and knocked.

Sierra opened the door, surprised to see Florence there. "Yes?"

"I think it best you lock your door tonight. And window, even though we're on the second floor."

"Why? Don't you think I'm safe here?"

"Girl, you're not safe anywhere until this is all over."

"You know, don't you." It was a statement, not a question.

"I didn't. I didn't know anything until you came back on the heels of 22 other women."

"Why don't you say something? Tell the truth! There's an innocent in jail for horrific crimes he didn't commit."

"I can't. He'll kill me too. Right now, he thinks I'll keep his secrets and he'll leave me be."

"So, you're just going to let another man be tried and possibly convicted for a crime you know he's innocent of? How could you?"

"He's just a Cheyenne. Who's going to care?"

Sierra was stunned with Florence's statement. "I will. Regardless of what he is, he's still human and has the same rights as everyone else. You know he's being framed. How can you, in good, Christian consciousness, allow that to happen and not speak up?"

"I'm not a strong person, Miss Hanley. Despite how I appear to run this place, I still value my own life, as you should value yours. Keep your mouth shut, your doors locked, and you might live another day too." She spun on her heel and headed to her office.

Sierra stood with her mouth agape. She couldn't believe any of it, and yet, it just happened. After several moments of mindlessly staring, she stepped back into her room and locked the door, then checked to make sure the window was locked as well. For a bit of final insurance, she put her chair under the door knob, even though she wasn't really sure it would prevent anyone who gave it a good enough push. Still, it eased her mind some, and at the moment, that was all that mattered.

She hoped Anna could obtain assistance and they'd all be back soon. Somehow, she had a feeling things would be moving very quickly, and Anna was the only hope she had to set things right.

Sierra's room was towards the back part of the house, so she couldn't see the jail or some of the other buildings about town. It didn't stop her from thinking about Stone, though. Her mind had been on him all day. They'd spent such a magical night together, and though she hadn't gotten any sleep then, she still wasn't tired. What happened? One moment she was lying in the arms of the most handsome and efficient lover she'd ever known, and the next her world had been flipped on its ear. Even though she knew she shouldn't have gotten together with him, that they couldn't stay together, that eventually she'd have to go back to her own time, he'd managed to find a way into her heart. She couldn't resist him. But now he was in danger. She might've screwed up history somehow, and as a result, he might die when it was obvious he was supposed to live.

She realized no one would've found those bodies if she hadn't tripped on Louise's hand sticking out of the ground. Bart's secret would probably still be safe. He wouldn't be fearing her or what she would testify in a court of law to accuse him and protect Stone. She knew the sheriff wouldn't listen to what she had to say, which is why she'd kept her mouth shut thus far. What sense was there to say anything when no one would believe her? Not because there wasn't any proof, but because it was easier to take the framing job against Stone, a Cheyenne Indian, then to believe a wealthy, seemingly model citizen was a serial killer. Hell, these people didn't even understand what a serial killer was, much less be able to recognize one in their midst. To the townsfolk he was generous, quiet, an entrepreneur bringing more work to the town, as well as the mines nearby. He was the vision of what the American dream was about. Started poor, rose to being wealthy and sharing his wealth with the less fortunate.

So, what made him want to kill all those women? What was it that set him off to murder so many? Why had he been so nice to her, apparently romantically interested, and then snap, trying to end her life too? Nothing made sense to her, and she wasn't sure it ever would. Even her psychology classes in college were of little help. She remembered reading some were just born that way; others abused and/or neglected to such a point that sadism was what made them feel important. Did he torture animals when he was young? Had he seen death early on and as such felt no empathy or concern for human life? Was he a victim of the human condition of the 1890s, where life was cruel and hard without the conveniences she was so accustomed to? Had he seen so much death that he just became immune to it?

Sitting on the bed, Sierra couldn't help but wonder how much she screwed up the past by being here. It wasn't like she planned on coming, though, or asked to travel back in time. If providence, or the fates, or whatever influence sent her through time itself, then they were just as culpable for the convoluted issues of screwed up timelines she was causing as a result of trying to live and survive in a place she certainly didn't belong.

Yet, she couldn't help but remember the sense of urgency to take her vacation in Colorado Springs, the feeling her destiny was here and she needed to fulfill it. If that was, in fact, the case, then maybe she *needed* to be here in order to set things right, even though they seemed so wrong to her. Nothing made sense, and her head spun with the what ifs and possibilities of each thing she said or did. She really could go insane trying to analyze it all.

As Sierra got ready for bed, she couldn't help but think of Stone. She wondered how he was doing in the jail. Were they treating him well? Giving him food? Making sure he was okay for his rest? Had they set up a date for his trial? Was he thinking of her? She hadn't heard him in her head since they walked back to town, which concerned her. Maybe she dreamed the conversation in her head. Or maybe he had to be near her, like old-time walkie-talkies, and mental telepathy was only good a few feet apart. She hoped he was okay. She hoped she'd be able to see him soon. Most importantly, she hoped she'd be able to prove his innocence and get the real culprit, Bartholomew Higgins, to pay for his sins. The question was, how? How would she make anyone listen to her? How would she be able to prove it? How was she supposed to accomplish any of this? More importantly, how was she supposed to get home?

Chapter 30

James Crandall paced as he waited for Governor McIntire to arrive at his offices. Crandall usually didn't get involved in the issues of smaller towns and villages unless the governor specifically sent him. Even then, he'd delegate the other Rangers. However, this was different. James didn't know for sure what was going on in Colorado Springs, but he wanted to investigate it himself. Miss Meyers' story was a bit far-fetched, and yet, because of this, he couldn't believe she'd make up something so elaborate.

Miners, Cheyenne and compromised local law sounded more like some fantasy novel than what was occurring in real life. He moved out west because there was a spot open for him that didn't deal with gangs, like Jesse James, Billy the Kid's gang or even the Reno Brothers. Granted, Sam Bass and the Black Hills Bandits were a bit closer to home than he cared to admit, but Texas, Nebraska and South Dakota were still far enough away he didn't have to give it much thought, and hopefully they would stay away from Colorado. The few that were a problem, the Rangers were able to handle and there hadn't been a major issue for the past couple of decades. At least with gangs. Indians had also been less of a problem with most of them being relocated to reservations. The miners were the newest concern, but so far, they were also easy to deal with.

James stopped as he heard a group of men getting closer. The door opened, and he waited patiently as Governor Albert Wills McIntire entered the room with some of his advisors. James moved out of the way so Albert could reach his desk and sit down.

"Nice to see you, Ranger Crandall. However, I take it this isn't a social visit."

"Good morning, Governor. Gentlemen. No, sir. It's not. I've recently been made aware of a potential issue in Colorado Springs."

"Miners fighting again?" Luke, one of the advisors, pulled off his hat to hang loosely from his hands.

"It's more complicated than that, from what I'm told."

"What are we looking at then, James?" Albert placed his elbows on the arms of his chair, clasping his hands in a steeple formation.

"A complete mess if this doesn't get resolved. How close are you to Mr. Bartholomew Higgins?"

McIntire thought about it, then shook his head. "I remember I finished signing off on some land originally owned by the Cheyenne, but they'd signed a treaty a few years ago. It was a land deal project started by Waite just before he left office. You know how slow the process can be when the office changes its personnel. Never actually met the man, though. Why?"

"It appears 22 women were found on that land you ceded over to him. A 23rd, from what I'm told, escaped. It is believed the Cheyennes who didn't leave the area are responsible for these women's deaths, except there is the possibility they're being framed."

"You're thinking Higgins is the one who might

be framing the Indians for his kills? Why would he kill all those people?" Luke sat down, putting his hat on his knee.

"That's one theory. There is also my concern the Cheyenne might retaliate if they don't think the one the local sheriff arrested is being treated fairly. On top of that, Higgins plans on bringing in some kind of mining process that will affect the land, which won't make the Cheyenne any happier. We don't need another Indian War because of misunderstandings about the gold in the area and those who are getting it."

"What are you proposing, Crandall?" McIntire knew this could become a potential threat if left unchecked, and he had only been in office for a few months. He didn't need to start his career with a bloody battle so close to his home in Denver.

"I'd like to go out there and investigate what is occurring. However, due to the multiple sections of these issues, I feel it would be beneficial if I have a couple of others meet me out there."

"You don't think it's going to be a simple

enough matter for you to handle alone?"

"Normally, I wouldn't even hesitate on dealing with this by myself, but the issues are expansive, and I can only be in one place at one time. There is too much happening simultaneously, and if a war breaks out between the Cheyenne and the miners, I won't be enough."

"Good point." Luke turned to McIntire. "We don't have anyone we can release today, but we can get a few more out there by tomorrow to give Crandall any assistance he might need."

"What's going on today?" James looked around, gauging reactions of the others in the room.

"I have that speech in the Senate today."

"Of course. I'd forgotten."

"Unlike you to forget, Crandall."

"Let's just say the Colorado Springs issue has me concerned."

"Then you'd best head out there and start the investigation. As soon as I've no more need for the heavy detail of Rangers, I'll send a couple more your way." Albert stood, holding out his hand.

James moved over to shake it. "Thank you, sir." Without any further ado, he bolted from the office and headed to Briley's Stables and Livery. There he got Anna's paint and his own mustang, having them hitched to a small wagon. Although riding the horses would probably be more efficient, he didn't wish to create further hardship for Anna's journey. Besides, he rather relished the idea of spending more time together, and in a wagon, it was inevitable they do so.

James made a quick stop at the restaurant they'd dined at last night before driving the wagon over to the boarding house. Anna was standing on the porch awaiting his arrival and seemed to light up when she saw him.

"Hello. Did you have a good rest?"

"Not really. I think I'm too anxious as to what might have happened since I've been away. And I'm worried I won't get back in time." She couldn't help but notice her paint was hooked up to the wagon.

James noticed her look and smiled. "I thought

this would be more efficient to get you back."

"You're coming with me?"

"I told you I would."

"Alone?"

"For now, yes, but others will come tomorrow. Governor McIntire has a speech in the Senate today, then a dinner. The Rangers need to be on hand for him. The rest are in other parts of Colorado handling issues that have arisen. Are you ready to go?"

"Yes." Bounding down the steps and through the short yard, she reached the wagon and let him lift her into the seat before climbing in himself.

Checking to make sure she was settled in, he slapped the reins to get the horses moving. "I'm not going to push as hard as you did yesterday. I don't think your paint will be up to it. Regardless, we should still be there by mid-afternoon."

"I'm grateful for your assistance and returning with me. I know my story must be a bit hard to digest, so your believing in it is appreciated."

"It's because it's so strange, it's hard to believe

anyone made it up. Besides, it's my duty to keep the peace between the miners and anyone else they may have a grievance with, especially if the distress is against the Cheyenne. We just dealt with them to a point they're no longer a threat. I can't have those relations dismantled and neither can the new governor. He doesn't need to start his career with a blotch like an Indian War on his record, especially after he just took office."

"Understandable. Then I'm doubly grateful you were the one who found me trying to sneak into the Capitol to meet with the governor."

James reached across and gripped her small, gloved hand. "So am I."

Chapter 31

A pounding on the door startled Florence. Moving over to the exterior opening, she unlocked the door, pulling it to find Bart standing before her. "What do you want?"

He pushed her aside to gain entrance into her office. "I want you to give her to me."

"Are you absolutely crazy? I can't do that, and I won't."

"I don't need your permission. It benefits you as much as it does me."

"How do you come to that conclusion?"

"You're in almost as deep as I am, Flo. If she starts talking, as she is bound to do, her talking could delay the mining operation, which you're also a business partner of. The chemicals are due to arrive tomorrow; we can start the mining process the day after at the latest. You can be rich on your own instead of leeching off me."

"I've never leeched off you. I gave you my hard-earned money that I saved for your investment."

"And riding my coattails in the process. You think I'm not going to implicate you, if they come after me. You think I'm not going to tell them you knew about it all?"

"It's a lie. Why would you lie to them about me?"

"Why not?" He grabbed her by the shoulders. "Just give her to me. Let me get her out of here before the house wakes up. I'll take care of the rest. No one needs to know. They will assume she either ran back to the Cheyenne or left because she was too embarrassed to remain here with everyone talking about her behind her back."

"You don't think they'll know she might've been murdered? They haven't forgotten how she was at the picnic with you before she was captured by the Cheyenne. Or that you insisted she was dead. Or that there were 22 other women found on your land."

"They'll believe anything I tell them to. I pay most of them enough and the rest are mules that will easily be led by their noses. She is the only obstacle

I have—*we* have—for starting the mining production."

"I won't give her up. It's too risky."

"It's riskier if she stays alive. I don't need your permission."

"I'm not letting you enter the house."

"How are you going to stop me?"

"I don't know, but I will."

"You're a fool."

"Maybe Bart, but I'm a smart fool who knows if you try and take her, she's going to make a ruckus and you'll get caught."

"Oh, so little faith in me. You think I didn't have that worked out. I have some chloroform from the good doctor. I'll wrap her up in some blankets. No fuss. No muss. No problem with her opening her mouth and the off chance someone might actually listen to her lunatic ravings."

"No. I'm sorry. I've protected you when we were in Pennsylvania, then Kansas and all those people went missing. I had a feeling you knew something, but I didn't think it was actually you.

When you came out here and things were quiet, I thought I was right and I'd misjudged you. Later, I hoped I was just being fanciful. I should've realized sooner when my girls started missing, but I just didn't want to believe it was actually you or that you had such sadistic tendencies, despite how you tortured those poor animals when you were a child. I'm never going to say anything against you, but I won't help you with Miss Hanley."

"I don't need your help, you pathetic leech." He pushed her backwards with a hefty shove. She fell against the bookcase. The top row of books jarred enough from her falling against it that a couple books dropped on her head. Bart didn't even look back as he burst through her office door into the house. He knew from secret past visits which room was Sierra's. Checking around to make sure no one else was awake and moving about, lest he be seen, he gently turned the knob to Sierra's room only to find the door locked.

His desperation was growing, and he shouldered the door, forgetting about any sound it might make. He shouldered it again, the wood starting to crack, but he also heard movement from the other rooms. He tried once more. If he could get in the room, he could shut the door and the mindless women wouldn't know what it was they were hearing. He could take care of Sierra, remaining with her corpse until the house was empty. Ramming his body against the door again, it still didn't give away and he knew it was too dangerous to stay behind. Growling, he headed back to Florence's office and used the shortcut it provided to head back outside, disappearing before anyone else was awake and could see him.

While someone was attempting to break through her door, Sierra sat straight up in bed. The noise startled her, but she was already awake. She couldn't sleep. At best, she might've dozed lightly on and off, but true sleep was unattainable. She was far too worried to settle down enough for her body to get its much-needed rest. Problem was, she'd had little to no sleep the day before. Not that she'd trade her experience with Stone for all the gold in the world! Her body still tingled at the thought of their night together.

She looked around in the darkness for something she might be able to use as a weapon should the intruder break through. Mistress DeVoe was right in warning her to lock her door and she was glad she put the additional stop by placing the chair under the knob. She couldn't think of anything in her room that might be used as a weapon. If she were smarter, she would've grabbed a knife from the kitchen downstairs, but she hadn't thought of it. Her own protection hadn't been a concern at all. Saving Stone and having Anna get away to retrieve help were more important. Covering for Anna was her next concern, and trying to talk to Stone was how she spent her time waiting for the night to be over.

The only thing she had was maybe her shoe as a weapon to hit him with. And, of course, her own training in defensive moves. Plus, she had her voice, and she wasn't above screaming bloody murder to get help. After the second attempt and the cracking of the wood, she moved to the back of the bedroom, farthest away from the door. Stupid as it seemed, even to her, she grabbed her heeled shoe and brandished it as a weapon. The door rattled again, but still held, and she heard rapid, heavy footsteps retreating while others awaking and moving about were noticeable. She didn't move from the corner she put herself in for several minutes. It was only when there was a knock did she jump and cautiously move towards it.

"Sierra? Are you alright?" Alice's voice was heavy with concern.

Relieved, Sierra put down the shoe, moved the chair away from under the handle, unlocked and opened the door, looking up and down the hall to see who else might be there. She was frightened. Being exhausted didn't help either. "Everyone okay?"

"Yes. I think so, though Anna isn't here. Her bed hadn't been slept in either."

"Oh. She stayed with me last night and just got up a little while ago. She wasn't feeling too well. I think that was partially my fault since I was too wound up to sleep. She was going to head over to the doctors to see if he could help her."

"This early in the morning?"

Sierra shrugged, trying to make light of it, knowing it was all a lie. Almost immediately, her conscience got the better of her and she pulled Alice in the room. "Look. I lied. Anna is on an errand to Denver to try and get a Ranger to come back. Sheriff Cosco is, I believe, corrupt. I'm trying to cover for her, so she won't get in trouble. Will you help me?"

Alice looked concerned. "Is it about those girls they found?"

"Partly, yes. Also about the Cheyenne, my attempted murder and so much more. Please. I don't want Anna to get in trouble for helping me."

"I don't like Mistress DeVoe much anyways. I'll say she is sick and resting in her room. That should give her a bit of time before the house mistress checks on her."

She pulled Alice into a hug. "Thank you."

Chapter 32

The sun was just starting to rise, but Sierra was already dressed and downstairs in the kitchen making coffee. No one would expect her down here, she normally wasn't up this early on her own, but a good case of worrying insomnia and an attempt to access her room kept her wide awake and alert.

It was nice, though, in the quiet kitchen. Nobody else was downstairs yet and the solitude was what she needed. Alice was going to help her cover for Anna and that was a huge relief. Taking a cup of coffee to the darkened lunch counter, she knew she needed to continue to remain hidden or be with a group of people. She wasn't quite ready for the group yet. Instead, she was content to enjoy the peacefulness before the day turned into mass chaos.

She wondered what might be happening at home. Was work missing her? Her family? Did the hotel realize she hadn't come back? How did they account for her missing from the train? Would she be able to get home? Or was she stuck in the past until she died? Which, if Bart had his way, would be sooner rather than later.

She began to hear movement, others coming into the kitchen to start preparing meals. The trains would be arriving shortly and go throughout most of the day. Looking at the schedule, there were seven planned. She wondered why the one at 6:30am tomorrow was circled in red. What was the significance of that particular train? It was the 835 from Kansas City, but there were no other trains highlighted on the schedule, not even the 835 listed on other days. Curious.

Florence came in, holding an ice bag to the side of her head.

"Mistress DeVoe? Are you alright? What happened?" Sierra set her cup down and jumped off the stool to approach the older woman and help her to a chair.

"Miss Hanley? You're uninjured?"

Frowning, Sierra nodded. "Yes, ma'am. I did as you warned me to. It saved me. It was him, wasn't it. Did he do this to you, too?"

Florence closed her eyes for a moment, moving

the ice over slightly. "I don't know," she lied, still protecting her him no matter the cost. "I was struck from behind." She knew she couldn't just say books fell on her head. It wouldn't be believable, considering he tried to break down Sierra's door. "I'm glad you listened to me and you're unharmed."

Knowing that Florence was a hard, strict person, seeing her concerned about Sierra made Sierra feel she might've misjudged Florence entirely. "Thank you. I'm sorry if he did this to you."

Florence shrugged her slender shoulders. "Not sure who did. I'm not really sure of anything." She put the ice bag in her lap, looking at Sierra. "Who exactly do you think it was?"

"Bart."

"Why? If anything, he liked you. Treated you well."

"At first, yes he did. He even saved my life. That's how we met, you know. He protected me from a train robber who already killed one man and was about to shoot me. I never wondered why he was even on the train to begin with. Or when he boarded. He just appeared out of nowhere."

"I heard the story. He saw the train stopped, heard a gunshot and snuck on board to stop the bandits. You said he saved your life. Why do you think he wants to take it now?"

"I don't know. Not really. I understand how it must sound. So strange and bizarre in accusing someone like Bart, who has been kind until recently." She picked up her coffee cup for something to hold, sipping it slightly. "I know you're in business with him. That the business is the leach mining for gold. I can understand why you want to protect your business partner. But, using sodium cyanide is dangerous and it'll kill far too many people. Those that don't die outright will be slowly poisoned, either through the animals they eat who have been drinking contaminated water, or by drinking the water themselves."

"How do you know so much about it?"

"Because where I'm from, it had caused those same issues and has been outlawed for the most part." Except in Alaska, which personally broke her heart. She hated the idea that something so pristine and beautiful could possibly to be destroyed, even with modern precautions. She'd done a story about this and her research for her report was horrendous. She'd almost forgotten but the foreman reminded her when he explained the process. As she was going through everything last she remembered even more. She couldn't forget the gold cyanidation and its effects.

"Where are you from again?"

"Illinois."

"Ah. The lead mines."

"Why are you in business with him? Can't you see what he's really like?"

"I'm in business with him because I want to be a free woman and not have to worry about my finances."

"I understand. It must've been a wonderful opportunity, but now that you see what he's really like, how dangerous he can be and how destructive his business venture is, how can you remain?"

"I don't believe he's as dangerous as you think. I don't understand how you believe someone who saved your life and cared for you is someone you believe is a monster." Even though Florence knew the truth, she'd do anything to protect him and his heinous crimes.

"Because, I've seen it with my own eyes. He tried to kill me. He tried to strangle me, and when I got away, he shot at me. He probably would've succeeded if not for the Cheyenne. A part of you must believe it too. You warned me to lock my bedroom door. You locked the downstairs doors and windows as well. I noticed that when I came downstairs. Why are you denying all of this?"

Florence put the ice bag on her head. How could she tell Sierra the truth? That she loved Bart regardless of everything he'd done? That he had a hard life? That at the age of five he watched his father die and it caused him to be off balance, so he turned into a monster? That she knew something was wrong with him, and she suspected he'd committed similar crimes in Pennsylvania, then

Kansas, before he came out west in search of gold? That she was relieved when he left? Or how, when he wrote and told her he'd become wealthy and to join him in Colorado, then he refused to admit he even knew her after she arrived? That he was ashamed of her? Or that he used his wealth to taunt her daily about her inadequate social and financial status? He made her realize she'd never find another husband to care for her. She thought he'd changed, focusing his hatred on her alone and not other women. No dead bodies were found, no women turned up missing that she knew of, until several months back with one of her girls.

She realized he had become more efficient at his habits, improved his technique at taking women so they wouldn't be missed as easily and at hiding them when he was done. He became better at keeping her in the dark and making her the fool in trusting him. However, despite everything, she wouldn't turn him in. Wouldn't go against him in any way. She'd lie to protect him.

"I locked everything up and told you to do the

same because this was your first night back and I didn't want you to be overwhelmed or concerned with others bothering you about your experiences."

"Hmm. Somehow, I just don't believe you, but if that's what you need to tell yourself to sleep at night and face yourself in the mirror every day, then good luck with that." Sierra headed back into the kitchen. She had work to do to help cover for Anna and get ready for the first train of the day.

Florence watched her go, pulling the ice pack from her head and gently using her fingers to probe the slight bump she had as a result of her confrontation with Bart. Maybe she should turn him in, but she just couldn't. No matter what, she loved him completely and sincerely. Somehow, some way, she was going to make this all okay.

Chapter 33

Bart paced his office. The sun was up, but he'd barely noticed. He lit up a cheroot, letting the puffs of smoke swirl around his head. His free hand clenched and unclenched. He felt like he was being backed into a corner and he was becoming a bit desperate. He should've gone back and hunted down Sierra and the Cheyenne who saved her. He should've made sure she was dead right from the start. He wanted to feel the life drain out of her as he had all the others, squeezing that last breath from her delicate neck, watching her eyes glaze over as she died.

He liked having the power of life and death at his fingertips. He enjoyed the thrill of the chase, only he had no interest in catching them other than as prey. Only Sierra had been one that was different, and he wasn't entirely sure why. Maybe it was because when he first met her, she was staring death in the face at the end of a pistol and remained unflinching. That had impressed him. She wasn't a quivering, cowering woman, but she wasn't so hard as to be manly.

Things changed for him when he was warned about her by Florence. They changed even more when Sierra started questioning him. She had become intrusive, inquisitive and a nag, everything he despised from the female gender. Why had she needed to ask so many questions? Why couldn't she mind her own business and stay out of his affairs?

His mother was a nag. Do this. Do that. Don't do this. Don't do that. It was annoying. His mother always wanted to know where he was, who he was with, and what they were going to do. She didn't say things like that to his sister, only to the men of the house. His sister got away with everything and he got the blame, which included all the whippings with a belt by his mother. He admitted to himself long ago he hated how his sister was the sparkle of his mother's eye and he was barely tolerated by all of them. Even his father would spend more time at the saloons just to get away from his nagging wife and the rest of his family.

After a particularly loud verbal argument about

his sister and how his father knew she didn't belong, his father stormed out of the house. When Bart could finally sneak away, he followed his dad to the local saloon. He wanted to know what was meant by his sister not belonging. At such a young age, it hadn't made any sense to him.

At least his dad could sympathize with him about the women of the house. Bart was never sure why his mother favored his older sibling, and yet his father seemed to tolerate his sister at best. Albeit, his father seemed to only tolerate him too, so maybe that was just his way.

He found his father gambling in the saloon and drinking heavily. Bart cowered down outside the window and watched. His father was winning but spending everything he won on liquor. Shortly thereafter, his father got into an argument. Before Bart could stand and get inside, his father had been shot four times in the chest. Several men just tossed him out into the street before going back inside, not knowing that his five-year-old son watched it all happen in front of his youthful eyes.

Bart ran to his father's side. He got there in time to see the light of life extinguish from his father. That last breath escaping his dry, whiskey-stained lips fascinated Bart. He wanted to see that play out over and over again. First, he tried with animals that he caught in his backyard, but it wasn't the same. His fascination grew as he , and by the time he was ten it was a full-on obsession. One his mother and sister didn't understand or want to. To them, he was just a deviant, troubled boy who had watched his father get gunned down for cheating at cards. If they only knew the truth. Bart liked killing, liked watching living creatures die by his hand.

When he was fifteen, his mother grabbed a belt to spank him because of some transgression he'd committed, but he turned the tables on her. Enough was enough and he was tired of being whipped for some petty infraction. Spinning rapidly, he captured the end of the belt and pulled with all his might. It caused his mother to stumble and fall at his feet. He kicked her back and pounced on top of her, wrapping his hands around her throat, using his weight to keep her down. Although she struggled, he had the upper position. He smiled with glee. This was much more fun than killing animals. So much more enriching and fulfilling.

However, his mother managed to hit him on the side of his head with the buckle part of the belt still in her hands just as his older sister walked in, quickly giving aide to their mother. Bart left the house then. He knew he wasn't welcomed there, but that didn't prevent him from remembering the look in her eyes as he choked her, giving him a thrill he remembered for days.

After a couple of weeks of failing to make it on his own and thinking of taking his mother's life for all her cruelty to him, he returned, begging for forgiveness. It was a complete ruse, though. He played the doting son as he bided his time, waiting.

When he felt the time was right, he snuck into his mother's room while she was asleep and killed her. He knew he couldn't afford to leave any trace behind and he'd seen the marks on her neck when he'd tried earlier, so he devised another way by placing a pillow over her face until she was smothered to death. But it wasn't as rewarding. Killing and watching her essence be snuffed out by his hand was far more entertaining than the way he killed his mother. Still, it was his first kill of a human. It had to be remembered, memorialized. Taking his pocket knife out, he took a lock of her hair. He was only fifteen. She may have been the first, but she was certainly not going to be the last. He'd get better. Just watch.

No one ever suspected the truth about his mother's passing, not even his stupid sister. And even if she did, she never said anything about it. His sweet, idiot sister had no idea how much he had enjoyed himself as he killed his bitch of a mother. He realized it wasn't going to stop there.

He was selective, though. It wasn't just any woman whom he chose. It was the weak ones that nagged, complained or demanded, whether from him or from others while they were in his presence, it hadn't mattered for naught. They reminded him of his mother and he killed every incarnation of her that he could, physically similar or not. At least at first. Recently, he'd gone for appearance more than attitude, just to have the power of life in his hands.

He'd thought Sierra was the exception. He thought he could be with a woman and not have her nag or control him. But she couldn't stay out of his affairs. She had to know everything and wouldn't let anything go. Then when she questioned him on Louise's necklace and his business dealings, he snapped. He wouldn't take the chance of getting caught because of her inquisitiveness.

A knock on his door broke the reverie of his life. Snuffing out the cheroot, he opened the door and let the sheriff in. "Cosco."

"Greetings, Mr. Higgins. I hope you are well."

"Fine. How did our prisoner do last night?"

"As restless as a cat. Pacing most of the night like a caged animal." He laughed. "I guess he is one, at that."

"Doesn't really matter, I guess."

"What do you mean by that?"

"I mean, I'm taking care of the situation as far

as he goes." His tone indicated the end of the conversation and Cosco was smart enough to take the hint and drop it.

"You said you needed me to do something, sir? In your note?"

"Yes. I need you to kill Miss Sierra Hanley."

The sheriff stared at him unblinkingly. Surely, Bart didn't just ask him to do what he thought he heard. "Excuse me?"

"Miss Hanley needs to die today before she can talk about her experiences to someone who might actually listen and attempt to save the Cheyenne. I want her dead. I know you're pretty handy with a shotgun. I suggest you use it as soon as possible. I'm sure she'll want to visit the Indian or take one of her daily walks with Miss Meyers. Perfect opportunities to take care of business."

"I uphold the law, for the most part. I don't go around killing innocent, unarmed women. Have you any idea the hornets' nest her death would cause?"

"I don't care. She can't be allowed to talk to anyone, especially about what really happened on our picnic."

"I was wondering about that myself. You swore she was dead then."

"I was pretty sure she was. But since she wasn't, she needs to be and it's your job to handle it."

"No."

"No? NO! I don't think so. Not if you want to keep those nice paychecks coming to you and not have your wife find out about all the extra you have spent in Pearl's Parlor House in Cripple Creek. What's her name? Mimi? Milly? I'm sure my memory will improve the longer Miss Hanley is still breathing."

Cosco wiped his hand across his now-sweaty brow. "You can't do that."

"I can, and I will. You think I'm going to let some piss-ant woman just take away everything I've been working for? You think I won't make sure my security, and thereby yours, is taken care of? I'm too public right now, so I need someone who would be the least possible person to take care of this issue for me. That's you. After all, who would suspect our good sheriff?"

Cosco felt like he was trapped. There was no way in hell he was going to go against the wishes of his employer, yet he wasn't sure he could kill an innocent, unarmed woman. There were too many things that could go wrong, not to mention living with his own conscience. Still, he didn't see a way out.

"Tell you what, Sheriff. Why don't you take the rest of the day off. You're not looking too well. A little pale, and sweaty. Use that time to get some rest and do what you need to do. Tomorrow, I'm sure you will feel better and everything will be as good as gold." Bart laughed at his own warped sense of humor.

"As you say, Mr. Higgins, I've not been feeling very well this morning. Think I will take the rest of the day off and get some rest." He bobbed his head as he backed out of the room. Maybe if he thought of Miss Hanley as a well-dressed deer, he could consider it as a type of hunting and it wouldn't be so bad.

Higgins held the front door open for the sheriff to depart, a satisfied grin on his face. Things were falling into place nicely. One problem down, now he had to instigate a way to take care of the next problem on his list.

Chapter 34

Bart moved to the window with his cup of coffee and stared at the commotion that was beginning to gather outside, slowly making their way to the jail. From his upstairs window he had a pretty good view of the proceedings of town activities. It's how he got so much dirt on so many people about their sneaky comings and goings.

With a satisfied, Cheshire cat-eating grin, he watched as Henry McAllister walked down the street, grumbling to anyone who listened. Henry had arrived shortly after the sheriff departed and was the answer to the second of Bart's recently acquired obstacles. Bart knew Henry well enough to know which issues would set the man's blood on fire, and Bart would be able to utilize that information for his own personal benefit. He just had to be smart about goading Henry without the man being aware he was being manipulated.

Although Henry left Bart's home with no one listening to him, he'd been able to rally others to his way of thinking as he walked the two blocks to the prison. Soon there was a huge crowd gathered around the jail, with Henry on the porch. From Bart's vantage point, he could tell Henry was inciting them nicely, working them up to a frenzy.

Problem two, done. Higgins mentally checked it off his to-do list. Pleased with himself, he headed down to his kitchen, knowing the rest would be handled efficiently. He could always manage to get Henry worked up over the littlest thing. Give him a few glasses of whiskey while they talked, and Henry was raring to go in whichever direction Bart had guided. Add to that the Cheyenne killed his family years ago, and he was ripe and ready to be picked. Yes, Henry was the perfect choice for this mission.

The sun was beginning to droop in the sky, coloring it in beautiful shades of orange, red and a touch of pink. The heavens almost looked more like a rich painting than actuality. Soon the sun would be down, making it the perfect time for the main event. It was just a little after seven. Most of the town's people were done working for the day and headed over to either the Eating House or the Saloon for dinner if they didn't make it themselves. A few were already enjoying a hearty liquid meal, but that would only enhance what Henry was attempting to accomplish as he fired them up with his speeches.

Bart had seen Cosco lying on top of the prison, keeping low. It was only because Bart's house was so tall he could see the roofs of many of the other buildings. Everything was going as planned. Well, mostly. True, he wanted to be the one who siphoned the life right out of that conniving little bitch Sierra, but he would make up for it later. When things calmed down a bit, he would take two women and make them pay for Sierra. And maybe one of them would be his business partner. He'd have to think on that one a while longer.

Regardless, Henry had this well in hand and Bart could fix himself another drink before returning upstairs to bring his chair over and watch the show from his private little window. He only wished he could hear everything going on as well, albeit, Henry was getting more and more boisterous with each passing moment. The crowd's responses were loud enough for Bart to hear even two blocks away.

Standing on the wooden porch, Henry really began to rant. "Are we really going to let this mongrel face our jail system?"

The crowd yelled back, "No!"

"Are we really going to let him use up our hard-earned tax money to feed him and keep him in the system? Can we really afford to?"

"No!"

"You worked hard for your money to be able to put food on your table, clothe your kids and make sure they have a roof over their heads. Now we have to take care of the likes of this Injun? He killed your friends! He killed your family! You can't let him get away with that, can you?"

"NO!" The crowd raised their fists, shaking them in the air. Some of the local miners raised their pick-axes instead of just their fists.

Sierra could hear the commotion outside and

ran to the door. She was about to run out when Alice stopped her. "Where are you going?"

"I've got to interfere. They might do something stupid, something rash. I can't take that chance. Stone is innocent of the crimes they are accusing him of, but he needs to be given a fair trial to prove it."

"Dear, there is no such thing out here. The law is what they make of it and nothing more. Here the law doesn't really exist, especially for the likes of Indians. It's whoever has the fastest gun, the most money or the loudest influence. Don't get caught up in the frenzy. They'll chew you up and spit you out as easily as if you were nothing more than a piece of fat on their steak."

"That's a charming analogy." Sierra gave a slight shudder. "I can't stay in here, though. I can't hide and hope this will calm down on its own."

"And if you go out there, you're only going to get hurt yourself."

"I'm not important, Alice. I won't stand by when there is an injustice going on right in front of me. I have to do something, anything. But I won't stand by. I'm sorry." Sierra didn't wait for any further comment but stepped outside and purposefully walked to the group that was gathered around the jail.

Once outside the doors, Henry's voice was more distinctive and clear. He was rallying up the townsfolk to take the law in their own hands.

"The Cheyenne have always been a problem. We got rid of most of them onto the reservations where they belong, but there are a few who wouldn't leave. Stone's one of them. He's killed our women. Who's to say he ain't gonna go after our kids next? We can't let that happen. We need to know our families are safe. We need to protect them."

"Yeah!"

"That's right!"

"Dem Injuns gotta go."

"We gotta keep our kinfolk safe."

Henry raised his fist. "Are we going to let this go on?"

"No!"

"Hang 'em!" And suddenly, the furious, worked-up crowd began to chant. "Hang 'em!"

Sierra rushed up to the steps, shoving past the others who were making their way to tear down the jail itself in order to get at the man who was inside. "Stop! Stop!" She was out of breath, but she blocked the door, her palms outward in order to protect herself and halt them from going inside. "He's innocent. You can't kill an innocent man. He didn't kill your wives, your daughters, your women. He found them."

"Then why didn't he report the find?"

"It was late. We were going to when the sun came up, but you beat us to it," she panted breathlessly

"Us? You're with him?"

"She's just trying to protect him."

"Don't let her fool you. She's with the Injun."

The crowd shoved her aside and rushed into the jail. There were sounds of a struggle before they dragged him out. He was bruised, with a cut lip and the beginnings of one eye getting swollen. She wondered why he didn't change or fight all of them. He certainly had the special strength of his kind, so what stopped him? It was then she remembered how they remained hidden from the humans, not giving them an inkling of what they really were. If he were to fight them off utilizing his strength or powers, they'd know he was something different, and that would endanger the rest of his people.

They moved past her and down the steps, dragging Stone with them.

"No. Stop!" Sierra tried to reach out and grab him, but they pushed him by too quickly for her to reach.

She stood and started to move with the group when someone caught her arm, pulling her around.

"Mistress DeVoe?"

"There is nothing you can do."

"I can try. Let me go." For a small, thin woman, she was amazingly and surprisingly strong.

"You can't defeat mob mentality."

"I won't let him die. I can't let them kill him."

Sierra pulled away, tearing the sleeve of her uniform in the process.

Running past others as she pushed them out of the way, the crowd was thick and difficult to move through. She wasn't fast enough to reach Stone before they put one end of a rope around his neck.

"Stop. You can't do this. He's innocent until proven guilty. He needs a fair trial. He's innocent." She was trying for anything to save him and get the madness of the mob to die down.

"We've judged him. He's been found guilty," Henry snarled as he tossed the free end of the rope over the limb of the tree and tied it to the horn of a horse's saddle.

"You're not the law; this isn't a judge and jury. I'll see each and every one of you brought up on criminal charges. Don't do this! It's not worth your lives and your family to kill an innocent man."

"You think an Injun is innocent? That *he* is innocent? Ain't such a thing as innocent when it comes to Injuns. They're all guilty. Have you seen how many helpless women we found at his personal grave site? He's a monster." Henry slapped the rump of the horse and it took off, hoisting Stone by the neck into the air, his legs kicking aimlessly in the air as he was being hung.

"NO!" Sierra screamed.

Chapter 35

Sierra continued to rush towards Stone but stopped, startled when a shot rang out. Stone flailed helplessly in the air for a split second before crashing in a heap on the ground. A second shot rang out and everyone turned towards the direction it was coming from.

Standing on a wagon, a rifle in hand and aimed at the mob, a man called out. "Colorado Ranger James Crandall. Move towards the prisoner again and I'll shoot you dead. I suggest, instead, you disperse."

Sierra was instantly relieved. She could see someone sitting behind Ranger Crandall, and though she couldn't see the person distinctly, she knew in her heart it was Anna.

Moving to Stone, she helped him up, pulling the remnants of the rope off his neck. There was a rope burn, but she knew it would heal with little to no scar as he hadn't dangled enough for it to permanently graft his skin.

"What are you doing? Get out of here." Stone

pushed her away.

She was stunned. She expected a lot of things, but having him speak to her in such a way, telling her to leave, wasn't among them. "I'm here to help you."

"I don't want your help." He pushed her away again and began walking straight towards the rifle-holding Ranger. His hands were held up in surrender and the crowd parted like the Red Sea to let him pass. When he reached the wagon, he turned himself over to Ranger Crandall.

Another shot rang out and the crowd screamed, running haphazardly and scattering about the area. James tried to figure out where the shot came from and who was firing. He looked past the crowd and saw a woman crouched by the tree who'd been helping Stone, her arms over her head. Assuming she was the one being shot at, he traced it back through the angle the shot would've come from just in time to see a man raise up enough to get another shot aimed. Crandall pulled his trigger at the same time as the man fired.

"Oh my god!" Anna said from behind Crandall. "That's Sheriff Cosco."

The sheriff was thrown back from the direct hit, his own shot missing Sierra and hitting the tree she was kneeling by, splinters of wood ricocheting into her hair. James kept his rifle aimed in case Cosco moved again. After a few minutes, he lowered his rifle, hopping off of the wagon. Checking once again, he reached in to grasp Anna by her waist and swing her down to the ground. "Go check on that woman the sheriff was shooting at."

"That's Sierra!" she exclaimed before hoisting her skirt and running to her. "Sierra! Are you alright?"

Sierra heard her name being called and lifted her head to see Anna. Just behind her was the Ranger, who saved Stone's life, and Stone, himself. Her gaze lingered on him for a split second, before she turned to Anna. "You did it! You got a Ranger to come back with you."

"I promised you I would." She hugged Sierra. "Did you get hit?"

"No. The bullet hit the dirt at my feet and then the tree behind me. I'm okay."

"I can't believe the sheriff was shooting at you."

"The sheriff? Where is he?"

"On top of the jail. Though James shot him before he could really get the second round off, and I don't think he's come up since."

"Maybe the sheriff was shooting at Stone and got me by mistake?"

"I doubt it. Stone was already at the wagon when Cosco fired."

"Then why?"

Anna turned around and saw James taking Stone back into the jail. Sierra watched him too. Stone kept his eyes straight ahead, but James turned slightly and gave Anna a wink, to which she blushed slightly.

Sierra watched the whole exchange between them. "Okay. So, tell me about your Ranger."

"My Ranger? What do you mean?"

"I saw that wink and your look. You two like

each other. I can tell. So, tell me about him. Is he nice?"

Anna couldn't help but smile and lower her eyes in bashfulness, but she raised them again to watch his backside entering the jail before she turned back to Sierra. "He's handsome, don't you think? And intelligent. I told him your story, what you wanted me to tell them, and he made arrangements to come first thing this morning. It took a whole day to get back here. I honestly didn't even think the horse would make it, but he telegraphed ahead to have a change of horses and brought a lunch from where we dined last night about half way here. In a day or two, when things have settled down, we'll go exchange our horses again. He wants me to go back with him, since it was the paint I borrowed and knew I was responsible for, but I think he also wants to spend time with me too."

"Yes. He's handsome. I'm thrilled he likes you a lot and wants to spend more time with you."

"I hope so. I like him, Sierra. We spent last

night at dinner and then the whole day on the journey here just talking. I've never been so comfortable with a man."

"Anna, my darling," James called from the roof of the jail. "Can you please find the doctor and send him up."

Anna waved an acknowledgement. "Why don't you go in the jail and make sure Stone is okay?"

"He doesn't seem to want to see me."

"It's probably a Cheyenne thing. His ego in looking helpless. Actually, that's probably also a man thing too."

Without waiting for a response, Anna went in search of Doctor Whalen.

Sierra started to head in to see Stone, but his words still stung. Anna was probably right, though. He was probably concerned she'd get hurt by interfering. Lifting her chin up, she headed inside and took a moment to look around.

The town was small enough there was no need for deputies unless they were sworn in for a particular cause, such as a posse, but they weren't a regular fixture. As such, there were only two cells, each containing a cot and a bucket. Outside the cell were a file cabinet and a desk. Along the wall by the door was a rack for gun belts. On it hung a rifle strap, a hat and a jacket.

Stone was sitting on the bed, his head in his hands. She stopped by the bars, her hands on them, watching him for a few moments. When he didn't move, she called to him. "Stone?"

His head snapped up. "What are you doing here? I told you to get out of here. Leave."

"I wanted to make sure you're alright? Did they hurt you?"

"It doesn't matter. It's not your concern."

"It does matter. It matters to me."

"I don't want to see you again, Sierra. How can I make that plain enough for you to understand?"

"You don't mean that. You're just upset because they almost killed you, or because you think you looked weak in my eyes because they tried to hang you. But I don't care. You don't look anything less than the chief and alpha I have come to know you to be."

Stone snarled, launching off the bed to be right in front of her face. "I meant every word I said. I never want to see you again. The next time I do, I might kill you. Stay. Away. From. Me. Do you understand?"

She blinked back tears. Nodding, she turned and ran out the door. He could see her running past the office window, and only when he was sure she couldn't see him again, he rested his head against the bars. Angry with himself and what he felt he had to do, he pulled his head back and slammed it against the bars. Then repeated the movement. The second time caused a trickle of blood to course down his cheek from a split just above his eye. Defeated, he sat back down on the cot and put his head in his hands once again.

It wasn't what he wanted to do. Just the opposite. His lion roared at what Stone was doing to push her away, but he didn't believe in the U.S. Government or their legal system. He was sure if the Ranger hadn't shown up, he'd be dead. And even though he knew Sierra was working to prove him innocent, he didn't expect to walk away from this unscathed. Somehow, they would find him guilty, regardless of what little proof they had. As a result, he had to set her free. He trusted her to keep the tribe's secret, but he knew her destiny didn't lie with him. He had to push her away for her own good, even though it killed him to do so, and he had to fight his lion with every ounce of strength he had.

Doctor Whalen and Anna headed upstairs. James stopped her from reaching the roof and escorted her back down. "There's nothing for you to see up there. I saw your friend leaving. She didn't look too happy. Maybe you should go check on her? I've got a few things to do here. I'll stop by later to make sure everything is okay."

"When did you want to speak with Sierra?"

"Tomorrow I'll talk to Miss Hanley and get her statement, then check on where all the bodies were found."

"You're not going to be doing this alone, are you? Is the sheriff dead? Why did he try to shoot

Miss Hanley?"

"Yes, the sheriff's dead. I don't know why he shot at Miss Hanley. Thankfully, he wasn't a very good shot. There should be some other Rangers coming tomorrow or day after. Don't worry. I'll take care of everything." He kissed her temple, escorting her outside. "I'll see you later."

"Until then, James."

He leaned against the post, arms folded as he watched her walk away. After several moments, James headed back upstairs. He knew he had to deal with the prisoner too, but one thing at a time, and the Cheyenne wasn't going anywhere.

Chapter 36

Florence didn't even knock as she entered Sierra's room to find Anna was also there. "What in God's name did you two think you were doing? Why did you bring that Ranger in? Do you have any idea what you have started?"

"No. What have we started? Maybe some real justice? Maybe the opportunity for things not to get even further out of control as they seem to be doing? Maybe providing resistance to the lynch mob out there?" Sierra stood, moving in front of Anna, as if to shield her.

"You're a fool. You both are. What you've put into motion can't be stopped now." Florence spun on her heel.

"God, I hope you're right, because the way it was going, injustice, murder, death, carnage, was not the way it should go. Something, anything, must be better than that. And Bart needs to be brought in to account for those women and for trying to kill me. Something also tells me he was behind the attempted lynching of Stone. He needs to pay for his crimes."

"And you think you and that Ranger are going to make him pay?" Florence looked over her shoulder, her hand on the doorknob. "He owns everything here. No one is going to go against him, and if they do, they're going to find themselves dead. Including that Ranger. Worse, you both are going to have to live with that. *If* he lets you live at all."

"You think he'll kill us like he did all those other women?"

"Probably. You're a loose end and he has no problems tying those up."

"Thank you, Mistress DeVoe. You just confirmed you knew about Bart's murder spree and everything else he's been attempting to do." Sierra folded her arms across her chest. Anna moved to stand behind Sierra, looking even more worried and concerned than ever.

Realizing she had been outsmarted, Florence left the room, slamming the door behind her. Only then did both Sierra and Anna let out the breaths they'd been holding.

"That didn't go so well," Anna mumbled. "Do you think he'll hurt James?"

Sierra turned and pulled Anna into a hug. "From what you told me about him and what I've seen, I think James will be able to handle himself. I'm more worried about Mrs. DeVoe at the moment. She's getting backed into a corner. People who feel they have nowhere else to turn usually become very reckless and fool-hardy. She's sort of the wildcard in this."

"What about Mr. Higgins?"

Releasing Anna, Sierra moved to sit down on the edge of the bed. "He's got to realize he isn't going to be able to sway everyone much longer. Unless he can bribe Ranger Crandall, he's got to know it's all coming to an end. Right? He, too, can become desperate. I'm not sure what he might do."

"What about the sheriff? Why do you think he tried to shoot you? Or do you think it was really bad aim for Stone?"

"I'm not sure. Stone was already at the wagon

when those shots rang out, but I'm not entirely sure he didn't miss on purpose." Sierra rubbed her forehead trying to comprehend everything. "Do you think Bart hired him to kill me? After all, you said he owned the sheriff. Maybe he considered it part of the sheriff's job?"

"It's certainly within the realm of possibility."

The women stopped talking when a knock on the door interrupted them. Sierra frowned, giving Anna a dubious look, then went to open it. Alice stood there with a tray laden with tea, cups and accompaniments. Smiling, Sierra took a step back and welcomed her into the room, shutting the door behind her.

"Tea. How thoughtful and just what we need."

"I slipped some whiskey in it. I figured we could also use the boost." Alice chuckled as she set the tray down, pouring the tea into each cup.

"Even better." Anna took a sip.

"I just got my first look at that Ranger who came to town. He's very good looking."

"I think Anna will whole-heartedly agree. She's

been smitten ever since they arrived."

Anna felt her cheeks heat up. "Yes. He is, but he is also kind and gentle."

Alice set the teapot down. "I guess he's spoken for then?"

Sierra nodded. "I believe so."

Anna shook her head. "No. He was just doing his job."

"His job doesn't entail him to be watching over you like he did. You can't fool me. His eyes followed you every moment, even if his feet couldn't."

Anna gave a wistful smile. "We talked the entire ride back. I don't think we stopped for the whole time it took to return. I really like him."

Alice patted her hand. "Sierra's right, I'm sure. He's smitten with you too. How can he not be? Now, about the Indian? And Mr. Higgins? And what is going on with Mistress DeVoe? She seems a bit out of sorts this evening."

"A lot is going on and I don't think it's safe for any of us at the moment."

"From who?" Alice queried the other two women.

"From all of them and who knows who else," Anna said quietly.

"Thing is, we don't know who to trust, Alice. Mr. Higgins has bought the loyalty of a good number of town's people. Ranger Crandall is an outsider, but if Higgins gets to him too, buys him off, I really don't know where any of us will be."

Anna gasped. "Do you think that's a possibility?"

"Maybe." Sierra gave her shoulders a slight shrug. "I don't know Crandall. I don't know what makes him tick. Does he have family that could be leveraged? Is he a greedy person? What does upholding the law first and foremost mean to him or is he open to bribery?" She faced Anna knowing if any of them knew, it would be Anna who would be able to answer those questions.

Suddenly, Anna looked highly uncomfortable. "I don't think he's that kind of person. I believe in him. He isn't greedy. He is kind and sweet. He went out of his way to make sure I was safe while he planned to come back here to help you, the Cheyenne and the town. He stopped the lynching. I don't think he'll be one where bribery will succeed."

Sierra patted her hand. "It's okay, Anna. If you believe in him and I believe in you, it's all good."

"What about Stone? Is he okay after the attempt at his life today?" Alice asked.

"I don't know. I'm sure all of this is weighing heavily upon him. He was very upset when Crandall returned him to his cell. I don't think he was very happy about the sheriff, though, or the attempt at my life."

"Did you get a chance to talk to him?" Alice took a sip at her tea.

"Not really. The Ranger just got there, and almost straight away shot the sheriff. There was a lot going on immediately upon his arrival and there's been little time to talk."

"Something's bothering you, Sierra. What is it?" Anna leaned forward.

Sierra set her cup down. She wasn't going to tell them how Stone rebuffed her, saying he never wanted to see her again, just as she'd never mention what Stone and his people could do. In truth, that wasn't the issue either, though. "I keep wondering why Mistress DeVoe is protecting Mr. Higgins. Why did they get into business to begin with? How did they know each other before they came here? I remember Florence said she was from Pennsylvania originally, then went to Kansas to train with Fred Harvey and his school before she was assigned here. I learned Bart was from Pennsylvania and moved to Kansas to get supplies before hunting for gold. Am I the only one who thinks this is highly coincidental, even though they both verbally deny it?"

"I hadn't realized." Anna was slightly shocked.

Alice looked a bit surprised, but overall was more relaxed in learning the information, which made Sierra wonder if the woman already knew.

"I hadn't put it together until last night and then I got to wondering. It just doesn't make sense to me to have Higgins include DeVoe in his business plans. There's no precedent, no cause, so I have to wonder why. Or am I making this more complicated than need be?"

Anna shook her head. "No. These are very good questions. Higgins didn't need to have Florence as a business partner. Unless he owed her or her late husband some sort of financial security."

Alice was quiet for a few moments. "Both of those are big states. Just because they came from the same ones, doesn't mean they knew each other beforehand. Maybe that's something they learned after they got here and realized it was something they had in common. Maybe Higgins is more sentimental than you give him credit for and that's why he offered to have DeVoe as his business partner."

"It could be, and like I said, I could be wrong in this whole assumption. It just seemed a bit strange to me." Sierra finished up her tea, setting the empty cup back on the tray.

"I think you're blowing some of the events out

of proportion. I'm sure it's nothing as dire as you're making it out to be, if in fact they even are really business partners," Alice commented.

Anna watched the two. She wondered why Alice didn't believe there was a business deal between DeVoe and Higgins. What was it she might know but wasn't telling?

Alice picked up the tray. "I'm going to turn in for the night. I'll take this back down and get it out of your way. Have a pleasant evening."

Sierra gave Anna a look that instructed her to remain quiet a bit longer as she stood to hold the door open for Alice. Once the woman was headed down the stairs with the tray, Sierra shut the door, moving to sit by Anna. In low hushed tones, she whispered, "I suddenly don't trust Alice. Maybe I'm being paranoid, but her swift defense of Higgins and DeVoe just makes me concerned."

"You got that also? I found it odd. She was concerned about James, then backed Higgins and DeVoe, not even believing there might be a partnership between the two of them."

"We need to find out more about their connection. I know there is something we're missing. I just don't know what it is."

"How can I help?"

"I've got an idea. How close are you to Ranger Crandall?"

Chapter 37

It felt good to be back in jeans and a shirt again and not the confining dresses Sierra had been forced to wear since she got here, though she was extremely grateful the prairie-style dresses and uniforms meant she didn't have to wear petticoats and corsets. She had Anna help her get a few other things to blend in with the night. She didn't know where she was getting the energy, but despite not sleeping for the past two nights, she was amazingly wide awake, which was good considering the dangerous excursion she had planned.

Anna found a black shirt and some black gloves in the train station's lost and found area. Although the shirt was a bit big, it didn't matter to Sierra, who just tied it off in a knot at the hem. Tying her hair up, she took a quick look in the mirror. "You're going to stay here tonight, right? And lock the doors behind me. Don't trust Alice or anyone with what I'm doing or where I'm going."

"I won't. Be careful. You're out way after curfew. The sun will be up soon."

Sierra laughed. "I'm sure curfew is the least of my worries. Not getting caught is more of the object."

"I was trying not to think of the worst situation you could find yourself in." Anna grabbed her arm. "I'm worried."

"I know, I am too, but I have to do this. If I'm lucky, the worst that will happen is I'll be sent to jail. Otherwise, I might be killed."

"Why do you have to be the one to do this? Let me talk to James."

"No, Anna. I can't get him involved. It's not because I don't trust him either. I need a neutral party in case I am caught. He's my only chance to get out alive."

Anna nodded, giving Sierra a hug. "Be careful. Please."

"I'm going to do my very best. Come on, you'll need to lock the doors behind me and I want to grab a knife on the way out."

"How are you going to get back in?"

"I hadn't quite figured that part out yet. I'm

still making this up as I go along. Any suggestions? I was originally thinking maybe the rear delivery door could be left unlocked. I can sneak in that way when I return. Tap three times quickly at this door, so you can let me in. Does that sound good? I hope to be back before Florence gets the rest of the house awake."

"I don't know. Not going out and doing this sounds better, but I asked you for help and got you into this. I can't think of anything better than what you've suggested."

Sierra sighed. "Actually, Anna, I was already looking into it when you asked for my help. It got me to trust you more, knowing you weren't a part of it because you didn't know what was going on. I'm sorry I didn't tell you the truth sooner."

Blinking, her mouth agape, Anna stood there in shock.

"Say something?"

Closing her mouth, Anna shook her head slowly. "You're very intelligent. I should've known you would've assumed something wasn't right and checked it out before I mentioned it."

"Still. I should've told you from the get-go. Please. Forgive me?"

"I do and I'm still not crazy about this idea of yours, but I understand your need to do this."

"You do?"

Anna nodded. "Yes. I'd do anything for James. You're doing whatever you can for Stone to prove him innocent. I don't think I fully understood that until recently."

"I'm glad you feel the same about James, that you found someone. Let's go." How could Sierra tell Anna about needing to do this for other reasons, not just Stone. Sure, Stone needed to be saved, but she had to get the information she did for her own piece of mind. Her curiosity is one of the things that made her a good reporter. Her mission was to set this time period right. Find out and prove who murdered those women. Stop the gold cyanidation of the land, stripping it bare and making it poisonous. Seeing Stone free was a bonus. His cold words of telling her he didn't want to see her ever again cut her deeply and she wasn't sure she could ever recover from it. However, it did explain why she went back to her own time. His words '*Don't leave me again*' might have meant something else, or maybe he only missed her because she *was* gone. Either way, she couldn't ponder it too deeply. It wasn't her destiny to be with him. Not here. Not now.

With Anna's assistance, she left the Eating House and stayed in the darkest shadows as she made her way the few blocks to Bart's home. The sun would be up shortly, so she didn't have a lot of time. Besides, she wasn't sure what time Bart awoke, so she had to be sure she was gone before he did so. Hiding among the bushes, she watched the house carefully for any sign of movement. After waiting several minutes, she scurried to the house, then checked the door. It was, of course, unlocked, as were most buildings during this era. She thought of the unlocked doors as being cocky for Bart. His way of saying he had nothing to hide and nothing to fear. She felt like the Pink Panther as she scurried about to get inside, constantly checking no one saw her.

Her heart was beating so rapidly, she was sure it'd pound right out of her chest. She'd never been inside his house before, so she wasn't sure of the layout of the property. Guessing, she moved from the foyer to the first room on the right. An elaborate dining room. Most houses would have the dining area and kitchen pretty close together. Not what she was looking for. She went to the foyer and listened for any movement upstairs, where she assumed his bedroom was. Not hearing anything, she continued across the foyer. The first room was a sitting room. Moving quickly, she found an office and library. She shut the door, pulled the dark drapes and set about finding a kerosene lamp she could light.

She continued to listen for any noise or movement, terrified she'd be discovered. She was, after all, breaking in to Bart's house. If he found her, she knew he wouldn't waste any time in killing her and he could claim it as self-defense from an intruder. She noticed there was a bit of space at the bottom of the door and quickly put a throw rug against the crack to prevent the light from seeping through. Feeling a bit safer, she opened his desk drawers, looking for anything which might help her prove he was the murderer. What she was looking for specifically, she had no idea, but she had to try. She'd know it as soon as she found it, if there was anything to find.

She saw the paperwork and ledger for the mining conglomeration he was about to start in a couple of days. Then she saw the 835 train scheduled from Kansas City. It was going to be carrying the sodium cyanide needed for the gold leaching project. That was why DeVoe had it circled in red; it was the train carrying all the necessary supplies to put the project in gear.

She felt even more nauseous than she had before she entered the abode. However, they already knew about the mining project. She needed to find something on the murders or on the business partnership between Higgins and DeVoe. Anything would be helpful. Anything to prove she wasn't stark raving mad. There wasn't much else in the desk and she worried anything personally incriminating would be in his room. There was no way in hell she was going to explore his inner sanctum, especially with him in it.

Looking around the room to make sure there wasn't any place else he might have hidden something, she happened to notice something about the floor. She couldn't put her finger on it exactly, so she examined it closer. This was the area from where she'd pulled the rug to block the rays of light of the lamp from seeping through the door. There was an outline, a thickening of the creases between the boards that looked odd. Her fingers lightly caressed the space and she realized it was a hidden hatch. It took her a few more minutes to find the release mechanism, but she managed to discover it. Cautiously, she opened the space. It wasn't deep, but it was long, and it was full of glass display cases. There had to be five, no, six of them. Each box contained 24 individual squares. It reminded her of those shadow boxes where one would store small trinkets or thimbles for display. Upon closer examination, she felt sick at what they contained.

Four boxes were totally full. One was empty. And one was almost completed. Each small square held a clump of hair and a label with a first name only. She wouldn't have understood only the almost full box on top had two names she recognized: Sophie and Louise. He'd kept a trophy of his kills, which means there were more deaths than just the 22 they found. Some looked quite old, and she realized this had been something that had been going on for decades. The idea he'd killed so many made her want to vomit. She had always heard about people like Gacy, Bundy and Dahmer, but to have actually known someone like that, even liked someone like that, was more than she could contemplate.

Hastily, she put everything back, her hands shaking in the process. She was about to shut the hatch when the office door opened and Bart stood there, pointing a rifle directly at her.

Chapter 38

Raising her hands slowly, Sierra backed away.

"How nice of you to pay me a visit. Saves me the trouble of going to your place again to try and kill you."

"So, you admit it then? That you tried to kill me? That I was going to be added to your sick collection? You killed all those women and more? That's what all these hair samples and names are, right? I'm surprised you didn't date them too."

Bart shrugged. "Hadn't thought of it. Thanks for the suggestion. Now, close the hatch and put the rug back on top. I think you've seen enough for one night."

"You weren't upstairs, were you." Sierra stated it matter-of-factly.

"No. I was at the saloon. Saw the light through the door when I came home. Smart to use the rug for the space at the floor, but you forgot the space at the top."

"Sorry. I'm not a good thief. My first attempt, actually."

He laughed. "How do you do that? I've never known a woman who can find the humor in the direst of situations."

She shrugged. "It's my defense mechanism? What are you going to do? Are you going to kill me right away? Others know where I'm at, and if I don't return back shortly, they'll come looking for me."

"Full of hubris, aren't you? Even if they come, they won't do anything."

"Are you sure? Sheriff Cosco is dead. I don't think you own Ranger Crandall and he has more Rangers coming. I don't think you can buy him off like you have most of the town. Besides, my disappearance will be harder to explain."

Bart moved closer to her, swinging the butt of the rifle up to hit her across the face, knocking her down against the desk. She curled up, wiping her bloodied lip as she peered at him through her hair splayed over her face.

"You like hitting women, don't you?"

"I like watching them go lifeless in my hands

more than hitting them."

"Why? You were so nice to me to begin with, and then this. Was I just prey for you the entire time?"

"Sit down." He waited until she complied, then moved to sit on the edge of the desk, keeping the rifle aimed at her the entire time. "Actually, no. I liked you, Sierra. I enjoyed spending time with you and found you braver than any woman I'd ever met or known. You were different, but then you changed. You became more of a liability, more of the things I detest in women. You became nosy and I wasn't about to let you turn into a shrew. Better to have you killed while you still have your beauty and your sense of self instead of losing it all to traditionalism."

"I'm not sure any of that makes any sense."

"It doesn't have to. It's my calling, that's all you need to know."

"Again, I ask, what now?"

Bart pulled the drapes open slightly. The sun was starting to rise and Sierra was aware Anna would know something went wrong. She should've returned by now.

"I ain't rightly sure, just yet. You see, my dear Sierra, you interrupted a delivery I'm having made in another hour and a half. I just don't really have the time to take my pleasure of watching you go lifeless under my hands and take care of your body at the same time. Yet, I certainly can't let you live. You know too much. You know, it was never supposed to be this complicated, but since you've been involved it's been one calamity after another."

"It's not going to get any better, Bart. I told you, I'm expected back, and if I ain't, the Ranger's going to come looking for me. They know this is where I came. How are you going to explain me disappearing again?"

Bart threw the rifle across the room and he launched himself at Sierra, gripping her by the throat, pulling her out of the chair and backing her up against the wall. Sierra struggled against him. He was fast and strong, the quickness creating such surprise she was momentarily stunned inactive. The pressure on her throat was relentless and she knew, despite his words, she'd pushed him too far and he was going to choke her to death if she didn't do something. Pinned as she was against the wall, he didn't leave her much room to maneuver, but she had to think this out, recall her training to utilize his strength against him or do whatever she could to break his grip.

Slamming her heel on his foot as hard as she could, he winced but barely let up. Then she remembered the knife she grabbed out of the Harvey House Kitchen. Releasing one hand from where she'd been trying to pry his fingers loose, she reached around her back to find the handle of the knife, thrusting it into his shoulder. She didn't know she'd chosen the same shoulder he had put an arrow in just a few weeks prior and had only removed the sling two days ago, just before she returned.

Bart gasped in disbelief at the hilt of a blade sticking out of his shoulder. He dropped his hands, taking a step back as he pulled the bloody knife out. He would use it on her, but before he had a chance, she gave him a swift hard kick to the groin which also pushed him further backwards.

She dashed through the office door, heading for the main door just as a knock came. Pulling the door open, she noticed Anna and the Ranger blocking the entryway, just as Bart came out of the office at the same moment. "I'm glad you're here," he called. "Arrest her. She broke into my home and just tried to kill me."

"Wait. He murdered those women and I saw the proof."

Anna stepped back, looking from one to another while James pulled Sierra out of the house by her arm. "You're under arrest, Miss Hanley. Mr. Higgins, I'll need you to come by the office as well to file an official complaint."

"Wait. Listen to me. Anna?" Sierra began to plead to be heard, but Anna just shook her head, and Crandall remained professional in arresting her, not listening to anything she had to say.

"You can tell your story to a judge, Miss Hanley. Come along quietly and no one will be hurt."

Realizing James was getting her safely away from the house, and therefore Bart, she quietly surrendered to the Ranger, who led her quickly away to the jail.

"What are you doing in here?" Stone frowned when they brought Sierra in, leading her to sit opposite the sheriff's desk.

"Is this really necessary?" Anna stood by James, resting her hand on his shoulder as he sat down to do the paperwork.

"Afraid so, darling. She broke into a private residence and stabbed Higgins. I have no choice at the moment."

"It was in self-defense. He was trying to kill me," Sierra blurted out, ignoring Stone. She still couldn't get the last words he said to her out of her mind. He really hurt her, but she'd be damned if she let him know.

"Where did you get the knife?"

"I brought it with me from the Harvey Eating House, just in case I needed to defend myself."

"Then he could claim intent. That you went there with the express purpose of killing him."

"Look at my throat. I'm sure you can see his fingers left marks."

A low growl came from the cell. Stone was furious Sierra was injured by anyone, much less someone the likes of Higgins.

Anna moved over to her and Sierra lifted her chin to expose her neck. Anna held a lit kerosene lamp for better illumination. She could see some redness, but she also knew it would take a couple of hours before the black and blue marks would be more pronounced. "James? She wasn't lying."

"I know. I also know I have to go through the steps so it doesn't look like favoritism, and I needed to get her safely away from him." He leaned back in his chair and looked at the two women. "I heard I've got reinforcements coming and they should be here in a few hours. As soon as they arrive, we can deal with everything, including whatever evidence you found, Miss Hanley."

"Sierra, please. I'm worried that he'll have time to move or destroy it in the interim. Isn't there anything we can do? Can't we go back before it's gone?"

"Not at the moment. I'm sure he'll move whatever evidence you discovered, but I've hired someone I'm sure can be reliable to watch the house, so he won't leave with the evidence without us knowing about it. We'll look very thoroughly for it as soon as possible." He leaned forward, taking a better look at the marks on her throat. "Are you okay?"

She rubbed her throat. "It's sore, but tolerable. I don't think I would've been alright if you hadn't shown up when you did. Thank you, Anna, for getting him. May I know who you hired to watch the residence?"

Ranger Crandall thought for a minute, then realized it didn't matter if they knew who it was or not. "A Cheyenne named Standing Elk. Seems the Cheyenne aren't too far away, and Standing Elk owed me a favor."

Sierra smiled. "We've met. I'm glad it's someone who can be so trustworthy."

Anna turned to retrieve a dress and apron she had brought with her and had left by the door when she came over to get James's assistance. "I told you I would. I just can't believe all of this is happening. I did bring you a uniform to change into. No sense in upsetting Mistress DeVoe more than necessary by having you caught in men's wear."

"Thank you. Is there someplace I can change?"

"There's an outhouse behind the jail. I'm trusting you not to try escaping."

"I won't, Ranger Crandall. I'll not be but a couple of minutes." With dress and apron in hand, she headed outside to change.

James walked over to the cell. "If we can find the evidence Miss Hanley discovered, you should be free by this afternoon."

"I'd appreciate it, Ranger." Stone moved to the bars of his confinement. "Can you do me a favor?"

"A little too soon to ask for that, don't you

think?"

"I just want to make sure Sierra will be all right. Higgins has a lot of sway, and I fear even if you do arrest him, he'll not serve time, or at least much of it, and will seek out Sierra for retaliation when he is free. I was just hoping you'd keep an eye on her to make sure she'll be okay."

James rubbed his five o'clock shadow on his chin. "I can do that. If not me, personally, I'll make sure there is a detail on her to keep her safe."

"I am indebted."

"You both realize she's not going to agree to any of this. She's pretty headstrong and independent," Anna piped in.

"I'm well aware, but I'm hoping she'll see reason when it comes to her very own life." Stone moved back from the bars to sit down on the bed once again.

Anna moved closer. "You hurt her, you know." She didn't give specifics; she knew Stone was cognizant of her meaning.

"It's for her own good." Stone didn't want to

be cold, but he needed to. Their being together was impossible for many reasons, none of which he'd go into with this woman who didn't know him or what he really was.

"That sounds selfish to me. You say you're doing it for her own good, but what she needs is you." Anna folded her arms, glaring at him.

"You don't know what you're talking about. I'm Cheyenne. She isn't. How can she come into my world and have a decent life? What can I possibly offer her? I certainly can't go into hers. Where does that leave us? Better to break her heart now, then later."

"He's right, Anna. He's making good sense and you have to see that too."

She dropped her arms and turned her back to the cell to face James. "I just want my friend to be as happy as I am."

"Like he said, I don't think she'll find it with him." James pulled her away from the bars to sit down. He leaned over her to whisper in her ear. "I'm glad I make you happy." He kissed her temple and stood back just as the door reopened with Sierra dressed in her Harvey Girl uniform.

Sierra wondered why they all looked slightly guilty, Anna's cheeks becoming a deep shade of red.

"You ladies should head back to the Eating House. Do your jobs, stay in a public group. Be careful." James held his hand out for Anna, leading her across to the door. "My men should be here, as I stated earlier. As soon as they arrive, I'll come and get you both."

"Thank you, Ranger." Sierra threw a longing glance at Stone who refused to even look up from his head-hanging-down seated position, his arms on his knees, his long hair covering his face. She quickly threw a smile up at James and departed, waiting outside for Anna to join her.

Before he let Anna go, he leaned down, his hand brushing back a strand of hair from her face. "Please be careful. I'll see you as soon as I can."

"Do you think the mob will be back to try and lynch him again?" Anna kept her voice low even though her concern was high.

"No. I've not heard of any rallying during the night. They all went home and slept on it. They know I'm here and others are coming, so I doubt they'll try. I can handle anything if they do. I'll keep him safe."

"How did I ever get so lucky as to find you to help?"

"I'm the lucky one." He leaned in further and gently touched her lips with his. She was his delicate flower and he wasn't going to do anything to harm her, including moving faster than she was ready for. "Three months?"

It took her a moment to figure out what he was asking her, then she smiled. It was a discussion they had on the journey back to Colorado Springs. "Yes. I have three months left on my employment contract."

"Once things settle down with this, I'm going to apply for sheriff here in the Springs. Then we can plan our future together, if you desire."

"I'd like that very much, James. Very Much."

He kissed her again, then watched her depart to meet up with Sierra, who was waiting for her at the bottom of the porch. He continued to watch them as they both walked back to the station. Only when he could no longer see them, did he close the door.

Chapter 39

Either Florence was so busy she didn't notice, or she was planning something that neither were sure about, but both Anna and Sierra returned to the house and started their duties with little to no comments about the fact they came from outside from anyone. Although, part of it might be that the two were known for taking walks together. Albeit, usually in the evening when it was cooler. They might've just assumed the women took an early morning one to get the day started off right.

Regardless, Sierra was grateful for the fact no one seemed to notice they were just coming into the house. She was also glad the dress she was wearing had a high collar to hide the marks Bart made on her throat.

Glancing at the clock, the train was due in twenty minutes. Anna went to make sure the serving bowls were ready while Sierra made sure all the carafes were set for easy filling once the coffee was done. The tables had been prepared yesterday after the last train departed, so they only had to deal with food and service preparation.

Before Sierra knew it, the train whistle blew as it was coming into the station. The girls all lined up, ready to greet the arriving customers. The first car let out, but the passengers looked a bit ill. Some were rubbing their foreheads or pinching the bridge of their noses. Others were holding their stomachs and groaning in pain or vomiting. Still, others seemed highly disoriented, unsure where they were or what they were doing there. Finally, a couple who were towards the rear of the first car were shivering, a light sheen on their bodies and their skin, their lips were tinted blue.

Florence moved quickly towards them, calling the girls into action to assist them into the train station's waiting facility, adjacent to the Eating House. "Sierra, Anna, Alice. Help me check out these other cars." She turned to the engineer. "Go get Ranger Crandall from the jail. I've a feeling he's going to be needed."

Alice, Anna and Sierra headed towards the second passenger car when the latter two stopped as

Bart came around the front of the train, wearing a sling. Sierra and Bart glared at each other, but Anna pulled Sierra towards the car. "He can't touch you at the moment. Remember what James said. Right now, this is more important."

Sierra nodded, though she didn't miss Florence going to talk to Bart. She knew Higgins was here to meet this train—the 835 from Kansas City. It had been marked red on the station calendar and noted in Higgins' notations. It then dawned on her what the problem was. "Wait! Alice. Don't go in there just yet." Sierra ran and stopped Alice from opening the door. "I think I know what happened. The car is filled with poison. We're going to need to air it out before we can even contemplate going in. Anna? Get some towels to wrap around our faces. We can't breathe it in."

Neither woman knew what she was talking about, but the fact Sierra seemed to be knowledgeable and compelling in her commands, they swiftly moved to follow her directions. By the time they moved away, Florence, Bart and James approached her to see what she was doing.

Quickly, she stepped back, appraising the situation. The third car was the cargo car. Behind that was the refrigeration car owned by Fred Harvey. Sierra didn't bother with the three of them, ignoring their questions as she moved to the refrigeration car. She looked around, but her assumption wasn't correct. There was no way the refrigeration car could've leaked into the cargo car and she assumed that was where the sodium cyanide was located. She then started to look underneath the cargo car.

"What are you doing?" James asked, also looking under the car, but unsure what he was looking for.

"I think the people in the front car were poisoned. I think the second car the same thing happened and that's why no one came out. They're all dead. Which means, it had to come from the third car. I think somehow, water got into the sodium cyanide and became hydrogen cyanide gas, which is highly toxic."

"How do you know this?" Florence moved behind them, overhearing the conversation.

"I told you. I'm from Illinois. We had similar situations with the lead mining there." It was a lie, but they didn't need to know that.

"There." James pointed at a couple of small drips from the underside of the car.

"The sodium cyanide must have mixed with the water. Where the water came from is unknown, but it's the only thing that makes sense. Those poor people." Sierra took a step back and glared at Bart. "This is your fault. You just had to be greedy, and now all these people are dead."

James must have felt she was about to charge him, for he grabbed her around her arms and held her back. Anna came running up with the towels to wrap around their faces. Sierra shrugged off James, grabbed a towel and headed to the door. Wrapping the towel around her nose and mouth, the others did the same. Opening the door to the passenger car, they stepped back to let it air out. Bart moved to the cargo car and opened the sliding door, stepping back to let the confined car air out as well.

Alice, who didn't have a towel about her face, began to cough excessively, feeling lightheaded.

"Anna, get her to the waiting room," James called out. He didn't want the woman he was beginning to fall for to be put in danger and this was a good reason to get her back from the toxic fumes.

James held the towel over his face and peeked in the passenger car. Everyone was unmoving, and he was pretty sure they were all dead. There were 32 in the car. Bart peered into the cargo car.

The sound of several horses' hooves pounding against the dirt road caused them to look up. Four men on various colored steeds rode into town. James removed the towel from his face and waved at them. They made their way to his side before one dismounted off his horse to speak with James.

The conversation was animated slightly, James pointing to the jail, then the train, in the direction of the Higgins House and finally at Sierra and Bart. One of the men then headed towards the jail, one went towards the Higgins home and the other two joined the group by the train.

Sierra noticed all of them wore the Ranger medallions on their chest. These were the reinforcements James had informed her were on their way. As they approached, James nodded to Sierra, then moved to Bart.

"Bartholomew Higgins?"

Bart turned to gaze at the new arrivals. "Yeah."

"I'm Ranger Duff. Would you come with me, please? We have some questions to ask you."

"You don't think I did this on purpose. I can't help it if some idiot put a block of ice in the hold with my cargo there too."

"I understand, sir. Please. Some questions?"

Bart grumbled, but followed Ranger Duff to the jail. It wasn't the ideal place to talk, but it was more private and definitely more secure than anywhere else in town.

"They're coming! They're coming!"

A woman screamed then fainted, a slight puff of dirt erupting around her as she fell onto the ground.

Some of the crowd scattered, going back to their homes, closing their doors and shutters. James, one of the other Rangers and the crowd around Sierra, Anna and Florence moved closer together as another group of horses made their way into the town.

In all their regalia, the Cheyenne were an impressive sight. James moved to the front of the group to meet them. They stopped, no one moving for several minutes. Finally, the horses moved to the side to make way for a steed from the middle to approach.

James moved to the rider and offered to assist her down. River accepted his aid and, once her feet touched the solid earth, James removed his hat, taking a step back. "Ma'am."

She noticed the star on his chest and then looked around until she saw someone she recognized, namely Sierra. Sierra moved towards the two of them, knowing what needed to be done. "Ranger Crandall? This is Novava'e. Their Medicine Woman, River," Sierra made the formal introduction. She knew having stayed with them for almost a month that respectful interaction was of extreme importance to avoid any misunderstandings. The fact James offered to help her down and removed his hat almost immediately impressed Sierra immensely. Her part done, she stepped back.

"Ranger. I believe I can aid you on your quest to discover the truth."

James raised his left eyebrow in questioning surprise. "What truth would that be?"

"The truth of what you seek."

Cryptic as always, Sierra thought.

James rubbed his forehead and looked around. There was so much going on simultaneously. "Shall we go inside so we can talk?"

"Yes, please."

James held his elbow out to escort her. The jail was small, made smaller with everyone already there, but he wasn't sure where else to go and have a conversation. He paused to speak with the other Ranger, who remained behind. "Mark, see to the passengers in car number two. Also, see about getting statements from those who are in the waiting room. Have the Harvey Girls help you. I believe they all know how to read and write."

Mark nodded and started barking orders to the others while James continued to lead River towards the jail. Sierra stayed by River's side. What surprised her was Florence also joined them.

At first, River turned to gaze at the Mistress of Harvey House, gasping in disbelief before quickly turning away.

How odd. Immediately, Sierra's newspaper reporter instincts went into overdrive. She wondered why Florence garnered such a reaction from the usually unflappable River. Did she know her? Had they met before? Had River seen Mistress DeVoe someplace else? So many mysteries with that woman, Sierra wasn't sure what to think.

Entering the small office and jail, Sierra wondered if Stone even moved since she last left him, as he was in the exact same position. Only when River entered did he look up in surprise.

Standing, he bowed his head. River ignored all the others gazing upon her as she walked up to the bars to rest her hand on his shoulder. "It'll be okay."

Bart stood up and growled. "What in damnation is going on?"

Ranger Duff pointed to the chair. "I suggest you sit down and relax, Mr. Higgins. It's going to be a long day, and the sooner you talk, the faster things'll move."

Bart pushed him out of his way. "I won't stay here another minute. You've no cause to hold me. The governor will hear about all of this."

"Which governor, Mr. Higgins?" James pulled a chair around for River to sit before moving towards Bart. "Governor McIntire doesn't have dealings with you other than signing the deed papers started by Governor Waite. I spoke with McIntire before I departed Denver. He told me to get to the bottom of the situation for justice. He didn't seem concerned whoever turned out to be guilty."

"Why are they here?" Bart grumbled, though

he neither sat nor moved towards the door.

"Ain't rightly sure about the Cheyenne. Whole group of them outside waiting. As for Miss Hanley, I still need to talk to her about some odd occurrences and her comments that you attacked her. Miss Meyers is here for Miss Hanley's moral support. I assume Mistress DeVoe is here for her girls. Now, why don't you sit down and finish making your statement to Ranger Duff."

Anna beamed at James and how he stood up against Bart. He was so commanding. Stone said nothing, but he watched closely to everything going on in the room.

Duff turned back to Bart and lowered his voice. "Tell me again how you were just out for a picnic and were attacked by the Cheyenne."

Sierra turned away, she couldn't even look at the man she thought she might have liked enough to consider staying once. And the man she *was* willing to stay for wanted nothing to do with her.

"Miss Hanley, please go to Mr. Higgins' house. Ranger Dan will be there to meet you and you can show him the evidence you found." Waving his hand towards the door, he indicated she needed to leave.

After a moment of hesitation, Sierra accommodated his request.

Florence held out her hand to stop her. "What evidence? What did you find? This can't be right?"

Bart stood again, about to fly towards Sierra. "That's a private house and you need a warrant to go in. I don't give you my permission to do so."

Duff drew his pistol and stuck it right in Bart's face to stop him from moving. James moved to stand toe-to-toe in front of Bart. Ranger Crandall growled low. "Actually, you attacked Miss Hanley. In your house. And you say she attacked you."

"She was an intruder. She's lucky I just didn't open fire and kill her outright."

"True, but either way, a crime was committed in your residence, which makes it a crime scene. As such, we have the right to investigate without a warrant or your permission."

"I knew I should've just killed you." Bart leapt

towards Sierra, pushing past Duff's gun and James's body. He gripped Sierra by her dress, but the other two men grabbed each of his arms and tugged him off her.

Sierra cried out when Bart gripped her. Once he was pulled away, she stood and quickly moved to the door. "I know where the evidence is that proves he killed those 22 women and dozens of others. He kept a trophy from each of them, a lock of hair. They go back for years. Maybe even decades. I saw the names of Louise and Sophie. The oldest, which might have been the first, was the lowest box I could find. Her name was Margaret."

A gasp from Florence caused them all to look at her. "Margaret?"

Bart seemed to shrink when Florence clutched her neckline, leaning heavily against the desk as if her legs could no longer support her. "Margaret?" she repeated. "How could you, brother? She was our mother. She loved you."

Bart was her baby brother. When their parents died, it was her responsibility to raise him, and she obviously didn't do a good job. It was her fault he was cruel and heartless, because she'd been cold and distant to him from the very start, never having wanted a brother to begin with. Her brother had slowly deteriorated since their parents died. She'd always suspected Bart had killed their mother, but there was never any proof and she hoped she was wrong. Her mother hadn't woken up one morning. They all assumed she died peacefully in her sleep, although Florence had suspected it was foul play. Her pose in the morning didn't appear totally natural, according to the doctor, who had spoken in whispered tones to the sheriff.

"No. She loved you. She barely tolerated me or Dad. She was happy when he was killed. I was only five and I felt alone. You and her were always together. I was an afterthought. Forgotten. Left alone. Hungry and having to fend for myself. Yes. I killed her with nary a second thought. I can do the same to you."

Sierra's eyes widened in total shock. She expected a lot of things, but learning that Florence and Bart were siblings was not something she'd even contemplated.

James pulled Sierra away from the bars and towards the door. "Go now. Tell your story to Ranger Dan and get the evidence."

Sierra didn't want to leave. This story was just unfolding and she wanted to know the crux of everything about to be said. However, she wasn't about to risk getting Ranger Crandall angry with her for disobeying, so she departed and headed for Bart's home.

"Matthew, why don't you talk to Mistress DeVoe while Duff is busy with Mr. Higgins." James turned to River. "Now ma'am, what brings you and the others to town?" James knew this was really close quarters, but he wasn't sure where else to talk and not be under the auspices of the other townsfolk who might even back Higgins, whether or not he was in the wrong.

"I think I can prove Mr. Higgins killed those women."

"I've been looking over the work the sheriff

had done before his untimely death. I understand these bodies were buried and none of them were scalped." James tapped on the desk with his fingers. "That's not the way a Cheyenne kills. I'm also aware the Cheyenne don't kill unarmed women one by one over the series of years. I don't believe any of you killed these women."

"Then why is Stone still locked up?"

"Because we haven't gotten proof yet to definitively set him free. Sierra just told us about the boxes. When we get them, then we can clear Stone and release him."

"What if I can also prove it?"

"How?"

River pulled a bag tied to her hip and carefully opened it up. The stench of decaying flesh caused all but River to pull back with a grimace.

"What is that?"

"The hand of the one known as Louise."

"How? Why? How are you in possession of it?"

"There were many bodies we were to watch

over until the morning light when we were going to fetch the sheriff. An animal attracted to the scent of the dead found her and gnawed off her other hand. We must have scared them off, for we only recently realized what must have occurred."

"Okay, but how does this prove it was someone else and not Stone or any other Cheyenne."

"My men, all of them, are outside. Free of their shirts, as is Stone."

"I noticed." James was beginning to lose his patience, which didn't help with Florence crying in the corner as she talked to Matthew, and the occasional outburst from Bart as Dan continued to ask him questions.

"Look at her hand, Ranger. Her nails. There is skin under there. Whoever attacked her, got scratched."

"She's been missing for almost two months, according to the records I have. Any scratch would've healed."

"True, but it could've left a scar. And I have a solution of herbs that will show if someone has been injured recently."

James leaned back in his chair, throwing the cover over the hand once again to help with the stench. "Thank you for coming all this way. Let's see what Miss Hanley discovered. It might be enough to prove Stone innocent. But, if not, we will certainly look into your solution."

River went to grab the hand, but James stopped her. "I think it best we include her hand with the rest of her remains."

"As you wish." River nodded to Stone, who hadn't moved from the bars since she walked in. She gave another intense gaze at Florence, sniffed the air, then departed the overcrowded building.

Stone also turned in Florence's direction and sniffed the air. Odd behavior, James thought, but who knew what went through Indian's heads. James went over to stand by Mrs. DeVoe and Ranger Citcar. "Matthew?"

Looking up, he stood. "Wait right here, ma'am. I'll be back in a couple of minutes." Matthew grabbed James by the arm and headed outside, taking a deep breath of the fresh air.

"This is so bizarre. She says she knew of Mr. Higgins' proclivity and was aware of the missing girls that go back as far as their home town in Pennsylvania, and later again in Kansas. She thought he was better when he invited her out here and no girls were disappearing. At least until several months ago when the first of five girls disappeared, though they were thought to have left with prospectors in the area who were moving on. She says because he's her brother, she never wanted to say anything against him. She believes it was partially her fault for not doing a better job in helping to raise him after their mother passed away, but she found his behavior too strange since the death of their pa that she didn't care to be around him much."

"So why is she squealing on him now?"

"Because of what Miss Hanley said about the oldest being Margaret. She believes that's their mother. She said she always felt their ma died unusual like, but she was still a kid herself and wasn't sure if she was just imagining it."

"You believe her?"

"Mostly. There's still something off, but ain't sure what. Could just be my imagination over that loon of a family."

"Could be." James noticed Ranger Mark Spindle headed towards them. "Go keep her company and see what else you can learn. I need to talk to Mark."

Matthew headed back inside the jail as Mark approached.

"What's the status?"

"The front car had 39 passengers. Two died, unable to breathe. The rest are sick, but Doc thinks they'll be okay with rest and no further exposure. The second car, all are dead. Miss Hanley was correct. Someone put a couple of blocks of ice in the cargo hold, not realizing the ice would melt and get the bottom of the crates containing the sodium cyanide wet, which in turn created the poisonous gas that spread to the other cars. Must've occurred last night. Seems most just died in their sleep. Four were babes. They ain't even had a chance."

"The bodies?"

"I had the telegraph office wire AT&KC HQ. They're aware of the situation and are notifying the families, at least those they can find. The rest will be buried in the town cemetery. They're pressing charges against Mr. Higgins for involuntary manslaughter and transporting a dangerous substance without the proper notifications."

"Without proper...? You mean they didn't know he was going to ship that stuff on their train?"

"That's what HQ is saying. They're going to let him hang for it on his own."

"I certainly didn't see that coming."

"Seems he was more promise than actual payoff, and if they ain't getting paid, they ain't gonna stand by him."

"I wonder how many people he was going to share the wealth with and how many are not going to stand by him now."

"Ain't sure, James. But I know I wouldn't want to be in his shoes."

"Okay, Mark. I'm sure there's still a lot to do. We have a few other messes to clean up around here." James nodded towards the group of Cheyenne. "They any problem?"

"Nothing I can't handle." Mark headed back to the waiting room of the train station. This was going to be one hellishly long day.

Chapter 40

Florence and Bart. Siblings. It totally shocked Sierra, who just couldn't contemplate they were related, much less brother and sister. Talk about being polar opposites, those two were nothing alike. However, it also made sense, explaining why he'd choose Florence as his business partner when she didn't really have anything to offer him, or why Florence backed everything he said, regardless of whether it was wrong or right. They were from the same area, first Pennsylvania, then Kansas. It explained how she knew he wasn't safe to be with, why she warned Sierra away from him, and why the two of them were arguing so much of late.

Approaching the house, Ranger Dan was waiting on the porch for her arrival. He stood, tipping his hat. "Ma'am."

"Ranger."

"Why don't we sit out here and you tell me your story before we head inside for this evidence Ranger Crandall says you found."

"Sure." Sitting on the bottom step, she told him

everything: from the moment she wore Sophie's dress, to agreeing to go on the picnic, to his trying to kill her, everything. Everything, that is, except the time in the Cheyenne village and the secrets they held. She told the Ranger how the Cheyenne went out to Harper's Creek to find what she tripped on, then discovered all the other bodies by noticing several plots of dirt had been disturbed, an Indian trick of tracking. She finished up her story with coming to the house and searching, only to find the trophy boxes filled with locks of women's hair all nicely labeled with their names. She mentioned Bart caught her, but before he could kill her, she escaped long enough for Ranger Crandall to show up, thanks to Anna.

"That's a hellava story, little lady."

"I know. It sounds rather unbelievable, even to me. But it's all true. I swear it."

Dan stood and held out his hand to help her up. "Why don't we see if we can find yer evidence."

"I'm sure he's had enough time to move it or destroy it, but I'll certainly help you look."

Entering the abode, they headed straight for the office. Sierra moved the rug and opened the hatch, but just as predicted, it was empty.

Dan knelt down and ran his fingers along the dirt walls, bringing his hands up to sniff them, before standing once again. "It's musty, like something's been sitting on it for a long while. Where do you think he put them?"

"I don't know. I'm relatively unfamiliar with his home. Maybe he has another secret hiding place, or maybe he destroyed them entirely. I just don't know. They had a glass window. I'll check the garbage and see if he threw them out."

"I'll search around here."

Heading to where she assumed the kitchen was, and therefore the garbage, she looked only to find nothing. The two of them searched the lower floor for an hour before giving up. Sierra was beginning to feel hopeless. "I didn't make it up. We have to find them to prove he's guilty."

"It's okay, ma'am. We'll find something. We still have the second floor to search."

"Sierra, please."

"Sierra then. You can call me Dan."

"Your name is Dan Dan?"

"Yeah. Ma parents had a sick sense of humor." He grinned.

She smiled back. "Second floor then?"

"After you, Sierra."

As they climbed the stairs, Sierra tried to think of where he could've hidden them. They weren't that small. Her foot hit the wood of the middle stair and it tipped slightly, causing her to lose her balance and fall backwards. Dan caught her, helping her upright. "You okay?"

"I think so. This step is loose." She pulled back, leaning down to examine it further. "Look! It's missing a couple of nails. Do you think?" She was too afraid to say anything further.

Dan helped to pry up the stair and there it was. Six shadow boxes filled with locks of hair.

"I can't believe we found it."

"You're more stubborn than a mule and won't give up," Bart growled behind them as he stood in

489

the foyer, his pistol in his hand and aimed right at Sierra's head.

"You can't possibly think you're going to get away with shooting us." Dan stood in front of Sierra, although there wasn't much space for her to go since the stair was in disrepair.

"Ain't too worried. The Ranger let me go. Figure you will too. I can pay you well. All you need to do is let me kill her and forget you ever saw those boxes."

"No can do. Why don't you just surrender?"

"Sorry Ranger. What did you say? No can do."

Bart cocked the pistol and took aim, but Dan was faster. Ranger Dan had his pistol drawn and fired before Sierra could even blink. Dan hit Higgins right between the eyes and Bart jerked his arm upward with the shot, missing Sierra entirely. She sat down heavily upon the stairs.

Dan ran down the stairs and checked Bart, kicking his gun away just to be sure. He felt for a pulse at the crook of his neck before looking up at Sierra. "It's okay, ma'am. I mean, Sierra. He ain't gonna be bothering anyone else ever again."

The door was kicked in, flying to slam against the wall. James stood there with both pistols drawn as he looked around, spotting Sierra, Dan and then Bart at their feet. He slipped his guns back into his holsters. "Everyone okay?"

"Yeah. How'd he get away from you, James?"

"Caught me unawares helping Mrs. DeVoe. Snuck out before we even realized it. I knew this is where he'd come. Sorry I was too late."

"Dan is an excellent shot. He saved my life. We found the evidence, though. Proof that Bart was the one who all killed those women."

"He won't be killing anyone else now." James moved to the bottom of the staircase and held out his hand, indicating for her to come down and take it.

Hesitating only a moment, she moved downstairs to grip his hand. He led her outside into the cool air. Suddenly, the house seemed oppressive and she was grateful to be outside. "You'll let Stone go?"

"Yes. As soon as we return to the jail, I'll release him. He can return to his village with the rest of the Cheyenne who came to town and are waiting at the edge of town limits."

"Thank you."

"Give me a moment." James poked his head back inside. "Take care of this. You can meet up with Matthew, who's still at the train station. I'm sure one more body to deal with won't be a problem compared to all those he killed today alone with his attempted gold cyanidation and the women they've yet to bury. God damn, what a freaking mess." James took his hat off to run a hand through his hair.

"I'll take care of this with Matthew. Go deal with the women. That's not a headache I relish having to handle."

"I actually don't mind it. It's a nice change of pace to smelly old men like you." James laughed as he shut the door. "Ready, Sierra?"

"What for?"

"Go back. I assume you'd like the pleasure of

releasing Stone yourself."

"No. You can do that. If you don't need me, I'd like to speak with River before she leaves."

"Of course. I'll go let Stone out."

"Thank you. For everything."

James gave her a smile and let her go to turn down the road leading to the jail while Sierra continued straight to meet up with the Cheyenne.

"River?"

"Here, child." River sat in the middle of a group of warriors. Most she recognized, some she didn't.

Sitting down by her, Sierra lowered her head in respect until River began the conversation. "He is dead. Mr. Higgins."

Sierra nodded. "Yes. They are releasing Stone as we speak. There's proof Bart is the one who killed all those women."

"And the destruction of our land?"

"The gold cyanidation won't be happening. Bart was funding it. He's gone. I don't think after the accident on the train today, killing so many others, anyone wants to even attempt it here. It's too dangerous. I believe the land is safe, as are you and your people."

"It's almost time, then."

"Time? For what?"

Before River could answer, Stone came up to them. Following him was Florence.

River stood, the others following suit as they waited patiently for them to reach River.

"He said you wanted to see me before you left?" Florence moved around Stone, speaking directly to River.

"You don't even know, do you? But you suspect."

Florence looked totally perplexed, probably just the way Sierra looked.

River sighed. "Mr. Higgins. He's only related to you through your mother."

Florence shook her head. "Yes. I knew that, although I think Bart only suspected it. The night my father died, they argued about me not being his. Afterwards, I was too scared to ask who my real father was. As time went on, I didn't think it was important enough to discuss it with my mother."

"You're from Pennsylvania, am I not correct?"

Sierra was totally fascinated, wondering how River knew all of this. Was it her spiritual ways, her Spirit Walker abilities or something else entirely? She wished she knew her history just a bit better to know where this might be going.

"Yes. I am." Florence was also curious.

"And you have felt different? Am I correct? You have felt stronger than you think you should be, find yourself dreaming strange dreams?"

She didn't answer right away, but managed to croak out, "How did you know? How *do* you know all of this?"

"I saw it, child. I sense it warring inside of you, wanting free."

"What? What do you see?"

"I see you're Seminole. I see you're special. You're more special than you realize."

"Is that what I've been sensing?" Stone spoke up.

Everything clicked for Sierra. "She's a Spirit Walker, isn't she?"

"Half. It's why she has had such a hard time accepting it and letting it embrace her."

"What are you all talking about? You said I'm Seminole? How is that possible? What's a Spirit Walker? What have you been sensing?"

"Sit down, let us talk."

They all sat around, the other Cheyenne keeping everyone else distant so as not to overhear anything not meant for their ears.

"General Jesup created a large army for the Second Seminole War. Many from Missouri and Pennsylvania. When the man whom you thought was your father arrived to fight, he met your mother. But, Margaret was already with a Seminole. She was going to stay with him, but he was killed in the War. She found herself alone and pregnant with you. She noticed Higgins watching her and figured if she could get him to sleep with her, he would provide for her. He'd help make her a legit woman and avoid two scandals. First, by being with a red man, and the second, being with a babe. If he died fighting, then she would've announced the baby and claim it was his. Either way, it would work to her advantage. What Margaret didn't know, what your true father didn't tell her, was that he was a special Seminole. He was a Spirit Walker, one who could change into their spirit guide as a gift from the Great Spirit."

"This is crazy. You're crazy. That isn't possible."

"What animal do you dream of?"

Florence looked uncomfortable. "A badger."

River nodded. "A badger is a solitary animal, preferring to be left alone in most aspects. But, they are also fighters, though whether you are fighting for the right battle or just being stubborn is up to the individual. He has been coming to you because he needs to connect with you to make you whole. Most likely, you have been fighting him, though. Haven't you?"

"They are just dreams."

"No," Sierra spoke up. "If River sees it, it's

true. Spirit Walkers are real. You need to give in to your destiny. Let them help you become what you're meant to be."

"Yes." Stone nodded. "We can help you find your way, aid you in achieving what you need to become to fulfill your place in this world."

"Half Indian? You're saying I'm a half-breed. No. I won't let that part of me ever be known. I'd be less than what I am now."

"No. You'd be more. Let them help you," Sierra pleaded. "Trust them, just as they're trusting you."

"Trust me?"

"They didn't have to tell you the truth about your family, or what you are."

"I wish they hadn't." Florence stood, steadily walking out of the circle of bodies.

Sierra stood to follow her, but River stopped her. "She will come around when she is ready, not before. She knows where we are and that we'll help." River lifted her eyes to the sky. The sun was getting lower. "Stone. Gather the others. It's almost time for us to return to camp."

He stood and followed her instructions. While he was busy with them, River looked into Sierra's eyes. "Your time is almost at an end, child. Say goodbye to those who have touched your heart." River brushed a strand of hair out of Sierra's face, then turned and headed to the horse waiting for her.

Sierra stood, watching as they all rode away. She wasn't entirely sure what River meant, but she had the feeling she'd never see River, Stone or any of the other Cheyenne again. The sun was gone by the time she turned back to the Harvey House.

She hadn't taken more than twenty steps when Anna came running up to her. "Sierra!"

"I'm right here, Anna. What's going on?"

"James. He's going to stay."

"What do you mean?"

"He is going to be the new sheriff of Colorado Springs. Taking over the position from Sheriff Cosco. He wants to stay close so when my contract with Harvey is up in three months, we can plan to be together."

"Anna!" Sierra hugged her. "I'm so happy for you."

"Thank you. I'm going to be Mrs. James Crandall. Can you believe it?"

"He's asked you already?"

"Yes. Just a little while ago. I said yes."

"That was fast."

"No, Sierra. It was a lifetime."

The two women walked towards the House. The lobby of the train station was still a hubbub of activity and Sierra's heart twisted at the thought of so many lives needlessly lost.

Anna headed to the kitchen to get some food. She realized with everything that went on during the day, none of them had a chance to eat. Preparing a couple bowls of soup, Anna brought them upstairs, calling to Sierra to open her door since her hands were full.

They sat and ate the soup, discussing Anna's upcoming nuptials.

A knock on the door disturbed their giddy chatter. Anna stood. "I'll take the dishes down."

She opened the door to reveal Mistress Florence. Slipping past her with the dirty dishes, Anna left Sierra and Florence alone.

"Mind if I speak with you?"

"Of course not, Mistress DeVoe."

Florence stepped inside and shut the door. "I'm sorry I wasn't able to convince you to not see Bart."

"You did warn me. I just didn't listen."

"I could've been more forceful. I should've been. I should've stopped him, or told someone, or done something."

"It's not your fault. You can't take the blame for his warped mind."

"Do you think those Indians were right?"

"River? Yes." Sierra wasn't sure how much she should mention, so remained guarded in her responses.

"I do know mother didn't really like those two. As I said earlier I suspected Higgins wasn't my pa, but that I was half-Seminole was a total surprise. Margaret must've followed him to Pennsylvania after the Seminole War, but she never loved him.

He was convenient for her and she had no choice. The world isn't kind to unwed mothers or half-breeds."

"Are you going to go meet River to learn more about your Native American heritage?"

"No. Not at this time. Maybe when I'm old, but this isn't the day and age to be part of that group."

"I suggest you go sooner than later. Talk to them. No one else needs to know. It's probably for the best to not tell anyone who or what you are."

"I hadn't planned to. I'll take the rest of your advice under consideration. I just wanted to apologize again about Bart."

"No need, but you will have to live with your own conscience for your responsibility in not reporting Bart, and thus saving all those lost lives." Sierra walked Florence back to the door. Once the house mistress left, Sierra closed and locked the door. This was the worst day ever and she was beyond exhausted. Yet, it was also a good day. She was able to prove Stone innocent, save the town from more women disappearing, stop gold cyanidation, and because of her, the Rangers were here, which included Anna's new love, James. In the end, everything worked out, but she was bone-weary. She got ready for bed, grateful to finally shut her eyes and put this day behind her.

Chapter 41

2018:

Sierra felt someone shaking her shoulder and slowly opened her eyes. It took her several minutes to realize where she was. She flung her arm out in surprise, hitting her elbow on the window and her leg on the seat in front of her. "What?"

"Sorry, ma'am. The train ride is over."

Sierra was stunned and confused. "Train ride?" Looking out the window, she could see the Cripple Creek Train Depot, but more important, she realized there were cars and neon lights and other modern conveniences. Was everything just a dream? Wasn't any of it real? Her heart tightened in sadness that everything she'd done wasn't reality.

"Yes."

"I'm sorry. I must've fallen asleep."

"I wanted to let you know, the train called ahead and that man you were afraid of has been arrested. The CCPD said the Springs picked him up and put him in jail. You're safe now."

"Safe. Yes. Thank you." Sierra's head was

spinning. She felt lightheaded and slightly nauseous. Slipping out of the seat, she headed off the train. She was totally lost, discombobulated from whatever she'd just experienced. How did she get back? Had she ever really been gone? Was any of it more than a fantasy? She had to find out what was real. She needed to get back to Colorado Springs as quickly as possible.

She made her way to the casino and scheduled herself for the next bus back. Pulling out her phone, she pulled up the internet, but sadly there wasn't much information on what she searched for. She truly didn't expect to find anything on the web about the Cheyenne Spirit Walkers. They were too secretive. She couldn't find anything on Anna Meyers or Florence DeVoe. She was able to find a small write up about the deaths of several women by Harper's Creek, and another on the deaths of the train from cyanide poisoning. But, truthfully, there wasn't much on either. Newspaper reporting has come a long way since 1895.

Putting her phone down, she sat back to look

out the window. She'd be in Colorado Springs in another hour. Then she'd have to figure out where they might have taken Stone. He'd be the one to let her know if it was all a dream brought on by things she'd read in the Cripple Creek Museums, or if she actually did, somehow, travel back in time and mysteriously return.

Anxious for the bus to get back to Colorado Springs, she tried to relax but was unsuccessful. As soon as the motorcoach pulled into the drop off area, she was out of her seat and out the door almost before it fully opened. Hailing a cab, she got back to her hotel and looked for the card of the officer who helped her months ago. No, just yesterday. The whole traveling in time and returning to when she disappeared was throwing her off immensely.

Remembering where she left the card, she grabbed it and stuffed it into her pocket before she headed back down to grab a Lyft. While she waited for the vehicle, she input the information of the police station. Sierra wasn't sure where Stone was taken, but she would start with the one she made the original report with and hope someone there could help her further.

A small beige Honda Civic pulled up and she climbed in. Since she already input the destination information, she just waited for him to get her there. "How long will the drive take?"

"About ten minutes."

"Thanks." Sierra sat back, but she was too anxious, moving back and forth as much as she could, despite the seatbelt restrictions.

The driver must've sensed her impatience as it didn't take quite as long as she thought it should. Thanking the driver, she dashed out of the car. She would confirm the pay and tip him after she got inside.

Running into the building, she stopped short at the information desk. "Please. I need to speak with an officer."

"About what, ma'am?"

"Someone being arrested in Cripple Creek by mistake. I was told he was brought to Colorado Springs after his arrest, because he was arrested here before." Not sure if she was rambling or making any sense, Sierra hoped it was the latter.

"Do you know what he was arrested for before or when?"

"Yes. Um. Yesterday. Oh! Wait." Reaching into her pocket, she pulled out the card from yesterday. "By any chance is Officer..." She paused, her mouth going instantly dry. How could this be?

"Ma'am?"

"Crandall. Is Officer Crandall available?" She managed to squeak out. Everything just got ethereal and unreal.

The desk clerk looked at the schedule. "He is on shift. Can I say who is here to see him?"

"Yes... Sierra Hanley. I mean, Hall. Sierra Hall." She felt woozy, the lightheaded feeling becoming strong once again.

Hearing the desk clerk call to the officer, she moved to sit down to wait. Her head was reeling from all the coincidences. It had to be more than that, though. It just had to be. Everything felt so real. Then something dawned on her. "Excuse me. Is there a bathroom I can use?"

"Sure. It's down the hall on the left."

"Thank you."

Sierra's heart pounded faster. Finally, she might actually have an answer to the question of whether or not it was all a dream. Locking the bathroom stall behind her, she pulled down her pants, afraid of what she might find and yet terrified of what she wouldn't.

Taking a deep breath to steady her nerves, she looked at her leg where the arrow hit her. Tears streamed down her face as her hand rubbed the puckered skin that once was smooth. The wound was still a bit pinker than the rest of her skin, the leg having healed but still showed signs of the trauma it endured. It was real. It was all real. She was actually in 1895 and she was wounded by an arrow. Nothing was a dream. It all happened. Sitting on the toilet seat, she let her nerves have control and sobbed. Just knowing she hadn't gone mad was such a huge relief.

Continuing to rub the mostly healed wound, she wiped her face with the toilet paper and flushed it before pulling her pants back up. When she felt she was ready, she went back into the waiting area. Officer Crandall was already there.

"Hello, Miss Hall. How are you doing today?"

"I'm well. Thank you."

"How may I be of assistance?"

"The man you arrested yesterday. I was told he was arrested again today in Cripple Creek and transferred here?"

"Yes. We have him in holding."

"Can you release him? I'm not pressing charges. Actually, his arrest today was a mistake. I just learned he's a friend of some friends of mine and they sent him to me to welcome me to the area. I only recently received their message, so you see, he isn't a threat."

"I'll need you to sign a release form."

"Of course. Whatever you need."

"Follow me, please."

"Do you mind if I ask you a personal

question?"

"No. Go ahead."

"Are you related to James and Anna Crandall?"

He stopped midway down the hall and turned to look at her. "They were my great-grandparents. Why do you ask?" He continued down the hall and led her to a seat alongside a desk.

"I was friends with them. I mean, my family knew them. He was a Ranger, then became a sheriff here in Colorado Springs, right?"

"Yes. He took over the job of being the sheriff when his predecessor was killed in a gunfight." Rummaging through his desk drawers, he pulled out some forms and started to write on a couple of them, filling in a few of the spaces, before he handed them to her to finish completing.

While she was writing out the forms, he called down to holding to have Stone Red Tree brought up from the cells.

The paperwork done, she passed it back to Officer Crandall. "Did your great-grandparents have many children?"

"They had three. Two girls and my grandfather. The men in my family were also officers here in the Springs. I merely followed in their footsteps."

"Were they happy?"

"I believe so. They were married for 61 years. I remember my grandparents talking about them and always smiling when they did so. They were very much in love. Did you know my great-grandmother was a Harvey Girl? I heard a few stories while I was growing up from my grandparents. I wish I knew more about them. Sadly, we lose a lot of those stories over the years."

"Very true. I'm so glad they had a good life. I remember…hearing…a lot about them myself. I knew Anna was a Harvey Girl and James was a Ranger but took over as sheriff, so he could remain close to Anna while she fulfilled her year contract with Fred Harvey. Thank you for telling me."

"I'll go check on Mr. Red Tree after I escort you back to the lobby. You can wait for him there. It will be a few minutes while he gets processed out."

"Thank you again, Officer Crandall. May I ask your first name?"

"Sere. It was a promise to my great-grandmother to keep the name somehow in the family in honor of a friend who brought my great-grandparents together."

Sierra hadn't thought she could get choked up any more than she had already, but his words and the meaning behind them left her too emotional to respond at first. She was glad they were walking so she didn't have to speak immediately. By the time they reached the front lobby once again, she was more in control of her emotions and voice.

"I can't thank you enough, Officer. For everything. I'm sure this is a unique case in general."

"Please know, he'll still have to come to court on the original arrest. Although you dropped the charges, he still resisted a police officer and he'll be brought up on that offense."

"When is his court date?"

"He has all the information as part of his

release yesterday. I believe it's in two months."

"Thank you again. I'll just wait outside on the steps. I could use the fresh air."

Chapter 42

Stone headed out the door. He wasn't entirely sure why he was released without a bail or notification to return to court, but he wasn't going to ask. He needed to find Sierra again, and he'd be starting from scratch, not knowing where she might be. He wasn't going to risk losing her again, even if she had no idea who he was or didn't remember him.

River made it a point to speak to Stone after they were back in the village once he'd been released from murder charges, thanks to what Sierra had found in Bart's home proving his innocence in 1895.

"Why did you let her go?"

"Who?"

"Sierra."

"Look at our lives, River. She's human, she's mortal and she's white. She wouldn't be welcomed by our tribe any more so than I would by her people. No matter how much we've advanced, hatred is still very strong among both our people."

"Yet, it was weak enough for you to tell her about who and what we really are. To have her belong to this tribe, you risked everything for her just to throw it away at the first challenge you came across. You wanted her with us so much, she trained with Sage in our ways."

"That was more your decision and the council's agreement. Why did you want her to know about us and go against our ways?"

"She needed to know, so she could help us the most, and for you."

"How is she going to help us now? She is back in her world, with the Harvey Girls and with the others like her."

"Still, she doesn't belong with them."

"And she doesn't belong with me. River! Don't you understand how hard this is for me? Why are you continuing to push this? She is better off without me in her life. She'll be happier this way."

"So, you did it for her? Broke her heart with your harsh words and denial of being?"

"She'll recover. She hasn't known me enough

to have her heart irreparably damaged."

"Can you say the same about yours?"

Stone pressed his lips tightly together, working his jaw to temper his emotions down. "I'm not the issue. I'm used to the hatred of whites, and them continuing to force us to lose our culture and heritage. She isn't."

"Then don't let her think she isn't worth your love."

"I'm not worth hers, River. I may have been harsh, but it was for her own good and I won't go after her."

"You're making a mistake, but I see in time, you too will realize it. And when you do, you'll be in a position to find her again."

Heading to her tipi, she left Stone standing alone in the middle of the circle. Eventually, he'd made it back to his tipi and regretted it, for the last time he was there, so was she. Shifting into a cougar, he paced, hissed and whimpered. He wouldn't admit it to any other, but Sierra had touched a part of him he didn't even think existed any longer. He wanted Sierra to be his and it killed him that she couldn't. He'd hurt her because he needed her to hate him. If she detested him, she'd be able to move on and then, maybe in a hundred years or so, he could as well. Life without her was going to be extremely difficult, but he didn't see any other choice.

How many years had passed before Black Mountain saw him sitting by the shore, staring at the water? Even though by 1945 the world had greatly changed, yearning for Sierra hadn't lessened. He wanted her as much now as he did 50 years ago. The respected elder sat down next to Stone and also stared at the water.

"The answers don't lie in the depths of the river, my friend. You still miss her, don't you?"

Stone bent a knee to rest his arm across. He didn't need to ask how the older man knew. He was wise. It had been a few decades since Sierra left, though no one knew where, except River, and each time he asked her, she would just say it wasn't time for him to know yet, but soon. Only soon was now over 50 years. A part of him suspected Sierra was dead, and River was just being kind by giving him false hope.

Despite how many years had passed, he hadn't gone one day without thinking about her, remembering her taste, her smell, her soft voice. He wanted her so badly, and he lost his chance. "Yes. I don't think that'll ever change."

"Because she's the one who got away?"

"Maybe. Probably. I did love her."

"You mean, you do love her. I don't think you ever stopped."

"Yeah. You're right. I never have. What am I supposed to do? Continue pining for her for eternity? I can't seem to let her go and move on."

"If you could find her again, would you stay with her?"

"Yes. Even old and filled with wrinkles as I'm sure she must be by now. I wouldn't care. I'd spend the last of her days taking care of her."

"And if you could have her join you in living an extended life, would you?"

Stone gave him a wary look. "I'm not sure she'd want that."

"But if she did, would you?"

Stone thought about it for a moment. Then shook his head. "Yes. It wasn't her looks I fell in love with. It was her spirit and soul. It was her attitude and bravery. I don't think one could lose those. So yes, I would if she desired it."

"You know there is a way. It's seldom done, for we don't usually find humans we wish to spend eternity with, but there is a ceremony to tie life forces together. As long as you live, she could as well."

Stone turned to Black Mountain. "I thought that was just a myth."

"I'm old not fanciful. I know, and so does River, how to accomplish the ceremony. You need only ask. She'd have to consent, but she's already aware of what we are. Half the battle is won."

Stone shook his head, turning back to the water with a defeated sigh. "It's been decades since she disappeared without a trace. I have no idea where to look."

"It's not where my son. It's when."

Stone gave him an odd look. "What do you mean?"

"Didn't you ever suspect? Didn't she tell you her very own secret?"

"No."

"She's from the future. Ma'heo'o brought her to 1895 to accomplish a mission that would've been devastating had Higgins succeeded in his plan. She needed to be the one to fulfill that destiny and end the tyranny Higgins had embarked upon to rule Colorado Springs, Cripple Creek and all the gold in-between. He was attempting to set himself up as king of Colorado. Ma'heo'o saw something in her that would achieve what needed to be done. In his great wisdom, Ma'heo'o did what was right, then returned her to her time. She hasn't even been born yet. And you will meet her when it's time. Be patient, my son. Then, you can ask her to join your life force to be with her for many centuries to come."

For the first time in decades, Stone had hope. The revelations Black Mountain provided were astounding but also made him elated. He felt freer than he had in longer than he could remember. He had something to look forward to, ameliorating his previous dour disposition. He'd wait. As long as it took, he'd wait and then he'd win her back.

Finally released by Officer Crandall, he plowed past the police department doors and down to the street; his feet were moving a bit faster than his own senses. He stopped short at the curb and slowly turned around, not believing what the rest of his body was screaming at him. Sierra was here, standing right in front of him, beautiful as ever. He was worried he'd scare her again, like he did yesterday, so he didn't move.

Bursting into a huge smile, Sierra knew he recognized her, but she still needed to hear him acknowledge her. The trip back through time still left her slightly addled and she needed multiple reassurances that her time in the past really happened. "Stone?"

She knew him. He bounded back to her, gripping her tightly in a hug, refusing to let her go lest she disappear on him again. "I'm sorry. I didn't know. I didn't know."

"It's my fault. I wasn't sure who I could trust and who I couldn't. Everything was and is so bizarre. I just returned. Hours ago, and yet, it's been years. I spent months in 1895 and yet, I only came to Colorado yesterday. I didn't know if it was a dream, or if any of it really happened. Nothing makes sense, but I don't care. I only want to be with you. I was afraid you wouldn't want me after having you arrested and the way you spoke to me in jail. My head is just swimming."

"I was harsh, because I understood how stubborn you'd be if you'd any inkling how much I didn't want to let you go. But it was a different time then. A couple like us would never have succeeded without being pushed to our limits. I waited for you. I want you to know that. I did wait for you."

"So, you knew then? That I was from the future?"

"No. Not at first. Not for about 50 or 60 years after. Black Mountain told me after he was tired of seeing me pine for you for so long." Pulling back, Stone gazed into Sierra's eyes. "He also told me to tell you, if you wish, we can join life forces and you won't age or die like a human. Your life will be with mine and will age in the same respect. As long as neither of us are killed, we can live for eons."

"If you asked me yesterday, when I was screaming for you to get away from me, I'd've said no instantly. But I've lived a lifetime in the past, and I don't want to be without you in my future. Today, you're my reason to live and I don't see that changing during my lifetime or yours."

He scooped her up and carried her down the street. She laughed. "Do you have any idea where we are going?"

"No. But it's the journey, not the destination, that matters. I'm with you. My heart is complete."

Epilogue

Standing in front of River and Black Mountain, Sierra and Stone held hands. Black Mountain laid a knife down near them. "When you are ready."

Stone released Sierra's hands. Picking up the knife, he took her hand and sliced it across the middle of her palm. Stone repeated the process with the knife to his own, before he clasped her hand, letting the blood mix between them.

"Repeat after me," Black Mountain said. Then in Cheyenne he spoke, *"Blood of our blood, mixed together. Force of our lives joined as one. Forever we'll be. One life. One heart. One soul. Ma'heo'o bless our union. Bless our lives joined together."*

Sierra knew this would be difficult, but she'd spent time with both River and Stone practicing the intonations to speak their language for this rite. While he spoke, River softly chanted. It was beautiful and fit the picturesque mountain valley setting they were standing in. Sierra repeated the words, and from the smiles she got from Black Mountain, River and Stone, she knew she learned well.

Stone then said the words and the formality was almost over. It was a lot better than those hour-after-hour wedding services she endured for her friends. Other than the two elders, the only witness they had to this ceremony was nature, and that was fine with her.

She knew there was one further thing to endure, and though it concerned her, she knew the outcome would be well worth the momentary pain and disgust she'd experience. As their hands were bound so she couldn't accidentally pull away, Stone grabbed her tightly around the waist. "Are you ready?"

She took a deep breath, tilting her head to expose her jugular vein. "Yes."

He waited until she closed her eyes, then elongated his teeth to their sharp, pointy tips. He licked her skin, sending a shiver down her spine. Keeping their mingled, bloody hands interlaced, he bit her just enough to cause her neck to bleed. Lapping up her life source, he pulled back.

When she opened her eyes, she couldn't help but notice how cat-like his had become. What she wasn't able to see was that hers reflected his in every way. She felt her mouth feel odd and realized her teeth were also elongating. When she felt them stop growing and the strangeness ceased, she opened her mouth for him to see. Stone nodded and tilted his head. She bit him on the neck, lapping up the blood. She could feel the changes within her own body, which seemed to become more alive than ever before. Everything was clearer, sharper, crisp. Every sense enhanced to take in all of her surroundings. Glad he was holding her, it took a few moments to adjust to all the new sensations.

Realizing River had stopped chanting and Black Mountain was removing the binding around their wrists, she turned to thank them. But Stone had other ideas. He scooped her up in a fireman's carry and bounded off to a secluded place by the river he had prepared for them earlier. They could thank the elders later. Right now, they had a multitude of years to make up for.

Bibliography

Fried, Stephen, *Appetite for America: Fred Harvey and the Business of Civilizing the Wild West—One Meal at a Time.* Bantam Books Trade Paperbacks, 2011.

Morris, Juddi. *The Harvey Girls: The Women Who Civilized the West.* Walker, 1997.

Poling-Kemps, Lesley. *The Harvey Girls: Women Who Opened the West.* Da Capo Press, 1994.

Dines, Glen, et al. *Dog Soldiers: The Famous Warrior Society of the Cheyenne Indians.* The Macmillan Company, 1961.

Gelo, Daniel J. *Indians of the Great Plains.* Routledge, 2018.

Grinnell, George Bird., and Joseph Fitzgerald. *Cheyenne Indians: Their History and Lifeways, Edited and Illustrated.* World Wisdom, 2010.

Lowie, Robert Harry. *Indians of the Plains.* University of Nebraska Press, 1985.

Timber, John Stands In, et al. *Cheyenne Memories.* Yale University Press, 1998.

West, Elliott. *The Contested Plains; Indians, Goldseekers, & The Rush To Colorado.* University of Kansas Press, 1998.

The Cripple Creek District. Arcadia Pub., 2011.

Dorset, Phyllis F. *The New Eldorado: The Story of Colorado's Gold and Silver Rushes.* Fulcrum, 2011.

Gallagher, Jolie Anderson. *A Wild West History of Frontier Colorado: Pioneers, Gunslingers and Cattle Kings on the Eastern Plains.* History Press, 2011.

Lee, Mable Barbee. *Cripple Creek Days.* University of Nebraska Press, 1984

Berkman, Panela. *The History of the Atchison, Topeka & Santa Fe.* Smithmark Publishers, 1994.

Pounds, Robert E. *Santa Fe Depots, the Western Lines: A Route by Route and Station by Station Look at the Depots of the Western Lines of the Atchison, Topeka and Santa Fe Railway.* Kachina Press, 1984.

ABOUT THE AUTHOR

Ms. Hawks has always been interested in writing in some form or other, including writing for a local newspaper. Deciding to become more knowledgeable, she headed back to school and received her Master's Degree in Ancient Civilizations, Native American History and United States History.

It was at this time she got involved in role playing on FaceBook, which gave her ample opportunities to grow and hone her writing ability.

She lives in the suburbs of Chicago with her three companions, all males... cats. She travels as much as she can to various Author/Reader conventions and loves to meet established fans and make new ones, some of which she considers friends more than fans. Check out her social media sites to follow her.

WebSite: AuthorLauraHawks.com

Twitter: @AuthorLHawks

FB Author page https://www.facebook.com/Laura-Hawks-249262585192270/?fref=ts

FB Fan Group: Hawks Flock: https://www.facebook.com/groups/508236979340885/

LAURA HAWKS

More From Laura Hawks: Demon Trilogy

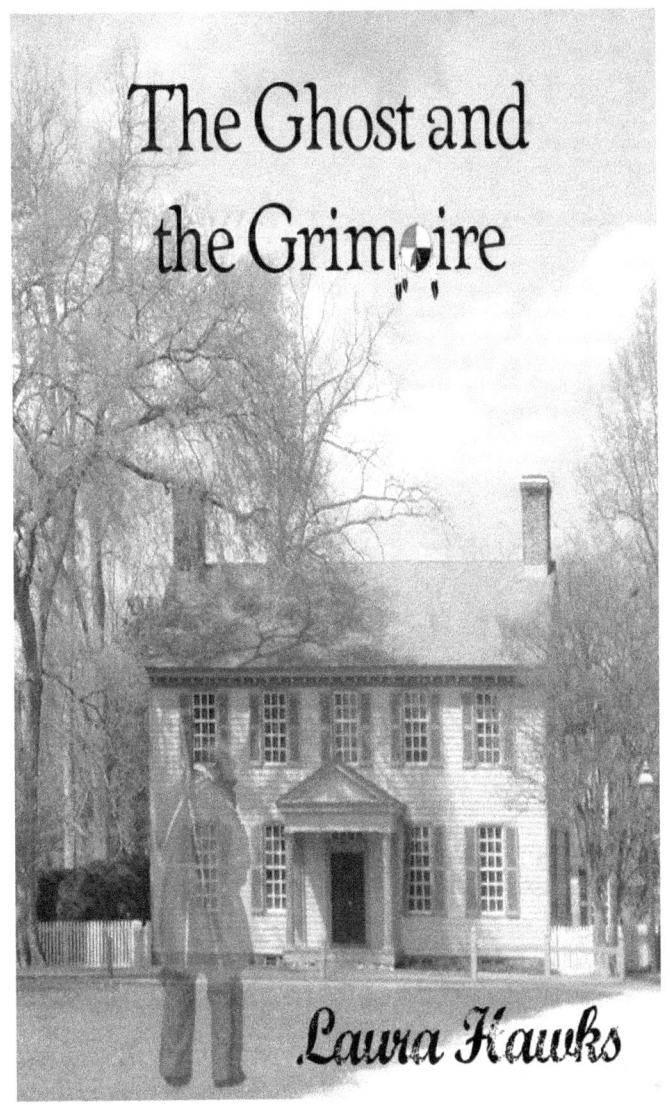

The Ghost and
the Grimoire

Laura Hawks

EGYPTIAN DESTINY
THE WEIGHT OF HER FEATHER

LAURA HAWKS

Spirit Walker's Thriller Series

Shattered Fairytales

Contemporary Suspense

LAURA HAWKS

FLAMING
RETRIBUTION